Praise for *Dragon*

post-1960s American identity yet often ignored… above all, Tran's
novel is a refreshing and entertaining story' – *New York Times*

'A superb debut novel…that takes the noir basics and infuses them
with the bitters of loss and isolation peculiar to the refugee and
immigrant tale' – *Fresh Air*

'A hard-hitting debut novel… [Suzy is] a mystery no one can solve,
particularly the people turning all their efforts in the wrong direction.
But while their efforts aren't fruitful, they're absorbing. And they
speak to the way everyone is a bit of an enigma to other people, no
matter how many words they put into the effort to be understood'
– NPR Books

'Transfixing… like such writers as Caryl Phillips, Dinaw Mengestu
and Edwidge Danticat, [Tran] is devoted to capturing the immigrant
experience and widening everyone's understanding of its particular as
well as universal truths' – *Chicago Tribune*

'A sophisticated mystery anchored in one woman's quest to make
amends with the daughter she abandoned, *Dragonfish* delicately
capsizes our notions of what it means to long for escape from the
prisons of our own making' – *Ploughshares*

'Like Gatsby, the characters in Tran's novel yearn for something
unattainable… This and the feeling that there will only be a tragic end
are what elevate *Dragonfish* beyond its bookstore genre'
– *Los Angeles Review of Books*

'Nuanced and elegiac… Vu Tran takes a strikingly poetic and
profoundly evocative approach to the conventions of crime fiction in
this supple, sensitive, wrenching, and suspenseful tale of exile, loss,
risk, violence, and the failure of love' – *Booklist*

www.vutranwriter.com

Dragonfish

VU TRAN

NO EXIT PRESS

First published in 2016 by No Exit Press,
an imprint of Oldcastle Books Ltd,
PO Box 394, Harpenden,
Herts, AL5 1XJ, UK

noexit.co.uk
@noexitpress

A CIP catalogue record for this book is available from the British Library.

ISBN
978-1-84344-826-6 (Print)
978-1-84344-827-3 (Epub)
978-1-84344-828-0 (Kindle)
978-1-84344-829-7 (Pdf)

2 4 6 8 10 9 7 5 3 1

Typeset by Avocet Typeset, Somerton, Somerset TA11 6RT
in 12.5pt Garamond MT
Printed in Denmark by Nørhaven

for my parents

Dragonfish

VU TRAN

Our first night at sea, you cried for your father. You buried your face in my lap and clenched a fist to your ear as if to shut out my voice. I reminded you that we had to leave home and he could not make the trip with us. He would catch up with us soon. But you kept shaking your head. I couldn't tell if I was failing to comfort you or if you were already, at four years old, refusing to believe in lies. You turned away from me, so alone in your distress that I no longer wanted to console you. I had never been able to anyway. Only he could soothe you. But why was I, even now, not enough? Did you imagine that I too would die without him?

Eventually you drifted off to sleep along with everyone around us. People were lying side by side, draped across each other's legs, sitting and leaning against what they could. In the next nine days, there would be thirst and hunger, sickness, death. But that first night we had at last made it out to sea, all ninety of us, and as our boat bobbed along the waves, everyone slept soundly.

I sat awake just beneath the gunwale with the sea spraying the crown of my head, and I listened to the boat's engine sputtering us toward Malaysia and farther and farther away from home. It was the sound of us leaving everything behind.

The truth was that I too thought only of your father. On the morning we left, I held you in the darkness before dawn and lingered with him as others called for us in the doorway. He kissed your forehead as you slept on my shoulder. Then he looked at me, placed his hand briefly on my arm before passing it over his shaven head. I could see the sickness in his face. The uncertainty too, clouding his always calm demeanor. He had already said good-bye in his thoughts and did not know now how to say it again in person. I did not want to go, but he had forced me. For her, he said, and looked at you one last time. Then he pushed me out the door.

If you ever read this, you should know that everything I write is necessary to explain what I later did. You are a woman now, and you will understand that I write this not as your mother but as a woman too.

On that first night, as I watched your chest rise and fall with the sea, I wished you away. I prayed to God that I might fall asleep and that when I awoke you would be gone.

PART ONE

1

IT WAS THREE IN THE MORNING and dark in my apartment. I stood half naked behind the front door, peering through the peephole at my vacant porch. My voice had come out small and childish and like someone else's voice calling from the bottom of a well.

'Who's there?' I said again, louder, more forceful this time. The porch light flickered but I could see only the lonely rail of my balcony, the vague silhouette of trees beyond it.

I grabbed my officer jacket off the kitchen counter and slipped it on. I steadied the gun behind me, then slowly opened the door and let in the cool December air. The hair on my chest and legs bristled. I stepped onto the porch. No one on the stairwell. No one by the mailboxes. A sweeping breeze from the bay made my legs buckle. I peered over my second-floor balcony. In the darkened courtyard, strung over the elm trees, a constellation of white Christmas lights swayed.

I returned inside and locked the door. I crawled back into bed, back under the warm covers as though wrapping myself in the darkness of the room.

The two knocks that had awakened me resounded in my head, this time thunderous and impatient and so full of the echo of night that I asked myself again if I had heard anything at all. Could a knocking in your dreams wake you?

Some minutes passed before I placed my gun back on the nightstand.

'No ONE out there to hurt you but yourself,' my father, a devout atheist, used to tell me. I never took this literally so much as personally, because my father knew better than anyone how selfish and shortsighted I can be. But whether he was warning me about myself or just naively reassuring me about the world, I have chosen, in my twenty years as police, to believe in his words as one might in aliens or the hereafter. They've become, it turns out, a mantra for self-preservation. Cops get as scared as anyone, but you develop a certain fearlessness on the job that you wear like an extra uniform, and people will know it's there like your shadow slipping its hand over their shoulder, and intimidated or not they'll think twice about hurting you. It's an armor of faith, a wish etched in stone. Go ask a soldier who's been to war. Or a priest. Or a magician. Without it, without that role to play, everything is a cold dark room in the night.

MY PHONE RANG at six the next morning, an hour after my alarm woke me. I was already in uniform, coffee cup in hand and minutes away from walking out the door. As soon as I answered, the phone went dead – just like the previous morning.

I went to the window and peeked through the mini blinds at the parking lot below. No one was up and about at that early hour, and the morning was still a stubborn shade of night. I made a fist of my left hand, unfurled it. My fingers had healed along with the pink scar on my wrist, but a warmth of unforgotten pain bloomed again. I stood there gazing at the lot until I finished my coffee.

Two days before this, I had come home from my patrol and found the welcome mat slightly crooked. Easily explainable, I figured, since any number of people – mailman, deliveryman, one of those door-to-door religious types – could have come knocking during the day. But once inside I noticed an unfamiliar smell, like burnt sugar, like someone had been cooking in the apartment, which I never do. In my bedroom, the pillows on the bed were in the right place but looked oddly askew, and one of my desk drawers had been left an inch open. It's always been the little things I notice. Show me a man with three eyes, and I'll point out his dirty fingernails.

The same smell greeted me the next evening as soon as I opened the front door. It followed me through the living room, the kitchen, the bedroom, the living room, the kitchen, fading at times so that I found myself sniffing the air to reclaim it, as I did as a boy when I roamed the house for hours in search of a lost toy or some trivial thought that had slipped my mind. Then the smell vanished altogether. Half an hour passed before I finally went to the bathroom and saw that the faucet was running a thin stream of water. I shut it off, more than certain that I had checked it before leaving that morning, something I always did at least twice.

I closed all the window blinds and spent the next two hours combing through all my drawers and shelves, opening cabinets and closets, searching the entire apartment for something missing or out of place, altered in some way. I knew it was ridiculous. Why would they go sifting through my medicine cabinet or my socks? Why move my books around? I suppose checking everything made everything mine again, if only temporarily.

That night I went to bed with my gun on the nightstand, something I hadn't done in nearly five months, since those first few weeks back from the desert.

I'd been trained on the force to trust my gut, or at least respect it enough to never dismiss it; but it crossed my mind that I was imagining all this, that in the previous five months I'd been glancing over my shoulder at shadows and flickering lights. You fixate on things long enough and you might as well be paranoid, like staring at yourself in the mirror until you start peering at what's reflected behind you.

When the phantom door knocks awoke me that same night, I lay in bed afterward and waited. I was that boy again, hearing the front door slam shut in the middle of the night and measuring the loudness and swiftness and emotion of that sound and whether it was my mother or father who'd left this time, and then waiting for the sound again until sleep washed away the world.

The lesson of my childhood was that if you anticipate misfortune, you make it hurt less. It's a fool's truth, but what truth isn't?

When I got home the following evening, I stayed in my car and stared for some time at the dark windows of my apartment. I was still in uniform but driving my old blue Chrysler. A drowsy fog crawled in from the Oakland bay, a cataract on the sunset, the day, which now felt worn. 'Empty Garden' played on the radio, a slow sad song I hadn't heard since my twenties. I remembered the old music video, Elton John playing a piano in a vacant concrete courtyard amid autumn leaves and twilight shadows. I sat back and scanned the complex of buildings surrounding me and thought of Suzy and the flowers that decorated every corner of our old house, and at the pit of me was not sadness or anger but the hollowness of forgetting how to need someone.

Three kids on bicycles glided past my car through fresh puddles left by the sprinklers. Some twenty yards away, an elderly man strolled the courtyard with his Chihuahua like a scared baby in his arms. In the building that faced me, three college guys were leaning over their balcony, smoking and leering at a pretty redhead who passed below them with a baby stroller. Then I saw a skinny Asian kid – a teenager – walk in front of my car, turn, and approach the window. He smiled and gestured for me to roll it down. His hands looked empty. He was wearing a Dodgers cap and an oversize blue Dodgers jacket zipped all the way to his throat. His smile was like a pose for a camera, and when he bent down to face me, he was all teeth.

I cracked open my window.

'Hello, Officer,' he said. 'Nice evening, huh?' He slipped me a folded note through the crack, and before I could say anything, he jogged away around the corner of the building.

I recognized the yellow paper, the Oakland PD logo, ripped from the notepad on my kitchen table. The words were neatly printed in red ink: *We've come from Las Vegas. Leave your gun in the car and come into your apartment. We just want to talk. Follow these instructions and no one will be harmed.*

That last line lingered on my lips as I refolded the note

and slipped it into my breast pocket, glaring again at the windows of my apartment. Why would they warn me? Why give me a chance to walk away? I considered calling in for help, but had to remind myself that if I hadn't told a soul about what happened five months ago, there was no explaining it now, at least not to anyone who could help. I could have driven away too, but I'd done that before and it had only led me here, to this moment. Or so I suspected.

And that was really the thing: whatever it was, I just needed to know. Nothing more exhausting than the imagination.

I pulled my gun out of its holster and made a show of holding it over the steering wheel before placing it into my glove compartment.

Walking away from the car felt like leaving a warm bed. I had lived in the complex for over two years, ever since the divorce, and liked it well enough, but only then, as I was trudging up the path toward my apartment, did I see how its tranquil beauty seemed like a postcard of someone else's life: the ivory stucco buildings leaning into shadow, hugged by tall trees and trimmed bushes and small perfect squares of lawn drowned now, even in winter, by the evening sprinklers. I began my climb up the stairwell. I noticed for the first time how craggy the stone steps were, how awfully they'd scrape at your skin if you were to go falling down the stairs.

Not sure what to do at my own front door, I knocked. There was no answer, so I slowly turned the knob. The door was unlocked. It opened into darkness. As soon as I stepped inside, the lamp in the living room clicked on.

There were two young Asian men standing side by side

in front of the TV set. The taller one spoke up in perfect English: 'Close the door, please.'

I remained in the doorway and gripped the doorknob, one foot still lingering on the porch. I remembered the last line of their note and took another step inside, nudging the door shut with my heel.

It's always difficult to tell with Asians, but the two of them could have been no older than twenty-five. The short one sported a goatee and slick hair and stood ashing his cigarette into my potted cactus, his wiry frame wrapped in a shiny black leather jacket. The other one, buzz-cut and sturdy in jeans and a bomber jacket, was a foot taller and moved that way, having just, without a word or glance, handed his binoculars to his partner, who dutifully set them atop the TV. I saw no sign of a gun on either yet, which bothered me more than if they'd already had one pointed at my head. They were not nervous, though they expected me to be. The goateed one, like their messenger outside, acted happy to see me; he had nodded when our eyes met, right after the lamp flickered him into existence. But it was the taller, stoic one who again spoke.

'You are Officer Robert Ruen.'

'Who're you? Why are you in my home?'

'I'm sure you can guess. You came up, didn't you?'

'Did I have a choice?'

He said something to the goateed kid that I did not understand, but I knew for certain then that they were Vietnamese.

Casually, the kid put out his cigarette in the cactus pot and approached me with a sly grin and his palms out like he wanted a hug. 'If you don't mind, Mr Officer, I'm gonna search you right now. Wanna make sure we all on even ground.'

I hesitated at first, not sure yet whether I should cooperate or play dumb and tell him to search himself. His pleasantness both irked and intimidated me. I put my hands on the front door and let him pat me down. He was half my size, but his hands were solid, with weight and intention behind them. Satisfied, he gestured for me to make myself comfortable on my own couch, which I did after quickly sniffing him and smelling nothing but cigarettes.

They'd been waiting for some time. A couple of my travel magazines lay open on the coffee table beside two open cans of Coke from my fridge, and the TV remote sat atop the TV instead of its usual resting place on the arm of the sofa. I was surprised they hadn't kicked off their shoes and made coffee.

The kid watched me as I, by force of habit, slipped off my loafers and set them neatly to the side. He chuckled lazily and turned to his partner. 'I think we dirtied up his carpet.'

His partner looked at his watch, then at my shoes. Again he spoke in Vietnamese. The kid threw him an exaggerated frown, but he repeated himself and was already silently unlacing a boot. A moment later they had both tossed their shoes onto the tile floor by the front door.

'Our Christmas present to you,' the kid said to me in his white socks.

'How did you get in here?'

'Through the front door. Simmer down, Mr Officer. We just waiting for a phone call.' He shut up for the moment, waiting like his partner.

On the wall behind them hung the samurai sword I had bought ages ago at a flea market for forty bucks. I had unsheathed it once or twice to admire it, and now wondered how sharp it actually was.

'Hey,' the kid said, struck by something. 'I got something else for you.'

Though I was going nowhere, he gestured for me to remain seated. He arched his brow mischievously at me, as if at some eager child at a birthday party, and reached into his jacket pocket. I held my breath as he pulled out another cigarette, which he put to his lips. From the other pocket, he revealed a silver flask. Holding out an index finger like a perch for a bird, he carefully poured the contents of the flask over the length of it. He raised it to his face and flicked his lighter. The finger ignited in a calm blue flame, which he promptly used to light his cigarette. He held up the finger like a candle, blew a lazy plume of smoke over it, and watched it burn itself out as he flashed his jack-o'lantern grin. I couldn't tell if he was trying to scare me, entertain me, or make fun of me.

His partner looked on with glassy, tired eyes. We exchanged an awkward glance before he looked away as if embarrassed by this brief talent show.

His cell phone chimed and he brought it carefully to his ear, nodding at the kid to take a post by the door. He spoke Vietnamese into the phone as he gave me another once-over. He moved into the hallway between my bathroom and bedroom, murmuring into the shadows. After a minute, he came back and handed me the phone.

The line was silent.

'Yes,' I said.

'You. Robert Ruen.' It was a declaration, not a question – an older man's voice, loud and somehow childish, the accent unmistakably Vietnamese. 'Say something to me.'

'What do you mean?'

'*You.* Your voice, man – I don't forget thing like this.'

It might have been his broken English or how quickly he spoke, but he sounded something like a puppet. He was smoking, sucking in his breath fast and exhaling his impatience into the phone.

'You've made a mistake,' I said.

'You got bad memory? You know who I am.'

'I have no idea –'

'Las Vegas, man. I know you come here. You think I'm dummy I not figure out?' He snorted and spat, as if to underline his point. 'In Vietnam, we say beautiful die, but ugly never go away. For policeman, you do some *bad* fucking thing. You know how long I wait to talk to you? I been dream about this. I see your face in my fucking dream.'

My houseguests were stirring. The tall one slowly unzipped his jacket, and the kid drifted behind me. I could still see curls of his cigarette smoke.

I spoke calmly into the phone, 'What do you want me to say?'

'Tell me.'

'Tell you what?'

'You fucking know.'

'I don't know anything about anything. Just what the hell are you talking about?'

He sounded like he was thinking. Then he replied, as if repeating himself, 'Suzy.'

The name drained me all at once of any effort to deny its importance. It was like he had slapped me to shut me up.

I think back on it now, and this was the moment I felt the full weight of the things I'd already lost – the last moment before everything that would later happen became inevitable.

I heard movement behind me. On cue, the goateed kid appeared at my shoulder. I did not see the gun until it was pointed, a dark hard glimmering thing, squarely at my temple.

The voice spoke again over the line. 'I ask you one time. Where is she?'

2

FIVE MONTHS BEFORE ALL THIS, I drove into Vegas on a sweltering July evening just before sunset. From the highway, I could see the Strip in the distance, but also a lone dark cloud above it, flushed on a bed of light and glowing alien and purplish in the sky. I was convinced it was a UFO and kept gazing at it before nearly hitting the truck ahead of me. That jolted me out of my exhaustion.

Half an hour later, the guy at the gas station told me about the beam of light from atop that giant pyramid casino, which you can spot from anywhere in the city, even from space if no clouds are in the way.

'Sorry, man,' he said like he was consoling me.

I must have looked disappointed.

The drive from Oakland had taken me all day, so I checked into the Motel 6 near Chinatown and fell asleep with my shoes on and my five-shot still strapped to my ankle. I slept stupid for ten hours straight and woke up at six in the morning, my mouth and nostrils so dry it felt like someone had shoveled dirt over me in the night. The sun had barely risen, but it was already a hundred degrees outside. Not even a wisp of a cloud.

After a long cold shower, I walked to the front office. The clerk from last night – an old Chinese guy who spoke English about as well as I spoke Chinese – was slurping his breakfast and watching TV behind the counter. He looked up when I knocked on the counter, but did not set down his chopsticks until he saw me brandish cash. I'd already paid him for last night's stay, and now I handed him a hundred for two more nights. He said nothing and hardly looked at me before handing me a receipt and diving back into his noodles. When I asked him where I could get some eggs, he mumbled a few incomprehensible words, his mouth stuffed, glistening. I felt like slapping the noodles out of his mouth but I turned and walked out before he could annoy me any further. Ever since Suzy left me, I'd learned to curb my temper. Let it sleep a little, save it for another, more necessary day.

In the strip mall across the street, I had some coffee at a doughnut shop and spent an hour thumbing mindlessly through a couple of Asian newspapers, waiting for the pho restaurant next door to open. I hoped they made it like Suzy used to – the beef thinly sliced and not too gristly, the noodles soft, the broth clear and flavorful. Turned out theirs was even better, which finally cheered me up, though it reminded me of something her best friend – a Vietnamese woman named Happy, of all things – once told me years ago when she was over at the house for Sunday pho. Suzy had been mad at me that morning for nodding off at church, as I often did since my weekend patrols didn't end until midnight, and though she knew I'd only converted for her and had never taken churchgoing seriously, she chewed me out all the way home, and with more spite than usual. So when she stepped outside to smoke after lunch, I asked Happy, 'What's bugging her lately?' Happy was her one good friend, her sole witness at our courthouse wedding and her emergency contact on all her forms, and they talked on the phone every day in a mix of English and Vietnamese that I never did understand – but she shrugged at my question. I chuckled. 'Just me, huh? I bet she tells you every bad thing about me.' But again she shrugged and said, very innocently, 'She don't talk about you much, Bob.' I'd long figured this much was true, but it burned to hear it acknowledged so casually. Suzy and I had been married for two years at the time. We somehow lasted six more years before she finally took off.

I sat in a front booth and finished off an extra large bowl of beef pho, four spring rolls, and two tall glasses of Vietnamese coffee, staring all the while at people passing by in the parking lot, including a bald Asian man who climbed into a red BMW. It could have been him, except Suzy's new husband looked more bullish on his driver's license and sported a thin mustache that accentuated the stubborn in his eyes. DPS listed a red BMW under his name – Sonny Van Nguyen – as well as a silver Porsche, a brand-new 2000 model. The master files at Vegas Metro confirmed he was fifty, five years older than me, and that he owned a posh sushi restaurant in town and an equally fancy rap sheet: one DUI, five speeding tickets, and three different arrests, one for unpaid speeding tickets, two on assault charges. He apparently struck a business associate in the head with a rotary phone during an argument and a year later threw a chair at someone in a casino for calling him a name. The last incident got him two years' probation, which was four months from expiring. It was Happy who told me he was a gambler, fully equipped with a gambler's penchant for risking everything but his pride. You should be afraid of him, Happy had said, but I knew it was already too late for that.

In my two decades on the Oakland force, I had punched a hooker for biting my hand, choked out a belligerent Bible salesman, and wrestled thugs twice my size and half my age. I once had a five-year-old boy nearly bleed to death as I nightsticked his mother, who had chopped off his hand with a cleaver, tweaked out of her mind; I'd fired my gun three times and shot two people, one in the thigh, the other in the palm, both of whom had shot at me and quite frankly deserved more; I'd been known to kick a tooth or two loose, bruise a face here and there, maybe even silently wish more harm than was necessary. But never, not once, had I truly wanted to kill anyone.

I WALKED DOWN Spring Mountain Road and quickly regretted not taking my car. Vegas, beyond the Strip, is not a place for pedestrians, especially in the summer. I'd pictured a Chinatown similar to Oakland's or San Francisco's, but the Vegas Chinatown was nothing more than a bloated strip mall – three or four blocks of it painted red and yellow and then pagodified, a theme park like the rest of the city. Nearly every establishment was a restaurant, and the one I was looking for was called Fuji West. I found it easily enough in one of those strip malls – nestled, with its dark temple-like entrance, between an oriental art gallery and a two-story pet store. It was not set to open for another hour.

Nothing surprising about Vietnamese selling Japanese food. Happy's uncle owned a cowboy clothing store in Oakland. What did startle me was the giant white-aproned

Mexican – all seven feet of him – sweeping the patio, though you might as well have called it swinging a broom. He gazed down at me blankly when I asked for Sonny. He didn't look dumb, just bored.

'The owner,' I repeated. 'Is he here?'

'His name's no Sonny.'

'Well, can I speak to him, whatever his name is?'

The Mexican, for some reason, handed me his broom and disappeared behind the two giant mahogany doors. A minute later a young Vietnamese man – late twenties, brightly groomed, dressed in a splendidly tailored tan suit and a precise pink tie – appeared in his place. He smiled at me, shook my hand tenderly. He relieved me of the broom and leaned it against one of the wooden pillars that flanked the patio.

'How may I help you, sir?' He held his hands behind his back and spoke with a slight accent, his tone as formal as if he'd ironed it.

'I'd like to see Sonny.'

'I'm sorry, no one by that name works here. Perhaps you are mistaken? There are many sushi restaurants around here. If you like, I can direct you.'

'I was told he owns this restaurant.'

'Then you *are* mistaken. I am the owner.' He spoke like it was a friendly misunderstanding, but his eyes had strayed twice from mine: once to the parking lot, once to my waist.

'I'm not mistaken,' I replied and looked at him hard to see if he would flinch.

He did not. I was a head taller than him, my arms twice the size of his, but all I felt in his presence was my age. Even his hesitation seemed assured. He slowly smoothed out an eyebrow with one finger. 'I am not sure what I can do for you, sir.'

'How about this. I'll come back this evening for some sushi. And if Sonny's not too busy, he can join me for some tea. I just want to have a little chat. Please tell him that for me.'

I turned to go but felt a movement toward me. The young man was no longer smiling. There was no meanness yet in his face, but his words had become chiseled. 'You are Officer Robert Ruen, aren't you?' he declared. When I didn't answer, he leaned in closer: 'You should not be here. If you do not understand why I am saying this, then please recognize my seriousness. Go back home and try to be happy.'

That last thing he said unexpectedly moved me. It was like he had patted my shoulder. I noticed how handsome he was – how, if he wanted to, he could've modeled magazine ads for cologne or expensive sunglasses. For a moment I might have doubted that he was dangerous at all. He nodded at me, a succinct little bow, then grabbed the broom and walked back through the heavy mahogany doors of the restaurant.

I felt tired again. Pho always made me sleepy. I walked back to the hotel and in my room stripped down to my boxers and cranked up the AC before falling back into bed.

People my age get certain *feelings* now and then, even if intuition was never our strong suit in youth, and my inkling about this Sonny guy was that he was the type of restaurant owner who, if he came by at all, would only do so at night, when the money was counted. My second inkling was that his dapper guard dog stayed on duty from open to close, and that he was willing to do anything to protect his boss. I had a long evening ahead of me. Before shutting my eyes, I decided to put my badge away, deep in the recesses of my suitcase.

When suzy left me, it was easy at first. No children. No possessions to split up. No one really to care. I was an only child, my parents both years in their graves, and her entire family was either also dead or still in Vietnam. After eight years together, I'd gotten to know maybe two or three of her friends, and the only things my police buddies knew about her was her name and her temper.

She gave me the news after Sunday dinner. I was sitting at the dining table, and she approached me from the kitchen, her mouth still swollen, and said, 'I'm leaving tomorrow and I'm taking my clothes. You can have everything else.' She carried away my half-empty plate and I heard it shatter in the sink.

The first time I met her, I knew she was fearless. I was responding to a robbery at the flower shop where she worked. She'd been in America almost a decade, but her English was still pretty bad. When I arrived, she stood at the door with a baseball bat in one hand and bloody pruning shears in the other. Before I could step out of the patrol car, she flew into a tirade about what had happened, as though I'd been the one who robbed her. I understood about a quarter of what she said – something about a gun and ruined roses – but I knew I liked her. That petite sprightly body. Her lips, her cheekbones: full and bold. Firecracker eyes that glared at people with the urgency of a lit fuse. We found the perp two miles away, limping and bleeding from a stab wound to his thigh. The pruning shears had done it. Suzy and I married four months later.

I was thirty-five then, an age when I once thought I should already have two or three kids, though I suspected she, at thirty-three, had given little thought to her own biology, let alone the passage of time. When I proposed, she agreed on the spot, but only if I was okay with not having children. She was not good with kids, she said, and having them would hurt too much, two reasons she repeated when I brought it up again a year later and a third time the year after that. I always figured she'd eventually change her mind.

Her real name was Hong, which meant 'pink' or 'rose' in Vietnamese. But it sounded a bit piggish the way Americans pronounced it, so I suggested the name of my first girlfriend in high school, and *this* she did give me, though her Vietnamese acquaintances still called her Hong.

When we married, neither of us seemed to have any worldly possessions beyond our clothes and the car we drove. It was like we had both, up until the time we met, lived our adulthoods at some cheap motel, so that we knew nothing about domesticated life beyond paying bills and doing laundry. We combined all our savings and bought an old townhouse near Chinatown that I repainted and she furnished – a luxury she'd apparently never had and one she indulged in with care and sincerity, down to the crucifixes that adorned every room and the two brass hooks on the wall of the entryway, the one for my coat a little higher than hers.

In our first year, we bonded over this novelty of owning a home, of living with another human being and building a brand-new life together with chairs and tables and dishes and bath towels. We were happy, I realize now, not because of what we actually had in common, but because we were fashioning this new life out of things that had never existed for either of us.

I'd stop by the flower shop every afternoon during my patrol to visit her. We had two days of the week together, and we spent it fixing up the townhouse, exploring local consignment shops, trying out every cheap restaurant in Chinatown, then going to the movies (Westerns and old black-and-white detective films were her favorites) or walking the waterfront, where the smell of the ocean reminded her of Vietnam. For a long time I didn't mind losing myself in her world: the Vietnamese church, the food, the sappy ballads on the tape player, her handful of 'friends' who with the exception of Happy hardly spoke a lick of English, even the morbid altar in the corner of the living room with the gruesome crucifix and the candles and pictures of dead people she never talked about. That was all fine, even wonderful, because being with her was like discovering a new, unexpected person in myself.

But after two years, I realized she had no interest in discovering *me*: my job, my friends, my love for baseball or cars or a nice steak and potato dinner. She hardly ever asked me about my family or my upbringing. She must have assumed, because of her silence about herself, that I was equally indifferent to my own past. She didn't know that until her I had not thought of Vietnam since 1973, when I was eighteen and the draft ended and saved me from the war, and that all of a sudden, decades later, this distant country – this vague alien idea from my youth – meant everything again, until she gradually embodied the place itself, the central mystery in my life. The least she could do was share her stories, like how happy her childhood had been and how the war upended everything, or what cruel assholes the Communists were, or how her uncle or father or neighbor had died in battle or survived a reeducation camp, or *something*. But she'd only say her life back home was 'lonely' and 'uninteresting,' her voice muted with hesitation, like she was teaching me her language and I'd never get it anyway.

Gradually, an easy distance settled between us. I found I loved her most when she was sick and had no choice but to let me take care of her. Feed her. Give her medicine. Keep her housebound, which she rarely was for more than a day. And since I'd apparently reached the limit of what she was willing to give me, I grew fond of any situation where she'd talk about herself, even if it was her waking in the night from a bad dream and then, in the grip of her fright, waking me too so I could lie there in the darkness and listen to her recount it.

She had bad dreams constantly. Recurring ones where I had cheated on her and hurt her in some profound way and she's beating me with her fists as violently as she can and yet all I'm doing is laughing and laughing as she throttles me in the face. Sometimes it's another man in this dream, though she'd never say who that might be – perhaps a lover from her past whose sins she was now mistaking for mine. Then there were the dreams where she's murdered someone. Not just one person but a lot of people. She doesn't murder them in the dream, she's only conscious of having done it and must now figure out how to cover it up. In one version, she has buried them under piles of clothes in the closet. In another, she has shoved them into the washer, the dryer, that large cabinet in our laundry room where she kept all the strange pickled foods I could never force myself to like. And the entire time, all she can think about it is that she has killed people and that her life is now over.

I remember her describing one dream where she's walking for hours through an empty furniture store and someone is following her as she makes her way across beautiful model bedrooms and kitchens and living rooms. Even as she climbs the stairwells from one floor of the store to the other, the person keeps following her, their footsteps loud and steady. I asked if she ever saw what the person looked like, and she said she couldn't make herself stop or turn around in the dream, and that all she wanted was for the person to catch up to her, take her by the shoulder, and show their face.

To church every Sunday, she brought along a red leather-bound journal, worn and darkened with age, and held it in her lap throughout Mass like a private Bible, except she never opened it. She said it was a keepsake from the refugee camp and that it made her feel more right with God at church, whatever that meant. At home, it lay on the altar beneath the crucifix. I opened it once. The first few pages, brittle and yellowed, were written in someone else's handwriting, the rest in Suzy's tiny Vietnamese cursive, which was already hard to read. I tried translating the first page with a bilingual dictionary but could get no further than the opening sentence. Something about rain in the morning and someone's mother yelling at them. Suzy once forgot the book at church and didn't realize it until bedtime. She wanted to go right then and there to retrieve it, insisting, 'Someone is always there!' But I refused to let her go. At dawn the next morning, after a long, sleepless night, she drove to church and came home with the journal clutched to her chest like a talisman, her eyes red from crying. She did not speak to me the rest of the day.

She could go an entire week without speaking. A way at first to punish me for whatever I had done to anger her, though gradually, almost every time, her silence outlasted her anger and became a retreat from me and into herself, an absence actually, as though she had gotten lost in whatever world she had escaped into. Her temper – that flailing beast inside her that she herself hated – would retreat as well, and the only thing left between us until she spoke again was what we had said and done to each other when we fought: about money we didn't have and the children we weren't having, about what to eat for dinner, about my poor driving and my poor taste in clothes and a million other things I can't remember anymore. I always played my part, stubborn and mouthy as I am, my own temper always burning brightest before hers exploded. She'd go from yelling at me to lunging at me, those eyes erupting out of her face as she slapped and punched my chest or seized my neck with both hands. Both of us knew she was not strong enough to hurt me, and on a certain level I think she went out of her way to avoid it, never throwing or breaking anything in the house, never once using anything but her hands and her words. Even as I held her wrists and let her scream at me, let her kick me in the stomach or the legs, it sometimes felt as though she were asking me – with her hateful, pleading eyes – to hold her back and tie her to the mast until the storm passed. Because inevitably she'd crumple to the floor and cry herself into a numb silence and eventually into bed, where she would begin withdrawing from me and the world.

Sometimes we didn't need an argument. She'd be talkative and affectionate in the morning, and then I'd come home in the evening and she'd seem afflicted with some flu-like melancholy that only silence and aloneness could treat. So I learned to let her be. I turned on the TV in the kitchen during dinner. I turned up the music in the car as she sat staring out the window. I spent more and more time with friends at the bar or at our weekly poker game. I slept in our spare bedroom, which was otherwise never used.

Once or twice a year, I'd startle awake in the middle of the night and find myself alone in bed, the house empty, her car still parked in the driveway. An hour later the front door would open and she'd be barefoot in her nightgown and a jacket, having taken one of her nocturnal walks through the neighborhood, God knows what for or where to. She'd crawl back into bed without explaining anything, despite my stares and my questions, and in the morning I'd notice the dirty bottoms of her feet, the stench of cigarettes on her clothes, the whiff of alcohol on her breath. One evening I came home from work and every single light in the house was on, and she was out back beneath the apple tree, curled up and asleep on the grass, empty beer bottles lying beside her with crushed cigarettes inside.

Then, after a few days, sometimes as long as two weeks, without any hint whatsoever of reconciliation, she'd crawl into my arms while I lay on the couch watching TV, roll over in bed and bury her face in my chest, join me in the shower and lather me with soap from my head to my feet. I never knew how to feel in these moments, whether to love her back or commence my own week of silence. Not until she started talking again, recounting some funny incident at the flower shop two weeks before, or describing some movie she'd seen on TV at three in the morning, would I then feel her voice burrow into me, unravel all the knots, and bring us back to wherever we were before the silence began. Then we'd make love and she would whimper, a childlike thing a lot of Asian women do, except hers sounded more like a wounded animal's, and that would remind me once again of all the other ways I felt myself a stranger in her presence, an intruder, right back to where we were.

And yet we still kept at it, year after year of living out our separate lives in the same home, of needing each other and not knowing why, of her looking at me as though I was some longtime lodger at the house, until I came to believe that she was both naive and practical about love, that she'd only ever loved me because I was a cop, because that was supposed to mean I'd never hurt her.

The night I hit her was a rainy night. I had come home from the scene of a shooting in Ghost Town in West Oakland, where a guy had tried robbing someone's seventy-year-old grandmother and, when she fought back, shot her in the head. I was too spent to care about tracking mud across Suzy's spotless kitchen floor, or to listen to her yell at me when she saw the mess. Couldn't she understand that blood on a sidewalk is a world worse than mud on a tile floor? Shouldn't she, coming from where she came, appreciate something like that? I told her to just fuck off.

She glared at me, and then started with something she'd been doing the last few years whenever we argued: she spoke in Vietnamese. Not loudly or irrationally like she was venting her anger at me – but calmly and deliberately, as if I actually understood her, like she was daring me to understand her, flaunting all the nasty things she could be saying to me and knowing full well that it could have been gibberish for all I knew and that I could do nothing of the sort to her. I usually ignored her or walked away. But this time, after a minute of staring her down as she delivered whatever the hell she was saying, I slapped her across the face.

She yelped and clutched her cheek, her eyes aghast. But then her hand fell away and she was flinging indecipherable words at me again, more and more vicious the closer she got to my face, her voice rising each time I told her to shut up. So I slapped her a second time, harder, sent her bumping into the dining chair behind her.

I felt queasy even as something inside me untangled itself. There'd been pushing in the past, me seizing her by the arms, the cheeks. But I had never gone this far. The tips of my fingers stung.

Everything happened fast, but I still remember her turning back to me with her flushed cheeks and her wet outraged eyes, her chin raised defiantly, and how it reminded me of men I'd arrested who'd just hit their wives or girlfriends and that preternatural calm on their faces when I confronted them, the posturing ease of a liar, a control freak, a bully wearing his guilt like armor. It made me see myself in Suzy's pathetic show of boldness. She'd never been as tough as I thought, and now I was the bad guy.

She spit out three words. She knew I understood. *Fuck your mother.* She said it again, then again and again, a bitter recitation. I barked at her to shut her mouth, shoving my face at hers, and that's when she swung at me as if to slap me with her fist, two swift blows on my ear that felt like an explosion in my head. I put up an arm to shield myself and she flailed at it, still cursing me, until finally I backhanded her as hard as I could, felt the thud of my knuckles against her teeth.

She stumbled back a few steps, covering her mouth with one hand and steadying herself on the dining table with the other until she finally went down on a knee, her head bowed like she was about to vomit. Briefly, she peered up at me. Red milky eyes, childish all of a sudden, disbelieving. I watched her rise to her feet, still cradling her mouth, and shamble to the sink and spit into it several times. I watched her linger there, stooped over like she was staring down a well. I didn't move – I couldn't – until I heard her sniffling and saw her raise herself gingerly and reach for a towel and turn on the faucet.

As I walked upstairs, I listened to the water running in the kitchen and the murmuring TV in the living room and the rain pummeling the gutters outside, and everything had the sound of finality to it.

In the divorce, she was true to her word and I was left with a home full of eggshell paintings and crucifixes and rattan furniture. It was a testament to the weird isolating vacuum of our marriage that she was able to immediately and completely disappear from my life. Her flower shop had closed down a year before and she had been working odd jobs around town: cutting hair, selling furniture, I rarely kept up. I had known so little about her comings and goings or the people she knew that once she was gone I had no way of even finding out where she was living. Even Happy had quietly disappeared.

Months later, after the divorce was finalized, with a little help from within the department I found out she had moved to Las Vegas. I sold the townhouse and everything in it and tried my best to forget I had ever married anyone. I went on a strict diet of hamburgers and steaks.

But two years later, a few months before my trip to Vegas, I bumped into Happy at the supermarket. Instead of ignoring me or telling me off, she treated me like an old friend, which didn't surprise me too much. She had always lived up to her name in that way, and actually looked a lot like Suzy without her glasses: a taller, more carefree version. She said she, too, had moved to Vegas for work and was in town for the summer to visit family. I asked her out to dinner that night. Afterward she came home with me. We shared two bottles of wine and I let her lead me to the bedroom, and it wasn't until we finished that I realized – or admitted to myself – my true reason for doing all this. With her blissfully drunk and more talkative than ever, I asked about Suzy. She told me everything: how Suzy had become a card dealer in Vegas and met up with this cocky Vietnamese poker player who owned a fancy restaurant and a big house and apparently had some shady dealings in town, and how she quit her job and married him after knowing him a month, and how everything had been good for about a year.

'Until he start losing,' Happy declared casually, sitting back against the headboard. She fell silent and I had to tell her several times to get on with it. She looked at me impatiently as though I should already know, as though anyone could've told the rest of the story.

'He hit her,' she said. 'She hit him too, but he too strong and he drink so much. Last month, he throw her down the stair, break her arm. I see her two week before, her arm in a sling, her cheek purple. But he too rich for her to leave. And always he say he need her, he need her.'

'Did she call the cops? Why didn't she go to the cops?'

I stood from the bed, my head throbbing from the wine and all that I was imagining. I knocked the lamp off the nightstand.

Happy flinched. She had put her glasses back on, as if to see me better. After a moment, she said, 'Why you still love her?' There was no envy or bitterness in her voice. She was simply curious.

'Who said I did?'

She checked me with her eyes as though I didn't understand my own emotions.

I tried to soften my voice, but it still came out in a growl: 'Is it just the money? What – is he handsome?'

'Not really. But you not either.' She patted my arm and laughed.

'You know what? I'm gonna go to Vegas and I'm gonna find this fucker. And then I'm gonna hit him a little before I break *his* arm.'

This time she laughed hard, covering her mouth and regarding me with drunken pity. 'You a silly, stupid man,' she said.

I RETURNED TO FUJI WEST at 8:00, as the sun was setting. I drove this time. The parking lot was half full, mostly fancy cars, and I immediately spotted the silver Porsche in the back row. Sure enough, it had the right tag. I rechecked the five-shot in my ankle holster. My hands felt bruised from the hot, dry air.

Inside, the restaurant was cool and dark and very Zen. Piano music drifted along the ceiling beams overhead. Booth tables with high-backed wooden seats, lighted by small suspended lanterns, lined the walls like confessionals. Candlelit tables filled in the space between the booths and the circular sushi bar, an island at the center of the restaurant manned by three hatted sushi chefs in white who resembled sailors. Flanking the bar were two enormous aquariums filled with exotic-looking fish staring out calmly at the twenty or so patrons in the restaurant, most of whom easily outdressed me.

I asked for a table near the bar and ordered a Japanese beer and told the hostess I was waiting for a friend. I'd barely wet my lips before Sonny's young Doberman appeared and sat himself across from me, as casually as if I'd invited him.

He was now dressed in a charcoal suit, set off by another beautiful pink tie, looking very ready to be someone's best man. He waved at a waitress, who swiftly brought him a bottle of Perrier and a glass with a straw. Pouring the Perrier into the glass, he said to me, 'So you did not like my advice.' His voice was gentle but humorless. He sipped his Perrier with the straw like a child. In the aquarium directly behind him, a long brown eel swam slowly through his head.

'My business with Sonny is important.'

'I'm sure it is. Except my father has no business with *you*.'

I drank my beer and tried to hide my surprise. I searched

his face for some resemblance of the hard man I'd already envisioned in my head. 'So you know who I am.'

'Miss Hong's friend Happy is also a friend of mine. She visited me recently and mentioned that she had been seeing you. That is, until last month. You stopped taking her calls. She got worried. She told me what you had been planning to do. She did not know how serious you were, but she wanted to tell me for *your* sake. She likes you, Mr Robert, and I suppose she has some womanly notion of saving you. She did not tell Miss Hong, of course, or my father. So only I know that you are here. And that is a good thing.'

'Because your father's a dangerous man?'

He eyed me sternly, drawing together his dark handsome eyebrows. 'Because my father does not have my patience.'

The hostess came by and whispered something into his ear, and Sonny Jr. looked to the front of the restaurant, where a large party had arrived, people in suits and dresses. He stood and gestured for a waiter, then gave him and the hostess rapid orders in Vietnamese. He glanced at me distractedly and went on with his instructions. He watched them walk away and continued watching as they saw to the party.

His father might have been a poker-playing gangster, or maybe a gangster-playing poker player, but for the moment Junior seemed nothing more than what he appeared: the young manager of a restaurant.

He turned back to me, adjusting his tie, his face once again as calm as the fish. 'You were a narcotics investigator once. Ten years ago, I believe.'

I took another swill of my beer. 'Nice detective work.'

'You did it for only two years and then returned to being a patrol officer. Why?'

'It didn't suit me. Why do you want to know?'

'Because the answer matters. You do not strike me as someone who gives up easily.'

'I didn't give up on anything,' I said, a little too loudly. His facts were accurate but told a meaningless story. He had no idea how good I was at prying into other people's lives, how tedious and occasionally thrilling the job was, or how enjoying it emptied me because I didn't care to know so much about people I cared nothing for. 'It just wasn't my cup of tea.'

He tried to puzzle me out, like he was readying a few more questions. But then he grabbed the linen napkin on the table and stood. He dabbed at his forehead with the napkin, pocketed it, and said, 'I have something to show you. It will behoove you to come with me.'

'I'm guessing this *something* is not your father.'

Instead of answering me, he nodded toward the front of the restaurant. 'You are free to go if you want. But I think you will regret it.'

I still hadn't moved.

'You're the police officer here,' he said. 'It should be me who is nervous.'

I felt vaguely embarrassed and downed the rest of my beer before getting up. As I gestured for him to lead the way, I noticed again how much taller I was. On our way to the kitchen, we passed two private tatami rooms, each being busily prepared by the staff for the swarm of guests out front. Foolishly or not, the presence of so many people eased my mind.

The kitchen was staffed by Mexicans and Asians, all in white uniforms. No one paid us any attention as we walked to the back, toward a door marked OFFICE. Junior unlocked it, and once we stepped inside he relocked it. He approached an enormous, door-size oil painting of a geisha walking up a dark flight of stairs. There was a clock on the wall beside it, which he set to midnight, then he turned the minute hand three revolutions clockwise and two revolutions counterclockwise. The painting slowly swung open from the wall like a door, revealing a passageway and a dark descending staircase. He walked down and with a glance over his shoulder said, 'It will close again in ten seconds.'

Visions of my own doom flittered through my head, but at that point I'd already talked myself into following. If he wanted to lure me into danger, he wouldn't be this obvious about it, even if he figured me for a complete idiot. The kid seemed too smart to underestimate a cop. He really wanted to show me something, and I wasn't ready yet to walk away.

We reached a long dim hallway and passed six closed doors, each with a keypad over the knob. At the end we stopped at a door that was set much farther away from the others. He punched a series of numbers on the keypad and something clicked. He pushed the door open completely before walking inside.

I heard soft oriental music. The room glowed bluish and shimmered.

It was no more than eight hundred square feet but felt cavernous, with a lofty ceiling and walls of glass surrounding us, behind them water and fish. I had entered a gigantic aquarium. The three walls before me each showed the flush faces of four separate tanks, framed in quadrants like giant television monitors, their blue-lit waters filled with stingrays and sharks and what looked like piranha and other menacing fish, swimming around beds of coral and white gravel. High above me were two ceiling fans, their slow synchronous spinning like the gears of a machine. I noticed then the small video camera perched in the corner, peering down at us.

On a large oriental rug in the center of the room stood a black leather couch, two dolphin chairs, and a glass coffee table. Sonny Jr. walked to the table and took a cigarette from the pack lying there, lit it casually, and approached the tank of stingrays.

I sensed something behind me. Haunting the hallway outside, in his oversize bib of an apron, was the seven-foot Mexican, his dull Frankenstein face looming beyond the top of the doorframe, nearly severed by it. Junior spoke Vietnamese to him and he stepped inside, bowing to do so, and propelled me farther into the room until I was standing by the black couch. He untied his apron and let it wilt onto the floor, then closed the door behind him.

I don't know why it had taken this long for my nerves to kick in, but as soon as the door clicked shut, I clenched my jaw. It struck me that the Mexican spoke three languages, including Vietnamese apparently, and something about this – the fact that he belonged completely to this absurd situation – was both comical and deeply troubling.

I said to Junior, 'Your father has expensive pets.'

'He is not here, Mr Robert,' he replied and ashed into an ashtray he held in his other hand – yet another overly formal mannerism. He gestured at the entire room. 'But I have brought you to meet his fish. You may already know that they are not… particularly legal. This one here' – he pointed at a whiskered creature over two feet long, with a golden, undulating body, glimmering in the light – 'is an Asian arowana. A dragonfish. Very endangered in the wild. They're supposed to bring good luck, keep evil away, bring the family together. Asians always love believing in that. Our clients will pay over ten thousand for a gold one like this.'

He glanced at me for a response. I gave him nothing. His arrogance with all this was confusing, but more than anything it was beginning to annoy me.

He watched the fish intently. 'You've heard of caliche?' he said with his back to me. 'It's a dense bed of calcium carbonate in the desert soil. Harder than concrete. They must often use special drills to remove it. Because of caliche, my father spent a fortune building all this. Being underground, you see, that's very important to him. He comes down here two or three times a week, sometimes for an entire day, to smoke and listen to music, to be alone with his fish, remove himself entirely from the world. For all his flaws, he is a man who values peace.'

'Maybe he just values a nice hiding place.'

'A person can hide anywhere, Mr Robert. Even right out in the open. You do, don't you? How long could you stand it down here, all alone, with nowhere to hide, with no one but you and yourself?'

I took a step toward him and heard the Mexican shuffle his feet behind me. I spoke to Junior's back. 'I've met your fish. Why else have you brought me here?'

He turned around, expelling smoke through his nostrils.

'I have brought you here to tell you a story.' He licked his lips and brushed ash from his breast. 'You see, my father appreciates these fish because they are beautiful and bring him a lot of money. But they also remind him of home – they *bring* home to him. It is the irony, you see, that is valuable: a tiny tropical ocean here in the middle of the desert; all these fish swimming beneath sand. The casinos in this city sell you a similar kind of irony, but what we have here is genuine and real, because it also keeps us who we are.'

'Who you are? You and your pops run a Japanese restaurant.'

'Be quiet, Mr Robert, and listen.'

He put out his cigarette and walked over to take a seat in one of the dolphin chairs. He grabbed a remote off the table and pressed a button and the music faded into the soft purr of the aquarium pumps. Unbuttoning his jacket, leaning forward with his elbows on his knees, he offered me the face of a boy but sounded like an old man.

'Twenty years ago,' he said, 'my parents and I escaped Vietnam by boat. Ninety people in a little fishing boat made for maybe twenty. We were headed for Malaysia. On our sixth night at sea we hit a terrible storm and my mother fell overboard. No one saw it. It was too dark and stormy, and the waters were too violent for anyone to save her anyway. I was seven at the time. I will not bore you with a tragedy. I will only say that her death hardened my father, made him more fearless than he already was.

'In any case, after nine days, our boat finally made it to the refugee camp in Malaysia, on a deserted island off the coast. The first day my father and I were there, a few ruffians in the camp made themselves known to us. My father was once in a gang back in Vietnam and had also fought in the war, so he was not afraid. He ignored them. A week later, one of them stole my rice ration. He slapped me several times, pushed me to the ground, ripped the sack out of my hand. For one last scare, he grabbed my wrist and ran a knife across it, barely cutting the skin. I ran to my father, bawling, and before he said a single word, he too slapped me. Shut me up in an instant.'

Junior peered at his hands for a moment, like he was studying his nails. His sudden sincerity felt real, except I couldn't locate its purpose.

He went on: 'He took me by the arm and dragged me to the part of the camp where the ruffians hung out, near the edge of the forest. There was hardly anyone around except three young men kneeling and playing dice outside their hut. One of them was the man who had attacked me. My father made me point him out, then had me stand under a palm tree. He ordered me to watch. On a tree stump nearby, someone had butchered an animal and left the bloody cleaver and my father grabbed it and marched up behind the man and kicked him hard in the back of the head. The man fell forward, dazed, and his two friends pounced at my father, but he was already brandishing the cleaver. They backed off. My father grabbed the man by the back of his shirt and dragged him to the tree stump. In one swift motion he placed the man's hand on the stump and threw down the cleaver and hacked off three fingers. The man screamed. Suddenly there were voices around us, faces appearing in doorways, from behind the trees. I heard a woman shriek. The man was kneeling on the ground, stunned and whimpering, clasping his bloody hand to his chest. His fingers – the three middle ones – still lay on the tree stump. His two friends could only stare at them. My father flung the cleaver away and bent down and muttered something in his ear. Then he wiped his own hand on his pants and held mine as we walked back to our shack. We stayed in that camp for three more months before we came to the States. No one ever bothered us again.'

Sonny Jr. stood from the chair and walked over again to the stingrays. He took out the linen napkin and wiped the glass where his finger had pointed at the arowana. 'I still occasionally have dreams about that afternoon,' he said, as if to the fishes. Then he turned to me thoughtfully. 'But I'm not telling you this story so that you'll pity me. I simply want you to understand what kind of man my father is. I want you, in your own way, to respect it. He *will* hurt you, Mr Robert. If he doesn't do it this time, he will find you some other time and hurt you then. No matter what.

'So please, think of this conversation – this situation between us – as an exchange of trust. I have brought you down here, an officer of the law, to see my father's illegal business. This rather foolish gesture should convince you of my good intentions. Please trust that I am trying to help you. I'm offering you the door now and trusting *you* to forget your plans in this city, to go home and not say a word of what you have seen. A man of your sentiments should appreciate the sincerity of this offer.'

I watched him neatly fold the napkin and place it back in his pocket. His fastidiousness seemed overdone, just like his words. He'd both shown me his hand and told me how to play mine, but it all still smelled like a bluff. The kid knew he was smart, and in my experience if you let people think they're smarter, they'll try a little less to outsmart you. Easier said than done though.

I walked over to the couch and sat down. I hadn't smoked since Suzy left me – another part of my detox plan, since smoking together was one of the few things we never stopped doing. But now I took a cigarette from the pack and lit up.

I squinted up at him. 'Why do you want so badly to help me?' I said. 'Is it really me you're protecting? Or is it your father? Because somehow I feel he's no longer the hard man you say he is. Maybe never was. And I'm guessing maybe you made up that dramatic little story just to scare me. But even if it's true, I've dealt with scarier people. Now why you've chosen to show me all this fish stuff is still a mystery to me – though I'd wager you just like getting off on your own smarts and impressing people. You've either read too many books or listened to people who've read too many books. Either way, it's not my fault that I can't understand half the things you say. But what I do understand is this…' I leaned forward on the couch. 'Your father is a thug. Not only that, he's a coward. He threw a woman down the stairs and broke her arm. Who knows what else he did or could've done or might do in the future, but men like him only have the guts to do that to a woman. You're a smart boy. You know I'm right. He's your father and you want to protect him. That's fine. It's admirable. But my business with him has nothing to do with you.'

I stood from the couch and walked around the table, stopping a few yards from him. 'I'd tell you to fuck off, but that would be rude. I *will* say that I have police buddies who know exactly where I am and who your father is, and if I don't say hi to them next week, they'll know where to come find me.' I took a long drag from the cigarette, flicked it on the ground. 'I want to speak with your father. That's it. All the rest of this doesn't mean a whole lot of shit to me.'

Junior glared at my cigarette on the floor, still curling smoke, then at me. I couldn't tell if he believed me or saw through my empty threat. From behind him, the stingrays swam languidly around his thin, stiff figure like a flock of vultures.

His eyes looked past me and he nodded and before I could turn I felt the Mexican's meaty arms clasp around me, crushing my chest so I could hardly breathe. My feet left the floor, my body seeming to spin like the ceiling fans above me, and I felt a fumbling at my ankle holster and soon saw Sonny Jr. with my five-shot, which he deposited in his jacket pocket. He said something in Vietnamese, and the Mexican shoved me to the floor, forcing me flat onto my stomach. With his knee digging into my lower back, he twisted one of my arms behind my shoulder and held the other to the floor before my flattened face. I could do nothing but grunt beneath him, a doll in his hands, the tile floor numbing my cheek.

I looked up and Sonny Jr. had taken off his jacket. From his pant pocket, he now pulled out a switchblade, which he opened. The Mexican wrenched my extended forearm so that my wrist was exposed. Junior kneeled and planted his shoe on my palm. He steadied the blade across my wrist.

'Wait!' I gasped. I struggled but could hardly budge under the Mexican and his boulder of a knee.

Junior slowly dragged the blade. I could feel its icy

sharpness slice the surface of my skin. It was like a crawling itch, not yet painful, but my jaw clenched so tightly that it ached. He lifted his shoe. A line of blood appeared across my wrist, swelled.

I suddenly saw Junior's open palm beside my face. He pulled back his sleeve and revealed the thin pale scar, like a bracelet, around his wrist.

'You and I,' he murmured, 'now share something.'

He wiped the blade twice on my sleeve, closed it, and returned it to his pocket. He stood and I could no longer see his face, but his voice came out bitter and hard, like he was shaking his head at me:

'I know exactly who you are, Mr Robert. The minute you arrived at our door, I knew. You are a man who has nothing to lose. But that does not make you brave, it makes you stupid. Happy told me you were a foolish man. What were you going to do – kill my father? Break his arm? *Yell* at him? Everything I have told you is true, and I meant every sentiment. Yet you are too sentimental to listen. You want to come here and be a hero and save your former wife from a bad man. You want to know how he has hurt her, and why. But in the end, the only thing you *really* want is to know why she would leave you for slapping her and then stay with a man who threw her down a staircase.'

The cut on my wrist was deeper than I had thought. I could feel the sting sharpening, the skin breaking as I bent my wrist and blood dribbled down my arm.

Junior's shoes reappeared before my eyes, a foot from my nose. He was now speaking directly over my head like he was ready to spit on it.

'Do you know why fish swim in schools? To protect

themselves. To move more easily. To find food and a mate. Now who do they choose to swim with? Their own kind, those they resemble most. Why do you think nearly every casino dealer in this city is Asian, and nearly every Asian dealer is Vietnamese? Because we enjoy cards and colorful chips? *No.* Because we flock to each other. We flock to where there are many of us – so that we will belong and survive. It is a very simple reality, Mr Robert. A primal reality.'

He bent down, speaking closer to my ear. 'What made you think she ever belonged to you? Or that *you* ever belonged with her? You call her Suzy, but her name is Hong. It has always been and always will be Hong. America, Mr Robert, is not the melting pot you Americans like to say it is. It's oil and water. Things get stirred, sure, but they eventually separate and settle, and the like things always go back to each other. They've made new friends, perhaps even fucked them. But in their heart they will always return to where they belong. Love has absolutely nothing to do with it.'

He sighed loudly and stood back up. 'That's enough. I'm tired of speeches.'

He lifted his shoe above my head and stomped on my hand with the heel.

I screamed out. The Mexican dismounted me. After a long writhing moment I forced myself to sit up. I held my injured hand like a dead bird. I couldn't tell if anything was broken, but my knuckles and fingers felt hot with pain, enough to distract me from my aching shoulder and my wrist, now smeared wet with blood.

Junior pulled out the linen napkin again and tossed it at my feet, then handed the Mexican my gun. He wandered back to the piranha tanks, snug in his jacket again and with his hands in his pockets. As if ordering a child, he said to me, 'If I ever see you again, I will do much worse. You will now go with Menendez here. He will take you back outside. Remember, you have seen nothing here. If necessary, I will hurt my new mother at your expense. I like her, but not that much.'

He nodded, and the Mexican led me out of the room by the arm, gently this time. Junior's voice crooned behind me: 'Go home, Mr Robert. And try to be happy.'

As I held my left hand wrapped in the napkin, the Mexican ushered me to another door, which revealed another staircase, which ascended into an office identical to the last one, except we stepped this time out of a painting of cranes flying over a rice paddy. The office opened into the pet store next door to the restaurant. We walked down the dark aisles, passing the droning aquariums and the birdcages and then the dog pens, where weary shadows stirred inside, their dry whimpers following us to the front entrance. Deep in the store, something squawked irritably.

I was released outside into a rainy, windy night. It was like stepping into another part of the country, far from the desert, near the ocean. I must have looked at Menendez with shock because he said, in a gruff but pleasant voice: 'Monsoon season.'

He handed me my five-shot, closed the door, and I saw his giant shadowy figure fade back into the darkness of the store.

I DROVE DOWN I-15 toward California in soaked clothes. My left hand lay throbbing in my lap, the three broken fingers wrapped tightly in the linen napkin and my wrist bleeding through the cuff of gauze and tape I'd used from my first aid kit. I could still move my thumb and index finger, but they too felt swollen and numb.

It was ten o'clock, half an hour after I left Fuji West. The rain had finally stopped, but on my way out of town I saw two car accidents, one of which appeared deadly: a truck on its side, the other car with no front door, no windshield, a body beneath glistening tarp. I had worked so many of these scenes in my time, and yet that evening they spooked me. In the desert night, rain falls like an ice storm.

I remembered another rainy night many years ago, when I came home from work all drenched and tired and Suzy made me strip down to my underwear and sat me at the dining table with a bowl of hot chicken porridge. As I ate, she stood behind me and hummed one of her sad Vietnamese ballads and dried my hair with a towel. I remember, between spoonfuls, trying to hum along with her.

I had often felt bitter in the moments I loved her most. What Junior said was only partly right. I did come to Vegas to save Suzy. Maybe whisk her away if she'd let me. I'd also had some hazy notion of punishing Sonny, though the farther away I drove from his son's threats, the more I understood that I had actually come to punish Suzy – to give her a reason to regret leaving me. She had stayed all those years only because I was not yet replaceable. She then found a man who would come to hurt her more than I ever could, but at least he felt right to her, in a way I never did. 'How can I be happy with children,' she once said, 'if I've never been happy with anything else?'

Sonny Jr.'s parting words flashed through my mind. What did he know about other people's happiness?

I took the very next exit and turned back toward Vegas, driving in the direction of their house. I had memorized the address, even looked it up on a map before the trip. It took me over an hour. By the time I turned into their neighborhood, the rain was coming down hard again and I could feel my tires slicing through the water on the streets.

Their house was two stories of stucco with a manicured rock garden and two giant palm trees out front. It looked big and warm. All the windows were dark. A red BMW sat in the circular driveway behind the white Toyota Camry I bought Suzy years ago. God knows why she was still driving it, with what he could buy her now.

I parked by the neighbor's curb and approached the side of the house, beneath the palm trees that swayed and thrashed in the wind. The rain fell in sweeping sheets, and I was drenched again within seconds.

On their patio, I saw the same kind of potted cacti that stood on our porch just two years before, except these porcelain pots were much nicer. And also there, like I was staring at the front door of our old house, was a silver cross hanging beneath the peephole.

The cool rain soothed my injured hand. I tightened the wet napkin, then donned the hood of my jacket.

I rang the doorbell and waited, shivering. I didn't know who I wanted to answer, but when the porch light flicked on and the door finally opened, I understood what I wanted to do.

He looked exactly as he did on his driver's license, except shorter than I expected, shorter than both Suzy and his son. He was wearing a tight white T-shirt and blue pajama bottoms, his arms tan and muscular, his mustache underlining the furrows of curiosity and annoyance on his face.

'Yeah?' he muttered sleepily and ran a hand over the hard, bald contours of his scalp.

I raised my gun. He snapped his head back and froze. He was looking at me, not the gun. There was a stubborn quality in his expression, like he'd had a gun in his face before, like he was trying to decide if he should be afraid or not.

'Open the door and raise your hands above your head,' I said. 'Then back up slowly until I tell you to stop.'

He obeyed and withdrew into the foyer, then farther into the living room as I followed him inside, leaving some distance between us. I left the front door open, and the porch light spilled into the darkness.

I turned on a small lamp by the wall and another one next to the couch, which flushed the room with a warm light that did not quite reach the high ceilings or the darkness of the open rooms behind Sonny, but it was enough to get my bearings.

Their house was furnished with all the fancy stuff required of a wealthy, middle-aged couple: the big-screen TV, the lavish stereo system, the large aquarium by the foot of the staircase. It was hard not to notice the tall wooden crucifix above the fireplace and the vases on every table, filled with snapdragons and spider mums, oriental lilies, bluebells and gladioli. I had learned all their names over the years.

Rain was drumming the roof above us. I must have

been a sight to him: pale and hooded, one hand swathed in bandages and the other wielding a gun, a stranger dripping water onto his wife's pristine white carpet. She used to yell at me just for wearing shoes in the house.

I caught a whiff of shrimp paste in the air, that nostalgic smell I would forever link to the Vietnamese.

'What you want?' He spoke in a quiet but strained voice. 'You want money, my wallet right there.'

He nodded at the table beside me, where his wallet lay by the telephone and some car keys. Behind the phone stood a photo of him and Suzy on a beach, in front of waters bluer than I'd ever swum.

'I got no other money in the house.'

His was a voice that liked being loud, that liked dancing around its listener. I could tell it took him some effort not to fling his words at me.

With the free thumb of my injured hand, I managed to pull the receiver off the phone and leave it face up on the table. 'Anyone else in the house?'

'Nobody here.'

'Nobody? Your wife – where's she?'

I could see him about to shake his head, like he was ready to deny having a wife, before he realized that he had all but pointed out the photo.

'She not here. She sleep at her mother house tonight. Just me.'

'I see two cars in the driveway.'

'What do that matter? I tell you it just me here tonight.'

'So if I make you take me upstairs, I won't find anyone there?' He looked stumped, like I had tricked him. He glanced, as if for answers, at the giant crucifix above the fireplace before returning his outrage on me. 'I tell you nobody here,' he growled. 'Take my wallet. My car. Take what you want and go.'

I kept my gun trained on him and walked over to the fireplace. Sure enough, on the mantelpiece, by a rosary and some candles, lay Suzy's red journal. I wondered if Sonny understood or even cared about its contents. The crucifix peered down at us, a contortion of dark anguish on the wall. I tucked the journal into my back pocket.

Sonny's eyes narrowed and he lowered his hands a bit. In the dim light, his shaved head made him look like some ghoulish monk. From the open door, I could hear rain slapping concrete, a violent sound.

'Tell you what,' I said, 'I'm gonna let you go. Walk out the front door. Call for help if you want.'

He threw me a baffled scowl.

'Go on. If no one's here, then you have nothing to worry about.'

Now his hands fell. 'What this shit, man? Who are you?'

I took a step toward him, and he slowly raised his hands again without adjusting his glare on me.

'Last chance,' I said.

'I'm not go anywhere, man.'

There was a calm now in the flimsy way he held up his hands, like I was an annoying child with a toy gun. He was ready to fight to the death. He didn't know, though, that he'd already won. He'd passed the test. Except how many more times would he save her like tonight? And what did that prove anyway?

I glanced up the stairs, at the dark hallway of doors at the top, wondering which room was their bedroom, which room might she be sleeping in, which door might she be standing behind right now, cupping her ear to the wood, holding her breath. A heaviness fell over me, like I no longer recognized that shrimp paste smell in the air or any of the outlandish flowers in this strange house – but I shook off the feeling.

I'd only glanced away for a second or two, but Sonny had already reached into the adjacent room and reappeared with a kitchen knife in his hand. He moved willfully, almost casually, and was coming at me like he either knew I wouldn't shoot him or didn't care if I did. I stumbled back a few steps, aiming at his chest, but I bumped hard into something and lost my balance, tumbling backward onto the coffee table, which met my back with a crashing thud.

He lunged on top of me, a rock of a man, and I managed somehow to grab his wrist in the crook of my bad hand, holding off the knife as best I could, but his other hand had seized my right wrist, his fingers digging into the bone so hard I thought it would snap and I lost my grip on the gun and it fell to the floor. He was dumb strong but I was still bigger, and growling through my teeth I heaved him off me and he pulled me with him onto the carpet. In our struggle I was able to get enough space between us to knee him in the groin, which knocked the breath out of him and freed my good hand. A glass ashtray from the table lay overturned on the carpet and I grabbed it and struck him across the temple. He grunted and still clawed at my arm, so I struck him a second time and was about to bring down the ashtray again. But he'd gone limp.

My lips were trembling, my mouth dry as I swallowed

that animal urge to crush his head. I snatched the knife from his hand and tossed it across the room.

I got up, backed away. I found my gun on the floor and trained it again on him. For a second, I thought he might be dead. In my fingers, I could still feel the thud of the ashtray on his skull. But he moved a little now, holding the side of his face with one hand.

Part of me was ready to shoot him while the rest of me rummaged through the consequences of walking away. I glanced at the dark staircase and nearly expected Suzy to be standing there, gazing down at me with horror. I hooded myself.

Sonny had raised himself on an elbow. He watched me slink toward the front door, ignoring the blood crawling down the side of his face, his eyes brimming with some unspoken promise. Behind him, in the aquarium, a pair of football-size fish were writhing around in the black water as though awakened by our violence.

I ran out into the rain, stumbling across the gushing lawn and through the surging water in the street to my car. My engine whined to life. As I sped past the house, I glimpsed Sonny standing on their front porch with his fists clenched at his side. I could have sworn a slimmer figure lurked behind him in the dark doorway.

I careened down the slick Vegas streets like an ambulance and passed cars one by one, my windshield wipers yelping back and forth. Only after I'd driven a few miles did I slow down. I turned on the radio. I reentered the highway. My body felt cool, and the rain was soothing on the roof of the car.

My bandaged hand, a claw now, began throbbing again.

I looked at it several times like it was some talisman, amazed that I'd been able to use it. Then I remembered Suzy's red journal in my back pocket and managed to pull it out. Cradled there in my lap, it too seemed miraculous and inexplicably precious. Stolen treasure with no value.

The Strip receded in the distance, a towering shining island in the night. I turned off the radio and let the rain drum in my ears. The night was a tunnel. I drove a steady clip down the highway and thought of nothing and everything all at once.

3

THE KID HELD THE GUN inches from my head, its proximity like a brace on my neck so that I could only stare straight ahead and lock eyes with his partner. They seemed disarmingly calm, my two intruders – and thoughtful, like they had heard what Sonny had said and were now, like their boss, waiting for my response.

When I was six, I watched my father grab my brown terrier by the collar and slam it headfirst against our porch wall. It had pissed on his shoe – this, after a month of him warning me of its messes around the house. It instantly went limp and he held it up and looked at it and walked to our curbside trash can. Hours later we heard scratching at our front door, and there it was, limping sleepily around the welcome mat. I remember the shiver that coursed through me when I saw its small head bobbing in the doorway, the same shiver I felt now as Sonny uttered Suzy's name. I realized that in the last five months, as I tried my best to close every door that led to Las Vegas, I'd been waiting all along to hear bad news about her.

I swallowed to keep my voice steady. 'What do you mean, where is she?'

'I ask *you*. Four days now she been gone. She just disappear?' He said 'disappear' the way an adult would say it to a wide-eyed child. *Poof! In a puff of smoke!*

'Wait,' I said. 'You think I know where she went, or you think I took her? I haven't heard from her since she left Oakland two years ago. Since she left *me*.'

'But you come here to Vegas, right?'

'Look, I heard you hurt her and I had to do something. It was stupid and you can come at me with what you think I deserve. But whatever this is with Suzy, I don't know anything about it. I told you – I haven't said a word to her in over two years.'

'How I know you not lie to me, huh?'

'I got no reason to. I know you think I do, but she left *me*, man. A long time ago.'

I heard ice cubes clinking in a glass, like him finishing off the last of a drink, like he was beginning to believe me.

'Sonny, can you please tell your boy here to point his gun at something else?' I could hear the kid breathing through his nose.

'Don't call me fucking Sonny. Give the phone to him.'

'He said to give you the phone.'

The kid snatched it out of my hand, said 'Yes' in Vietnamese a couple of times, then backed away from me. I had to blink several times, breathe out, like the gun had been a hood over my face.

He handed the phone to his partner, who listened intently without saying a word. A minute later he hung up.

'We're leaving. You're coming with us to Las Vegas.'

'What for?'

He slipped on a pair of black leather gloves, then turned away all of a sudden, seized by hacking coughs. He recovered himself, wiping his mouth with renewed calm. 'Your clothes. Change them.'

The kid was kneeling on the floor, tying his shoelaces with his gun on the carpet beside him. He peered around my apartment, then up at me. 'This a sad place, man. Not even a Christmas tree?'

IT WAS DARK by the time we got on the 580 going south, toward Vegas. As I sat in the backseat of a morbidly tinted Lexus with the kid beside me and his partner driving in front, I felt more a guest than a captive. No guns pointed at me, my hands free, the car doors unlocked. It was like I had asked them for a ride. Their remaining gesture at seriousness was their silence, though the kid was soon singing under his breath, tapping his fingers to some beat in his head.

It dawned on me that I'd been spared for the last five months – that Sonny had known all along who I was and where I lived and for some reason had decided to do nothing, because whatever this was now, whatever he was planning for me, it didn't smell of him settling a score. What actually troubled me was that he was dangling Suzy over my head, certain that I'd be desperate to find out what happened to her, that if my escorts had stopped the car and let me out, I would have climbed right back in.

Around midnight, we stopped at a McDonald's drive-through by the highway. For the first time since we left, the quiet one spoke, regarding me in the rearview mirror. 'You eat meat?'

I watched him order for us, the way he passed the kid his food without asking him what he wanted.

'You're all brothers, aren't you?' I asked the kid.

He stopped smacking his food and checked for a reaction from his partner up front.

'You old enough to drink?' I continued.

'Hey, man, I'll be twenty-three in December.'

'And he's the oldest, right? What, twenty-five?'

He looked away, chuckling like he didn't care, and stuffed his mouth with some fries. In the rearview mirror, his brother was ignoring us, driving and chewing his food evenly.

'Behind us,' I said, gesturing at the third brother trailing us in my Chrysler, the one who had handed me the note in the parking lot. 'He's younger than you both. Looks like he got his driver's license last week.'

The kid made a face. 'Come on, man, we don't look that much alike.'

'You don't need to. I can still tell.'

He tried to suss out my meaning, his grin a defensive one now. He couldn't see what I saw: the older brother's authority, unquestioned, almost paternal. It was a right of kinship wielded by Asian siblings, whether they looked alike or not – a right I would have envied had I a brother or sister.

Hours later, as we traveled deep into the night, I was watching him sleep when he opened his eyes, like he'd only been meditating, and stared at the back of his brother's head.

I noticed something in his hand. Before we left my apartment in Oakland, they had me call the station and leave a message for my sergeant, explaining only that I would be out of town indefinitely for a family emergency. Then they made me pack a small duffel bag and change into civilian clothing. Before we left, they took one of my credit cards and also my badge, which I could now see in the kid's palm. He was caressing it slowly with his thumb.

He peered at me. 'How many people've you killed, Mr Officer?'

'I've lost count.'

'Come on, you ain't young. How you be a cop in Oakland for so long and not kill nobody?'

'We don't *kill* people. We defend ourselves when necessary and sometimes people die. It's part of the job. It's not exactly intentional.'

'Man, it's intentional if you killing them before they kill you.'

'All right. If that's how you want to see it.'

'So come on, how many you shot? How many you killed?'

'I've never killed anyone. You look disappointed.'

'No one, huh? But I bet you wanted some of them bitches to die, right?'

There was a vulgar sincerity in the way he kept nodding at me as though, despite the difference between us in age and profession, we shared some secret affinity because of the hardware we carried.

'Sure, I wanted a few assholes to not make it. Do I have to give you a number? Tell me yours.'

He looked up as if sifting through his memory. 'Shit, I –' His brother snapped at him in Vietnamese, three or four clipped words and a glare in the rearview mirror, his sudden scowl as startling as his tone. The kid fell silent and sheepishly turned to the window.

The brother glanced at me before returning his eyes to the road, as if returning to a reverie, as if the night saddened him.

IT WAS DAYLIGHT when I awoke, with the kid driving now and the brother seated next to me, facing the window. His coughing had awoken me, but the car was coasting in funereal silence. I sat up and saw that we'd arrived in Vegas, crawling along I-15 in early-morning traffic. Still following us, nearly riding our rear bumper, was the youngest brother in my Chrysler.

I yawned, and this time it was the kid glancing back in the rearview mirror.

I said, 'Your baby brother been driving all night long?'

'Don't worry, he's a fucking vampire. He doesn't sleep till the sun's out. We drop you off, and his ass is going to bed.'

'And where are you dropping me off?'

'You think I know?'

Next to me, the eldest brother lit a cigarette and massaged his cropped hair as he gazed out the window, cut off in his own quiet like he was the only person in the car. I could tell that he rarely concerned himself with any of his brother's white noise. He rolled down his window halfway and ushered in the buzz of traffic and a frigid morning breeze. It had slipped my mind that winter comes to the desert. I put on the rumpled jacket I had used as a pillow. The car was so darkly tinted that the white light from his open window looked alien to my bleary eyes, the color of emptiness.

I asked him for a cigarette and he obliged, lighting it for me without a word, without meeting my eye. The quiet ones do this. They exert control by giving nothing out, and it's this blankness that makes them unpredictable, as dangerous as the loud ones are obvious. But this kid's silence also made him somehow genuine. The one person so far who wasn't *trying*.

I opened my window and zipped up my jacket, blew smoke into the harsh light. The one time I'd smoked since Suzy left was that last time here with Sonny Jr. But it soothed me now, as it used to in the morning, back when I'd smoke a pack and a half a day, starting with the one I'd put to my lips the moment I got out of bed: before I brushed my teeth or even looked at myself in the mirror, standing by the bedroom window and slowly waking myself in the sunlight, amid the drifting curling smoke, those five minutes like a silent prayer to prepare myself for whatever the day might bring. Suzy sometimes joined me by the window. We'd share the cigarette.

I realized now why I had quit. It wasn't to get healthy. And it was only partially to rid myself of the nostalgia for my old habits with her. I was at work the day she left the house; she took all her clothes and only the possessions she had acquired before we met, which amounted to some Vietnamese music cassettes, a few books, and a collection of small framed watercolor paintings of Vietnam landscapes. And of course the red journal. Everything else remained: our furniture, the jewelry I'd bought her, all our photographs together, framed and unframed. I came home that evening to a fully furnished house that felt as empty as her half of the bedroom closet. To my surprise, her crucifixes still hung on the walls and her porcelain figurines – the various Jesuses and Virgin Marys and Saints this and that – still peopled the shelves, as if in knowing my resistance to religion she had purposefully left God's presence to save me. Or mock me. I found myself sinking into the sofa and not quite believing that she'd actually gone through with it, abandoned me. I remember smoking a cigarette on the front porch that night, watching the fog amble in from the bay, and deciding that after a carton a week for three decades – since I was fourteen, for God's sake – *that* cigarette would be my last one. I was quitting not because I wanted or needed to, and definitely not because I thought it would be easy. I was quitting to punish myself.

We were approaching the southern end of the Strip. As the brother lit up another cigarette, I flicked mine out the window and gazed at the mountain range of hotels that bordered the highway. At night, I remembered, amid giant digital screens flashing promises and exaltations, these same hotels towered over the city like monuments, some with mirrored walls that – as you traveled past them – trembled in the wash of glitter and dancing light, as though the city were too alive, too troubled with hope, ever to fall asleep.

But now, in the desert dawn, there was a lifelessness to the way the valley's light fell across the Strip and to how the shadows pooled beneath the hotels like melted paint. Framed by the Martian mountains in the distance, the Strip looked like an artist's rendering of some alien civilization, with buildings erected from every culture and time in history, every possible mood, and with no consistency save their garishness and size. In the daylight, everything looked faraway, out of reach. If people came here to lose themselves, did they ever come to find anything?

As traffic picked up, I closed my window and let its tint darken Vegas once more. I wondered then if peace was a thing that one achieved or that one could only be given.

Last time I took this road, I felt like I'd just escaped a burning house that I'd ignited in the night, that had singed my backside and sent me fleeing my own shadow. I didn't understand it then, but I admitted it to myself now: I had wanted all along to kill Sonny. There was no logic or morality behind it. Just an overwhelming desire to *do* something to him, at least hurt him badly, and maybe then things would feel right again. Except they never did, because they never do, not for people like me. I was back on the highway, steering blind, hoping for a clear path beyond the horizon.

This had become my life since Suzy left: a constant fumbling toward peace that lies only and always in the distance.

4

WE TOOK THE HIGHWAY SOUTH of the Strip until the city turned into a succession of clay tile roofs and stuccoed strip malls lined with palm trees. It was typical suburbia, distinguished by a pervading newness as bright as the sunlight. You could almost smell the sawdust and drying paint.

We approached a large park. Softball fields and basketball courts. Picnic tables. More trees and shade than I'd seen anywhere in the city so far. By the entrance, crowning the treetops, a giant digital screen flashed the words SUNSET PARK! HAPPY HOLIDAYS!

After some distance inside the park, we appeared to reach its end at a gravel lot that yawned into a vast desert of brush and dirt mounds. We parked. The brothers got me out. We were still deep in the suburbs, but this felt like the edge of the city, the point where it surrendered itself entirely to sand and dust and silent sunlight and people vanish by simply walking into the distance. A few lonely cars peppered the lot. My Chrysler was not among them. For the first time since leaving Oakland, I regretted ever getting out of that car.

But I only had to turn around to see life again: the tops of pine trees ahead and then, as we mounted a short grassy hill, the enormous pond that glistened beyond them.

It was like stumbling upon a man-made oasis, burnished gold in sunlight. The pond was around fifteen acres, its grassy banks dropping over a short brick wall that encircled the waters like the coping of a swimming pool. A few people sat at picnic tables bundled in their coats beneath shady pines, watching the ducks, the pigeons flapping about like seagulls, the toy boats buzz-sawing across the glimmering water.

As my two escorts scanned the area, I spotted the small island at the center of the pond, a mirage within a mirage, adorned with a giant Easter Island head that loomed out of a grove of palm trees.

The older brother pointed at someone in the distance. As they flanked me, we walked toward a chestnut tree with a large branch overhanging the water. Beneath the tree, wrapped in a dark coat, sat a hooded figure in one of two lawn chairs. He held a fishing rod in his lap, its line in the water. I wondered if Sonny was a man who ate the fish he caught or threw them back.

As we came closer, the figure turned his head, and I realized it wasn't Sonny at all. Even under the hood, Junior's angular, elegant face was easily recognizable. His expression did not change when he saw me. He just sucked at his cigarette and returned his attention to the pond. His father was nowhere in sight, and I couldn't decide if that relieved or disappointed me.

With my two escorts hanging back, I approached the empty lawn chair beside him, stepping into the shadow of the chestnut tree.

'Please have a seat,' Junior said without turning to me. He was wearing a long black duffel coat and leather gloves, holding the fishing rod indifferently in one hand and smoking with the other. As stoic as a mannequin.

He called out something in Vietnamese to the brothers. The older one approached him and said, 'Are you sure?' Junior gave him a look. Without another word, the two brothers made their way down the sidewalk that skirted the pond.

Junior peered at me now with raised eyebrows. I could see my own awkwardness in his calm, dignified demeanor. It reminded me of my first and only time going to confession, at Suzy's request, and not knowing what was too sinful to divulge to the priest and what was not sinful enough.

'It's good to see you again,' he said.

'Is it?'

'It is. So long as you cooperate this time.'

'I don't know anything about Suzy.'

'I know.'

'Does your father know it?'

'We both know it now. We had to be sure first.'

'About what? That I wasn't hiding her? That I hadn't stolen her back?'

'Given your last visit, we thought anything was possible.'

A moment passed before I realized I was silent out of shame. My recklessness months ago had cost me the right to be above suspicion in anyone's eyes, least of all theirs.

'So why am I here now? Is it penance you want?'

Junior unhooded himself. His pale skin was flawless, his hair slicked back, not a strand out of place. Such symmetry seemed to sharpen his admonishing air.

He said, 'I am here today in my father's place because I insisted on it. Because I know he is a man who remembers everything and forgives nothing. You should be glad to see me, Mr Robert. And you should be grateful – to my father and to me – that up until now you have been shown some mercy. Do you understand?'

He noticed my left hand, which I'd been absently clenching and unclenching.

'Of course I do,' I said, more meekly than I wanted to. If I had been spared, I doubted that kindness was behind it. Still, Junior's tone confused me. It struck me that his most inscrutable habit was his insistence on his own sincerity. Like last time, I found it difficult to trust, but even more difficult to dismiss.

I searched along the banks, the picnic tables, the random vague figures who might resemble his father, watching us from a distance. About fifty yards away, the brothers sat smoking on a bench with their sunglasses and their obviousness trained on us.

'Listen,' I said to Junior. 'I respect everything you're saying. Believe me, this situation between me and your father, between me and you – none of that's lost on me. But you guys've had a gun to my head for a day now. Someone needs to either shoot me or explain what the hell's going on.'

Junior reached down and stubbed out his cigarette in the dirt. He took off his gloves, dropped them in his lap like he was ready at last to speak truthfully.

'Miss Hong disappeared four days ago. The last time my father saw her was Saturday night when she was sleeping in bed. Sunday morning, she was gone. As you must know, she never misses Sunday Mass for anything. She took her car and her purse and left everything else. Her clothes, jewelry, books, everything. She and my father have had their problems, and she's had her reasons for leaving in the past. But nothing explains her leaving like this.'

He looked at me like I had contradicted him. 'Understand something, Mr Robert – my father has made mistakes, some much worse than others. But he loves Miss Hong more than anyone in the world. He wants her back. And he wants you to help him.'

I must have looked sufficiently perplexed because he raised a quelling hand and added, 'We have reason to believe she's still in town, and I'll explain that shortly – but that is why you're here.'

'What makes you think I can help him?'

'Don't be stupid. You know your value to us. You know my father wants nothing to do with the police. The *real* police anyway. What he has is you, and you are in debt to him.'

I felt like telling him his idea of a cop was as real as Dick Tracy, but he reached into his coat pocket and pulled out a photograph, which he handed to me. I tried not to blink. It was a surveillance image of me standing in Sonny's living room with a gun over his prostrate body. The camera must have been hidden on the crucifix and lurking above our heads the entire time. It wasn't a very clear image, but I was unhooded, my face recognizable, teeth bared like a dog's.

Junior took out another cigarette. 'We have the entire video. I'm sure you understand all the implications here. Unlawful restraint. Burglary. Aggravated assault with a deadly weapon. Losing your badge would be the least of your worries.'

He held the unlit cigarette with his thumb and forefinger

like the handle of a teacup, his hands as slender and delicate as a woman's. I felt a sweet, savage urge to shove him into the pond.

I gave him back the photo, but he raised his hand. 'That's yours to keep.'

'You could have hired a private investigator,' I said. 'This is Vegas. Plenty of them here, and you have plenty of money. I'm not a detective anymore. I write traffic tickets, man.'

'Mr Robert… do you really think we brought you here for your professional talents?'

'What if she refuses? Suzy's more stubborn than I am. She wouldn't come back to me, and now you want me to convince her to come back to your father. Maybe it's better that she stay away from him.' I waited a breath for a reaction. 'Why would I let her go back to something she had reasons to leave?'

He leaned back in his chair as if he had anticipated the question. He was still holding the unlit cigarette like a forgotten pen. 'She's been unwell for a year now, especially these past few months. We think this has something to do with her disappearing. It's impossible to know unless we find her. My father – he's afraid she might hurt herself.'

I winced and he saw it. He already knew that I was only too familiar with what he was saying.

'Has she?' I asked. 'Since she's been with your father?'

'He does not always tell me those things. What I do know is that she had an episode two months ago. My father called me in the middle of the night. He's not one to ask for help, but that night he didn't hide his concern. She had gone out walking again. The front door was left wide open and it was raining outside, and her car was still in the garage. He'd been driving around the neighborhood for an hour. I came over at once and we searched for her together on foot. We shined our flashlights in everybody's backyard, calling out her name in the rain. My father was not angry like I had expected. When he's worried, his voice is calm, and he kept calling her with that calm voice.

'Around three in the morning, we found her at the elementary school a few blocks away, sitting on a swing in the playground. She was drenched and barefoot, shivering in her nightgown. It's possible she was drunk. I never got close enough to be sure. As soon as she saw us, she got up and started walking away and ignored our calls. We ran after her. She struggled when my father caught up to her and screamed out a few times before suddenly falling silent. They didn't say a single word to each other. He wrapped her in a raincoat and we walked her home in silence. She was sick in bed for almost a week and said hardly anything to anyone.

'After she got better, she started going to the movies every Thursday evening. She told my father that she just wanted to be alone in a dark theater for a few hours, then maybe have dinner somewhere by herself — that the routine helped her. It turns out she's been visiting this hotel downtown called the Coronado. There's no telling how long she's been making these visits. She checks herself into a room on the twelfth floor, always room 1215. It's reserved every week in her name. She arrives around seven and doesn't leave or even open the door until midnight, when she comes out and makes her way home. My man is positive that the room is empty before her arrival and that she is alone the entire time. For all we know, she naps for those five hours. My father wanted to confront her immediately, but I convinced him to wait, let a few weeks pass, see if something happens that we can't ignore. Until then, what is the difference really between a movie theater and a hotel room? Maybe this was something like church for her. Something she can do every week to feel whole or normal or whatever again.'

Junior had been rolling the cigarette between his fingers and now peered at it as though he didn't know what to do with it. 'I was wrong,' he said. 'It was three weeks ago that we found out about the hotel. Now she's gone. It's partly my fault, I suppose.'

He fell silent for a moment as if reflecting on the accuracy of this confession. I could have believed now that he was sincerely, humbly, asking for my help.

'The truth is, Mr Robert, she will not run away from you if it comes to that – or do anything foolish. You may find that hard to believe, given your history with her, but you're the only person who can do this.'

The confidence with which he spoke of my marriage should have annoyed me, except that it was comforting to hear someone acknowledge what I'd only known as a private regret.

'You also want to find her as much as my father does. He needs someone who will care how this all turns out. Think of him what you will, but he wants no harm to come to her. He wants her back because he wants to take care of her, something you, frankly, never did very well. It might displease you to hear this – but my father knows that Miss Hong still loves him. She has always loved him. Long before she ever met you. Perhaps one day that will all be explained to you.'

He crossed his legs, satisfied that he'd said enough to convince me. He finally lit the cigarette, sighing smugly, and switched the fishing rod to his other hand.

'We checked, and she has again reserved her normal room at the Coronado. Something about that room is important to her, so we're hoping she comes tonight, or sometime today. We booked the room next door under your name and with your credit card. Room 1213. Check-in is at noon, so you should be going shortly. You will wait for her there – until tomorrow, if necessary. If she does come, talk to her. Persuade her to come home. Tell her whatever you need to tell her.

'If you will, consider this a favor. Bring Miss Hong back to my father, and you can go on your way. He'll forget everything, and we never have to see each other again. I'm offering you another deal. Hopefully this time you will accept for her sake, if not your own.'

He offered me a cigarette, his eyes disarmingly warm, conspiratorial. I shook my head, which seemed to disappoint him. He waved the brothers back.

I was still processing everything he had said. In particular, about me not taking care of Suzy, about her knowing Sonny before me, her still loving him. Every time he called her 'Miss Hong,' I felt like clocking him. It didn't matter if he was lying.

A feeling passed close to me then, distressing in a way I could not yet understand, like some shadow of a painful memory flitting past me while I wasn't looking.

Junior's fishing line jerked and his body awoke. He stood

and took hold of the rod expertly with both hands, tugged at the line a couple of times with his cigarette clamped between his lips. He started reeling it in as the brothers approached. The kid rushed over to the bank as Junior's fish burst out of the water, floundering violently, a foot-long trout. As Junior held up the rod, concentration petrifying his face, the kid grabbed the line and then the fish itself. It took him a few seconds, but he took hold of the convulsing trout with both hands, looked over at me, and kissed its belly with an exaggerated smack.

Junior ignored the kid's antics. He gestured for him to unhook the fish and throw it back. 'My father comes here about once a week. It's the only place you can fish in the city, outside of Lake Mead, which isn't a real lake either. They stock this pond with about thirty thousand trout a year. Catfish, too, and bass.'

Junior eyed the shimmering waters. He said, seemingly to himself, 'I have never eaten a single fish I've caught here.'

The kid finally managed to unhook the fish, and it jumped out of his hands and flopped on the ground before tumbling back into the pond. He stared at the rippling water and wiped his hands on his jeans with an infantile smirk.

Junior sat back down and placed the rod on the ground. Beside his chair was a small blue cooler. He reached into it and pulled out a small but bulging manila envelope. He handed it to me and flicked his cigarette into the pond, which drew some glares from fishermen nearby.

I was struck by how openly he was doing all of this, as if no one would find this scene curious, the two brothers in their FBI shades and him in his stylish fishing gear, pulling envelopes out of a cooler like beers. Why, I wondered, were we not having this conversation at his restaurant or some dusty office with the curtains drawn?

'Inside the envelope,' he said, 'you will find a cell phone and five hundred dollars in cash for the room and any expenses you might have. Stay alert. Check Miss Hong's room as often as you can. Stand guard outside if you have to. And keep the phone on you at all times in case I call. The boys here will escort you to the hotel. You will find your car parked on the fourth level of the garage, in lot 4B. I will give you back your keys after this is all over. Just know that it's there, and that despite everything, we *do* want you to drive home on your own.'

'And if she doesn't come?'

'We'll cross that bridge when we get there. For now, start with the hotel room.'

The brothers approached me, my cue to embark on the job I'd been given.

When I stood, Junior gestured at me with yet another unlit cigarette between his fingers. 'My father would not want me telling you this, but you should know that it was Miss Hong who pleaded for you. In fact, she promised him that if he left you alone, she would never leave him. She swore her life on it. For you. That is the only reason my father's men didn't come to your doorstep months ago.'

He lit the cigarette, turned from me, and expelled a profound cloud of smoke into the morning air.

He had spent our first meeting convincing me that I had no business being with Suzy. This time I was the only person who could save her.

That feeling rose in me again, though now I understood what it was, why it distressed me so. The job I'd been given was to be my punishment.

5

THE ENTRANCE TO THE CORONADO HOTEL was canopied by a blanket of lights so brilliant, even at noon, that I imagined it singeing my hair. Two valet attendants, bow ties choking their necks, stood glumly below the raised lance of a giant bronze conquistador who welcomed guests. Like the other casinos downtown, the Coronado revealed its age during the day, with its big-bulbed signs flashing sixties glamour, its flat crusty walls a world away from the mirrored splendor on the Strip.

When the brothers dropped me off, the kid handed me my duffel bag of clothes through the car window along with my credit card and my badge, which he pulled out of his own pocket. 'Don't lose yourself, Mr Officer,' he said. 'We'll find you.' He winked at me as the tinted window swallowed up his face. Slowly, their hearse of a Lexus rolled down the street.

I walked at once to the parking garage where my Chrysler, as promised, stood pristinely in lot 4B. I checked the undercarriage and could find nothing suspicious. To my surprise, the door was unlocked. Inside, my Glock lay where I'd left it in the glove compartment, and my backup fiveshot was still nestled comfortably in its holster beneath the driver's seat. Except for the seat having been adjusted for its recent driver, everything else seemed normal. I pocketed the Glock after checking the clip.

At the registration desk, I waited in line behind an overweight family besieged by luggage and cigarette smoke, the two parents puffing away as their three snickering sons took turns punching each other in the arm. Twenty minutes later I reached the desk, which stood before a mural of the two resident shows, some white-haired comedian I vaguely knew and a magic act involving a python and exotic birds. The girl gave me my room, reserved under my full name, and the credit card the brothers had returned to me matched their records. When I asked whether a Hong Thi Pham or a Suzy Ruen had checked in, she claimed she couldn't divulge that information, so I asked for directions to their gift shop. It took me another fifteen minutes to find the shop, the clerk's directions as helpful as a compass in a maze. For about thirty bucks, I bought an obscenely expensive pack of cigarettes, a razor and shaving cream, and some ibuprofen.

'Don't be taking that with alcohol, baby,' the small black lady behind the counter said with an admonishing smile. 'Bad for the tummy.'

I must have looked as worn-out as I felt.

My room was on the twelfth floor and looked clean and inoffensive: a queen bed, a private desk and loveseat, framed prints of Old World maps and Spanish galleons, maroon velvet drapes that covered an entire wall like a theater curtain. There were other stabs at luxury, like the gilt mirror above the bed and the glass doorknobs, but flop down on the stiff mattress and sniff the vague odor of bleach and cigarettes and you knew how many stars the hotel was.

A door connected my room to Suzy's. It seemed fantastical to me, a portal into another world. I tried the knob. It was locked. I knocked several times and heard nothing but the heater blowing in my room.

Next thing I did was place the Glock in the drawer of the nightstand, right on top of the Bible. I went to the notepad on the desk. *Suzy*, I wrote, *I'm next door in room 1213. I'm here to help you. Please let me. Robert.*

I stepped out into the hallway and slid the paper under her door. For a moment, I wondered if it was possible she had forgotten my handwriting.

In the bathroom, the harsh fluorescent lights emitted heat. I shaved, showered, and changed into a pair of jeans and a white button-down shirt that I'd only ever worn to church with Suzy.

I brewed myself a pot of coffee and popped three ibuprofen before sitting down with a cigarette and everything Junior had given me.

The cash in the manila envelope was all new hundred-dollar bills, which I pocketed. The cell phone looked brand-new too, a disposable. I checked the outgoing and incoming calls and saw that the phone had not yet been used.

I looked again at the surveillance image Junior had given me. Seeing it this time, with only myself as judge, reminded me of how enraged and terrified I was that night. How entwined those two emotions could be.

I thought of Junior's story about Suzy and the episodes she used to have with me. Sonny and I, it seemed, shared an affliction. We were in love with Suzy and afraid of her at the same time, and though I'd like to think he and I went to different places once our marriages went bad, I couldn't help wondering where I would have gone had Suzy stayed with me a little longer. I'd arrested plenty of people over the years who had violated restraining orders, who'd hunted down ex-lovers and begged for love with threats, their fists, a gun. At that point there's no difference between a plea and a threat, between loving someone and hurting them. At that point, love doesn't matter.

My parents came to mind, all those years of them openly resenting each other for reasons never explained to me. My father died when I was sixteen, two years after he abandoned my mother for an identical woman: same age and height, same dark curly hair, same everything except she wasn't my mother. When he was dying in the hospital and the cancer in his lungs had muted his once sonorous voice, I asked him why he left her, and he said that love just dies sometimes, and when it does, you can't save it anymore than you can revive a corpse. The words rasped in his throat, but I could still hear his confidence, his certainty. He had never lost it, not for a second. I suppose I had always admired him for this trait. Everything else about him was cold and cruel.

I thought again of all the reasons Suzy had to leave me and wondered how many Sonny had given her.

One thing I was sure of: when and if I found her, delivering her was out of the question. They couldn't possibly expect me to discover the real reasons why she left, as I surely would, and then just hand her over like a lost puppy. I suspected Junior already anticipated I'd feel this way, which unsettled me all the more. Why would he give me the chance to disobey him yet again?

Other half-formed questions flitted through my head. I

dropped my cigarette in the coffee just to hear the satisfying hiss.

On the room telephone, I dialed Tommy, my old partner during my time in narcotics. He was a lieutenant now and had been working homicide for the last decade. Before I met Suzy, we used to go out drinking and I'd spend all night watching him start fights and chase ass. Nowadays he played the devoted husband and father, something he once drunkenly swore he'd never do, not even if life put a gun to his head.

'Yeah?' his dull voice muttered over the line. His idea of answering the phone was to communicate his displeasure at being called.

'Tommy. It's me.'

'Where've you been hiding? You were MIA at Laura's birthday a few weeks ago.'

'I know, I'm sorry. I still have her present, actually. I'll give it to you next time I see you.'

'Uh-huh.'

'I got a favor to ask. That call you put in for me to Vegas Metro six months back? On a Sonny Van Nguyen? I need a narrative on one of his assault charges. Incident at a casino. He threw a chair at some guy.'

'This again?'

'It's N-G-U –'

'I know how to spell *Nguyen*, Bob. We live in California, for fuck's sake.'

'Two more things. Can you run a tag for me?' I read him the plate for Suzy's Toyota. 'I'm also curious about priors on 2121 E. Warm Springs Road, 89119. Anything in the last six months.'

'Jesus, you running a federal investigation?'

'Just some questions that need answering. You still have that Vegas contact, right?'

'You know, man, if you want to play detective, just apply to be one again.'

'Look, I know you're busy, but if you can do this asap for me, I'll owe you forever. I'll call you back in an hour.'

'Yeah, yeah. Get out of the house, man. Go visit an old friend. Call him for something other than a favor.'

He hung up. Peevish and sensitive as always. I hadn't told anyone yet about Suzy moving to Vegas and remarrying. But Tommy knew something was up. He knew five months ago and either didn't want to pry or didn't care enough to. Probably the latter. The world is full of people who care but never quite care enough.

It was half past noon. How many hours would I have to wait? How many was I willing to wait? I tried to imagine Suzy's face once she saw me. *I'm here to help you*, I'd say and put up my hands like someone surrendering, like I'd always done at some point in our arguments. *I have money saved*, I'd say. *We can jump in a taxi and get out of town, away from this desert, back to California and back to the ocean, and then we can go wherever you want to go and forget everything that happened here and you won't have to say a single thing to me except yes I'll go with you.* Was this what she had wanted to hear all those years ago? Could she already be there next door, sitting in an identical room, on an identical bed, staring – as I was – at the door that separated our adjoined rooms?

I fell back on the bed, letting my head sink into the pillows. Some faraway sound startled me awake an hour later. I jumped out of bed and went to the adjoining door and tried knocking a few more times. I put my ear to the door, as though waiting for an echo.

A glass of water cleared my head a bit, and I called Tommy back.

'Yeah, I got your info,' he said, his voice less irritable now. 'No priors on the address you gave me. And no activity on the tag. Sorry if that disappoints you. That casino incident, however, is a little less boring.'

'Go ahead.'

I heard him sip some hot coffee while a baby started crying in the background. I'd caught him on his day off. He was probably still in his pajamas and sitting in his kitchen with the morning newspaper. I could see Laura sitting across from him, trying to nurse the baby.

'Looks like your guy Nguyen was playing poker downtown two years ago and got into an argument with another player at the table. White twentysomething male who tossed a hundred-dollar chip at his chest and called him a Chinaman. Very creative. Anyway, Nguyen went at the kid and tried to strangle him. Kid had fifty pounds on him but apparently didn't fare very well. Casino security rushed in to break things up and managed to pry Nguyen off him, but he got loose and picked up a chair and flung it at the kid's head. Knocked him out cold. Kid was fine but suffered a mild concussion, cut to the head, bruises to the neck. Your guy was held by security until Vegas Metro came and arrested him.'

'The casino blacklist him? Which one was it?'

'Let's see...' I could hear him flipping through his notes. 'The Coronado. I've been there actually. Years ago. One of those old downtown joints on Fremont Street. Ain't no models waitressing there. And yeah, he got himself a criminal trespass. Immediate arrest if seen on the premises. That goes the same, by the way, for his son.'

'His son?'

'Yeah. A Jonathan Van Nguyen. Twenty-eight years old. Runs his daddy's restaurants. He showed up during the melee and tangled with security. One of the reasons his father got free and was able to throw the chair. The casino didn't press any charges on the son, but they did ban the both of them. Anyway, Nguyen Senior pled out and got two years' probation, which actually expires in three months. I doubt he wants to make trouble any time soon. If he's been throwing chairs at people lately, he's probably doing it in private.'

Tommy let my silence go for a few seconds before saying, 'Exciting enough for you?'

'That's what I needed.'

'Sure that's all you need?'

'Of course.'

'Should I be asking *you* anything?'

'Sounds like you already are. I'm just curious about the guy.'

'Uh-huh.' I could hear him nodding doubtfully at me. 'We should have a drink at McGee's next week. I'm off Wednesday night. You free?'

'I'll call you. Thanks again, man. Really.'

'Bob…' he said soberly. 'Call me, right?'

'Of course.' I hung up.

I took a swig of cold coffee but spat it back into the cup, retching a little as I smelled the cigarette still floating there. I rinsed the cup and my mouth in the sink, then poured myself a new cup. I downed it in three gulps.

I put on my jacket and stuffed its pockets with the cell phone, the surveillance photo, and my badge, which now felt unfamiliar and useless.

In the hallway, I knocked on 1215 and waited five seconds before moving on.

The hotel was lined with mirrors: along the hallway, in the elevators, across the walls of the casino floor, which appeared much bigger and deeper than it really was. I saw myself everywhere I walked. I saw every person multiplied, refracted like a kaleidoscope of faces and bodies, a constant illusion of life so that this place never felt empty, even when it was.

I wandered through the throng of afternoon gamblers, hunched over table games amid a cigarette haze, the air alive with their chatter and the melodic jangling of slot machines. Nearly every dealer I passed was Chinese, Filipino, Vietnamese – just as Junior had said. I wondered how many of them had actually come from somewhere far away, and how many were right at home.

The poker room stood in a lonely corner of the casino – an open space sectioned off by a wooden rail. A few onlookers were leaning on the rail and watching the action. Only half of the eight tables were occupied at the moment, populated by college-age dudes in baseball caps and sunglasses, their white-haired elders in plaid and khakis, and the solitary middle-aged woman with her purse in her lap. The place was like some sad foodless cafeteria, fluorescent lights shining down on worn green felt and flimsy chairs, on pale faces staring hungrily at one another behind their towers of poker chips. Sonny must have spent hours on end at these tables, drinking coffee and cheap booze, stepping outside the rail every half hour for a smoke break. Hardly the high roller I had imagined.

I took a seat at the bar nearby and ordered myself a beer and lit a cigarette. For the first time since pulling up to my apartment the previous night, I felt at ease. Neither Sonny nor his son could touch me here. At least not yet. What gave me pause was that Suzy had apparently chosen this place with the same thing in mind. She must have had a very good reason for not wanting to be found, for holing up every week in the one place in town that could protect her.

The bartender served me my beer. 'Got the good juice tonight, brother?' He had slicked grayish hair and a sincere Latin accent. He wore his maroon vest and bow tie as proudly as a soldier.

'Don't gamble.'

'Smart man then.'

'Not smart. Just unlucky.'

'Everybody think they unlucky. Even lucky people say they unlucky.'

'We all complain, don't we?'

'Not me, brother. Vegas been good to me.'

I nodded for him and his stubbornly winning smile. 'Anything exciting ever happen over there?'

'The poker room? What you mean, *exciting*?'

'I don't know – people getting into fights. Getting thrown out.'

He looked over at the room and shrugged, rummaging through his Rolodex of memories with his hands on the bar. 'Nah, I don't remember nothing like that. People lose and yell at each other, yeah. Sometime they come over here and yell at me too.'

'No one ever gets caught cheating or anything?'

'Nah. Other gamblers, sure, but not poker players. I been working at casinos in Cali and Reno too. Poker players are honest, brother. They wanna win your money, not steal it. They too smart and proud for that, know what I mean?'

'I guess I've watched too many Westerns.'

He chuckled. 'I from Columbia. People bring guns to go gamble. Here in Vegas – people cheat you, but they cheat you honestly.' He let that sink in, then patted the bar genially as he walked off to see to another customer. He was a service provider indeed. How often did desperation trudge up to his bar and beg for a drink and a dose of his ready optimism?

A tapping noise made me turn my head. Nearby, an obese guy in an oversize T-shirt sat between two slot machines, a plastic bucket of coins in his lap and a hand on each machine, tapping them like tribal drums. Every now and then, he stopped to wipe his face with a towel. I wondered if he knew it was daylight outside.

Around me, the air felt artificial. Time was artificial here too. No windows or clocks. No sense of progression outside of what you gain and what you lose. That thought made me anxious, like hours had passed without me knowing it.

I finished my drink and left a tip for the bartender and pulled out another cigarette for the long walk to the elevator.

Back in my room, I turned on the TV and stretched out on the bed with my shoes on. It was a little past two. I realized I hadn't eaten since the highway stop at McDonald's the night before. I muted the TV, perused the room-service menu, and reached for the phone. A woman's voice greeted me. But I hung up on her.

A door had opened in the next room.

I grabbed an empty glass off the nightstand and rushed to put it against the adjoining door. Nothing but silence for a long time. Then a door clicked shut. Was someone arriving or leaving? I stepped out into the empty hallway. I went to put my ear against 1215.

My first knock was gentle. The knock a maid would make. After some moments, I knocked again, louder this time but still polite. I could feel her standing behind the other side of the door.

'Suzy?' I said, leaning in. 'It's me. It's Robert. Please open the door.'

I took a step back so that I could stand in full view of the peep hole. I would have stood there for hours if I had to. But then the knob turned.

The door opened halfway, revealing the face of a young woman who stood partly behind it, staring out at me, cautious but unafraid. She was Vietnamese, in her early twenties, and wore faded jeans, cowboy boots, and a tight brown leather jacket zipped all the way up like she'd just come in from the cold. No jewelry and no makeup, though she needed neither.

Her boyishly cropped hair muted the resemblance at first, but it was impossible not to recognize the cheekbones and the dark glaring eyes, the shade of familiar stubbornness there. She even had the same long, proud neck, that way of holding up her chin like she was ready to stand her ground against anything. I felt a childish urge to blink and see if she'd disappear, wave my hand in front of her so that something might change.

But my eyes did not lie. Suzy stood there before me, twenty years younger, both something found and something I had lost.

'Who're you?' she said. 'And who is Suzy?'

PART TWO

On our second night at sea, you disappeared. I awoke and found your shorts by my side and had to keep from screaming your name. Where could you have gone with all the sleeping bodies around us? I'd seen a few mothers tie string from their wrists to their child's wrists, and I cursed myself for my laziness.

Then I saw you, and it was like seeing a ghost. You were outside the boat looking in, calmly holding on to the gunwale as though you were ready to let go, as though you were levitating. I grabbed your arms and hauled you back inside. You were naked from the waist down. I looked over the gunwale and realized that you had been squatting over the sea, balanced on some wooden trim along the side of the boat, all to avoid the boat's latrine, which apparently frightened you more than falling into the sea.

You flinched when I touched your cheek. I must have been glaring at you as if I was ready to spank you. But my heart was pounding. If you had fallen overboard, no one could have known. The night would have swallowed you whole. Your presence now seemed such a miracle that I was overcome with shame at having ever wished you away. I loved you more in that moment than at any other moment in your life. I cradled your head, smoothed your brow, and wondered what had possessed me those last few days. Don't ever do that again, I told you, but I was saying it to myself. I held you fast until you slept and did not close my eyes until images of your death faded into the night.

There are things that people do poorly for lack of talent, and things they do poorly for lack of desire. Then there are those things that all the desire and talent in the world cannot make possible, cannot make fit, no matter how often you pray and how hard you pretend.

On the day you were born, I lost my voice. Words came out like gasps, and during labor my pain had no sound. The nurse held my hand.

Your father had been gone for five months, vanished without a word, and no one knew if he had fled the country or been imprisoned or if he was even alive.

You must have sensed it. A baby's cries at birth are full of vigor, but yours were weak and willful, a stubborn crying, as though you were already disappointed in me and mourning him.

When I held you for the first time, you refused to nurse. You struggled in my arms and kept crying softly. Even when my voice came back, I found I had nothing to say. I remember a deep, instant love for you that felt like a locked room inside me. It's only now as I write this, as I say these words to myself, that I begin to understand it.

I wonder what you remember of our fifth night, when that strange tragedy began. It was a moonless night, the darkest so far of our trip. A woman began wailing and awoke the entire boat. Where is my son? she shrieked. My son is gone!

The engine stopped and lanterns were lit. People were already looking overboard. Although a few men stood ready to jump into the sea, we all knew there was no sense in it. We had only just stopped the boat, and the calm black waters around us showed no sign of anything. If the boy had fallen in, it was already too late.

People were consoling the mother, restraining her. Like me, she had no one else on the boat but her child.

I remember him. He spent most of the first day retching into a plastic bag as she stroked his hair and patted his back. The yellow stains on his T-shirt were still visible the last time I saw him. He was your age, your height, thin and sickly, and his disappearance cruelly echoed what might have happened to you three nights before. What I had miraculously avoided, this woman was now suffering.

People searched every corner of the boat. There was no trace of the boy. The captain finally restarted the engine, which got the woman screaming again. No! No! You can't leave him behind! I must find him first!

Somehow you had remained asleep through all of this. But now you were wide awake and clutching my shirt. Why is she screaming? you asked me. I had no idea what to say and could only turn you away and cover your ears, but you peeled off my hands and repeated your question until I finally snapped at you. Even as the shadows obscured her, you kept staring.

She wept for hours. We could hear her over the boat's engine, moaning in the darkness. No one could comfort her, and no one could sleep, not even you. As her fits turned hysterical, my pity for her was replaced with something like hatred. At one point I even considered quieting her by force, but at dawn she suddenly stopped, exhausted apparently, and people at last were able to fall asleep.

It rained late that morning. Everyone's mood improved. We collected rainwater in as many containers as we could find, and the storm was cool and soothing after days of scorching weather.

I watched you sit nearby with two older kids. It surprised me, since you rarely played with other children, or with anyone for that matter. But then you went still as you faced the stern of the boat. I figured you had grown bored, as you often did in the company of others. You were drenched in the rain, your hair matted on your forehead, your eyes salty.

Someone screamed. By the time I turned around, I caught only a flash of the woman's head and arms disappearing overboard in the haze of rain. You must have seen everything, her climbing onto the gunwale and standing there for a heartbeat, for one final breath, before leaping into the sea.

Two men dove in after her. The boat again was stopped. The storm had gotten worse and it took some effort just to get the two men back on board. Neither had seen or laid a finger on anything.

The boat was quiet for hours save the sound of the engine and the old women reciting their rosaries. I prayed alongside them, but only for the boy.

I remember the minutes after it happened, when people peered overboard and waited breathlessly for the swimmers to come back up with the woman's body, and all I could think was how melodramatic it was, how cowardly. She had no right giving up. To come all this way, and then to do that.

It turned out, of course, that she died for nothing. Hours later, someone below decks lifted the tarp that covered the fuel store and found the boy wedged between the twenty-gallon cans, lying amid a pile of filthy gasoline-soaked rags. He had a burning fever and could barely move or make a sound. Who knows why he had wandered down into the hold that night, or how he even got there, weak as he was. He must have passed out beneath the tarp, hidden from people lying arm's length from him, and deaf to his mother wailing his name for hours.

He was carried above deck where two older women forced water down his throat, cooled his forehead with a damp rag, and rubbed hot oil over his chest. I prayed for his recovery, yet dreaded it. What would we say when he was strong enough to ask for his mother?

He ended up surviving the boat trip somehow, despite hardly moving for the final four days. Once we made it to the camp, he disappeared onto the floating hospital, that white ship moored off the island's shore, and we heard three months later that he recovered and was sponsored by his uncle in Australia.

He'd be a grown man now, with children of his own and stories about his childhood that he might not be able or willing to tell. He's probably forgotten what his mother looked like. I still remember, more than I want to, her writhing in the arms of a consoler, tearing at her white blouse until the neckline ripped, her long equine face crumpled behind the tangles of her hair, mouth ajar and eyes clenched shut, that howling mask.

She must have felt she lost everything when she thought her son was gone. Until then, she had only lived for him. What was she now to herself or to the world if she was no longer a mother to anyone?

It was shame that welled inside me after they found the boy that day. I imagined myself losing you, and realized that I could not have done what she had done. I would have mourned you for the rest of my life, there is no doubt, but your death would not have been, back then, the death of anything inside me.

As I write down these thoughts, I wonder if you can read Vietnamese, if any of these words make sense or if they are as foreign to you as the sound of my voice. It is the only way I can speak honestly to you because it is the only language, the only world, in which I truly exist. I wish that weren't so. I've always wanted it otherwise. My suspicion is that you've grown up to see things as an American would and that you live your life for yourself alone. It saddens me that you might be so distant from the world I still dream about every night, but I feel envy for you too and a strange relief.

A few months ago, I came across the jade rosary your father gave me when we first got together, tucked away and forgotten in an old cigar box of trinkets I saved from the refugee camp. I had clutched that rosary all nine days we were at sea. You once wore it like a necklace, sitting startled on our bed in Vietnam and gaping at your father, who took the photograph. It was black and white, bent and tattered from the trip across the ocean. I discarded it years ago, along with all the others.

I have wondered often if you've grown into some version of me or become someone entirely different, someone better. In my mind, I can only see you as your five-year-old self. Your pursed lips and cracked *brow. Your eyes always bruised with thought. When you were angry, curious, you glared at people until they either looked away or scolded you. When you were pensive, you wandered into yourself like a lonely old woman.*

People said that you resembled me in every way, that even at a month old, you already had my eyes, my cheekbones, and most of all my temper. Something about our likeness to each other bothered me back then. It was as though you had come into the world to remind me constantly of myself.

Your grandmother always said that I was the most stubborn, the most selfish, of her three daughters. Growing up, I never shared sweets or toys with my sisters and constantly argued with them, sometimes hitting them since I thought it was my right as the oldest. I talked back to everyone, even your grandfather, a former soldier who had cut men's throats and spent days on the jungle floor listening for enemy footsteps. He spanked me often for my loose mouth, though secretly, I believe, he admired it.

He used to hit us with a wooden rod as thick as his finger. We'd stand before him in the family room, arms crossed, and confess our offense, and after he told us how many rods we deserved, we would have to turn around and face the wall and await them. If we uncrossed our arms or tried to dodge them, it would earn us an extra blow.

One time, when I was ten, I refused to bow and apologize to him after getting five rods for breaking the porcelain Jesus on our family altar. I had been running in the house, but only in order to rush and answer my mother's call. Why am I being punished for an accident? I demanded through my tears, I didn't break Jesus on purpose! My outburst startled him, but only for a second. A sixth rod nearly buckled my legs. When I still refused to bow, he hit me twice more until I bled through my shorts.

106

That night, when everyone had fallen asleep, I retrieved the rod from its home atop the bookcase and brought it out to our front porch, where I set it on fire with his matches. I watched it burn, then stomped on it. I left it there on the porch in three charred pieces, right by his smoking bench, fully aware that he was always first to rise and that smoking was the very first thing he did. When I came out the next morning, the mess had been swept away. He must have suspected that I had done it, but he never said a word. Two days later I saw a brand-new rod atop the bookcase.

Your grandmother liked to say that I was the fearless one in the family, that I would challenge the Lord if I ever met him. It was a compliment, but also a criticism of my temperament, which I suppose made her blind to everything I was actually afraid of.

The rosary also reminded me, of course, of your father. Not that I still yearn for him. I am not so romantic as that. It's just the way of memory and loss. We never truly forget the things that have passed out of our lives. We merely move further away from them in time, until they become either less important than they actually were or more profound than we might have ever imagined.

Had your father lived, I would never have left you. What happened on the island would never have happened. And of course I would not be writing these words. I know it sounds ridiculous to attribute all these things to one event, to one person, but that is how I have always seen it.

He was a farmer's son, your father, and a captain in the air force. He grew up raising ducks and pigs, and by the time he met me he had authority over hundreds of men.

I was seventeen the first time he arrived at our house in his perfectly pressed olive uniform, accompanying a fellow soldier who was pursuing one of my sisters. They drank tea with your grandparents for two hours.

It was not his uniform or his stature that impressed me. Everything about your father was easy. The way he smiled and sat back in his chair and seemed to know everything about every topic. The way he asked questions as though your grandparents were the most interesting people in the world. They soon ignored his friend and started boasting to him of my sisters' talents at school and in the kitchen, and of my skill at cutting hair. Your father nodded politely and never once looked at me. Although he was only twenty-four at the time, he seemed as old to me as your grandfather.

Two days later he returned alone with a tin of French biscuits. He was on his way to work at the Saigon airport, yet still spent an hour visiting with my parents. They spoke mostly about religion, your grandmother's favorite subject, and about the war, your grandfather's. I understand now that what impressed them, what impressed most everyone who met your father, was the certainty of everything he felt. He offered it to people not as a criticism or a play for superiority, but as a gift, as though he were a soldier offering safety, a priest offering forgiveness.

For more than two weeks, he stopped by every few days on his way to work. Always in uniform, always with a gift of cookies or candy, and never noticing me as I served him his tea. My parents wondered if he was interested in any of us. We soon just figured he enjoyed the company. He even started talking to me and my sisters, though he showed none of us any special attention. Everyone agreed that he carried a casual kind of loneliness.

Then one day he came with a carton of American cigarettes for your grandfather and a bundle of expensive silk for your grandmother. But instead of sitting down with them on the couch, he remained standing and asked them if I could accompany him to Saigon for lunch. His *manner was as casual as if he was asking for a glass of water, despite everyone's surprise, not least of all my own.*

I thought his interest in me had come out of his visits, but at that first lunch in Saigon, he asked me questions as if he had been storing them up for those last two weeks. He confessed that he had loved me since the moment he stepped into our house, which frightened me at first, that someone could just love you so completely before you'd had a chance to return any of it. I realized that befriending your grandparents had been your father's way of ensuring that he was the best man for me in their eyes, and that he already knew that my love for him was inevitable. I should have been offended, but something about that moved me deeply.

He gave me the jade rosary that afternoon, a peculiar first gift, particularly as a profession of love. I suspect now that he already saw me as a creature of faith. He had no idea how wrong he was.

We married five months later, in late 1974, when I was eighteen. I moved to his base in Pleiku, and despite the distance from my family and my home, despite my inexperience in almost everything, I was somehow never too afraid. In no time at all, he taught me how to take care of him, how to love him and be loved by him, how to believe in this entity we'd become as man and wife, even though I wondered where his own understanding of these things had come from. It was as though he'd been a grown man and a husband since the day he was born.

We set up a simple home in the barracks, with two twin beds pushed together and a modest bathroom and kitchen your father built himself. He worked at his office during the day, but we spent our evenings together, reading the newspaper or an old novel to each other, or hosting his officer friends, who came for my cooking and stayed for mah-jongg and poker. Your father rarely lost. On the weekends, we walked to town to see a movie and always enjoyed the ones with Charles Bronson or Alain Delon, who both talked very little and always got the job done. On Sundays we strolled up the hill, along a path that skirted a mango orchard, and went to church.

I struggle now with the idea that those days could've lasted much longer, perhaps even forever. That's the naive and sometimes dangerous urge in all our memories. What might have been is a vast and depthless ocean that surrounds the tiny island of what actually happened, what was actually possible. You can either die of thirst on that island or wade out into all that endless water.

When I became pregnant with you, just a few months into this life with your father, it was as though I had uncovered a startling secret about myself. It should have felt natural, invigorating, as it would for any woman, but for me it was like a sudden and incurable affliction. I had only recently been given a brand-new version of myself to walk around in, and just when I started to feel comfortable inside it, I was forced into yet another version that seemed not only alien but unbearably permanent. Once you became a reality inside me, I knew I could never go back to being anything else.

Your father, however, immediately wrote his family and went about building a new crib and a bigger dining table, and three or four times a day he playfully caressed my flat belly as though the bump was already there. Before you ever actually existed, you were already the center of his life.

His joy was brief. When I was three months pregnant with you, we moved back to Cat Lai to await the Communists. He had already decided long ago, without telling me, that he would never flee the country, that as the oldest son he would stay and bear his responsibility to the family.

On the day Saigon fell, as your father's family and I sat in the basement with the buried gold and listened to the radio and the screaming missiles overhead, your father put his ear to my belly and, to you or to me or perhaps to himself, murmured a lullaby in the darkness,

The lights in Saigon – some green, some red.
The lights in My Tho – some bright, some dim.
Go back now to your books and learn patience.
Nine moons I shall wait for you, ten autumns I shall wait for you.

By noon that day, he was nothing more than a farmer's son.
But the Communists knew everything. He was immediately forced
to attend their weekly meetings in the town square. He had to bring
his own chair and mosquito net, as well as the reeducation booklet
they provided. Not once did he look afraid. You would have thought
he enjoyed studying the booklet. Each time he went, I refused to
say good-bye, so he started leaving me with a kiss on the cheek and
these grinning words in my ear: If anything happens, I'll kill a
hundred men to get back to you.

On the night of his fifth meeting, he never came home.

That was the first time your father died. For the first two years of
your life, I did not know if I should miss him, mourn him, or hope
for his return. He existed in some hazy region between death and
life, where thinking of him was like choosing between a memory and
a ghost. What made it worse was that I could not look at you, as you
began teething and walking and settling into your own personality,
without also thinking of his absence for all of it, and then hating him
for believing any of this was avoidable. So I tried not to think of him
at all, until gradually you became a marker for when my life changed
from something solid and hopeful to something as unknowable as the
sea at night. Perhaps that was when I started blaming you for making
me erase him from my life.

Twenty months after his disappearance, the family received a letter.
He was alive. It was his handwriting but not him completely. We
could tell that they had inspected every single word he wrote, all 155
of them, informing us of what we had both hoped for and dreaded all

along. He had been taken to the camps, but they would not let him tell us where or when he would ever come home. Only that he was working hard and honoring his reeducation, whatever that meant. Months passed without any more letters, from him or the authorities. We were left again to imagine the worst.

Finally, at the end of that year, a second letter arrived, this time from the government. He was to be released early for undisclosed reasons.

You were three years old when he returned. He was many shades darker now, his skin leathery and his eyes sallow and dry. He had lost so much weight that he seemed both smaller and taller. What struck me hardest was his smile. I had never seen him smile weakly as if he was uncertain of his happiness, embarrassed by it.

The first time he met you, he held you for a full minute. He wept quietly into your chest, the first time I had ever seen him cry. He was a complete stranger to you, and yet you did not struggle out of his arms as you did with everyone else. You stared at him wide-eyed and with understanding, as though his tearful smile was the first genuine thing you had ever encountered in your life. That night, you slept between us, cradled in his arms.

I asked him many times what had happened in the camps. He'd only say that they worked him hard and fed him next to nothing, and that they had little mercy for slow learners. It was clear from his reticence that he had rejected his reeducation and that that had cost him much more than he was willing to share.

One night, months after his return, I awoke to him crying in bed. The second and last time I saw him cry.

You two must leave, he whispered. Things will get worse.

But I refused to consider it. Not without you, I said.

And that was when he confessed that he was sick. They had diagnosed him in the camps and told him he had a year or less to live.

That's why they had released him early. He was not strong enough to make the trip with us. He'd be a burden. He could even get us killed.

I could barely get the words out. I told him anything could get us killed, and if I were ever to leave without him, it would only be after he was gone. I'd wait until then, no matter how long it took.

He shook his head and stared at the ceiling. He could not bear the thought of his daughter seeing him die.

You must go now for her, he said. I'll never forgive you if you stay.

Your father died three weeks after we arrived at the refugee camp. He had held on a year longer than anyone expected. I was holding your hand when I read my mother's telegram. I crumpled it and tossed it away, saying nothing to you, and started for the beach with you in tow, and once there we continued walking along the shore, through the sand and over the rocks, past the jetty and up the tree-lined cliffs as though we were actually headed somewhere, silent the entire time as you tugged at me and said you were tired and didn't want to walk anymore. But moving was the only thing I could do. The words could not come to my lips, for you or for myself. We walked in an hour-long circle until we came back to our hut and I fell onto the pallet and went instantly to sleep.

I sometimes forget how young your father was. He had always seemed like a much older man, someone I had to catch up to. In the end we were only together a year before he disappeared, and for one more year after he returned. I have spent so much more time missing and remembering him than I ever spent knowing him. Though how long does it take to truly know anyone? Had your father lived, had he crossed the ocean and returned to us, to me, would I still love him now?

His favorite meal was one he cooked himself. A simple pork dish sautéed in fish sauce with a little sugar and pepper and minced ginger. After eight days at sea, when none of us had eaten or drunk anything for days, after we had lost three more people, two of them babies that had to be thrown overboard, our boat stopped dead in the water. We had no more oil or grease for the engine, so the captain mixed some pork fat with gasoline, which got the engine running again except the oil smelled so good that people could hardly stand it.

You said, That smells like Father.

This is the part I've never told anyone. I swear it is all true.

We met a man on the island. He had been on our boat. A man named Son, whose presence you might remember even if you've forgotten everything else about him. On our sixth night at sea, a storm rocked and flung us against each other for hours, thrashed us with blinding choking rain, and in the end took his wife. She had been thrown from the boat when it heeled and nearly capsized, and in the calm after the storm's passing, whispers traveled of how he had tried to save her but she had slipped from his hands and tumbled into the sea. He was still onboard somewhere with their young son. We heard no moaning or crying of any kind. I imagined him staring silently at the tranquil sea and reliving his last glimpse of his wife as she vanished under the waves.

She was the second woman drowned in less than a day. She had not flung herself and she had not gone willingly, but she and the other woman quickly became one person in my mind. At that point, there was no room left in me for separate tragedies.

Two months into our stay at the camp, with nothing to do one afternoon, I decided to take you to the untainted beach on the other side of the island. The main beach at the mouth of the camp was always crowded with swimmers and barterers and supply boats from the mainland. But this other beach was over an hour's walk from camp and cut off from all facilities, so few people went there unless they were young, in love, or in need of time alone. The easiest path there was along the base of the mountain, which skirted the shoreline, and we were walking the path that afternoon, about halfway to the beach, when we came upon a wall of trees. You saw something and stopped us, and when I followed you through the trees, I saw that we had discovered a small promontory that overlooked the shore.

You pointed him out to me. We stood at the edge of the promontory, with a quiet view of the untainted beach in the distance and a steep path below us that led down to a small rocky cove. There was a platform of rocks at the bottom, and he was sitting on one of the rocks with a fishing pole he'd made from a tree branch. I'd seen men in the camp sneak out into the open waters on makeshift rafts, or with nothing but a life vest made of empty plastic bottles, risking their lives to catch fish they would then barter around camp. Son's brand of fishing had no industry. He was there for the silence.

You asked me who he was, and though I had never actually set eyes on Son, not even on the boat, I knew immediately. You can't live elbow to elbow with thousands of people without hearing stories. Son's boy was only a few years older than you, and in their first week on the island, some man had improperly touched the boy and threatened him with a knife, so Son confronted the man with a cleaver and hacked off three of his fingers. He left him the thumb and part of the pinkie. That's what I heard. The man deserved it, I suppose, and everyone agreed that Son was merely protecting the one thing he had left in the world. But still, people kept their distance. The Malaysian police jailed him for two weeks, and some said they shaved his head as punishment. We knew he had already done it himself to mourn his wife's death.

Let's go down there, you said.

I hushed you, afraid that he might hear us. But you kept tugging my hand. It had been so long since I'd seen that kind of recognition and vigor in your eyes. Your father, of course, had also shaved off all his hair months before we left, lest you see him lose more and more of it every day.

I want to fish! you insisted.

I was about to cover your mouth when Son turned and saw us. He yanked his pole out of the water and marched halfway up the path until he was a few meters below us. I wanted to flee but stood transfixed by his childish outrage. He seemed embarrassed for some reason, and angry that he could not hide it.

Why are you watching me? he demanded. His voice rang across the empty promontory.

I pulled you close to me, behind me a bit, as you squeezed my hand. I shot back at him, This is not your island! We can be here too if we want!

You were watching me, he insisted and glanced accusingly at you too.

Why would we watch you? We're here for the same reason you are.

He was taken aback, unsure of what I meant.

I added, And we'll come back here as often as we want, whether you like it or not! I pulled you from the edge and decided it was better to return to camp. We would save the beach for another day.

As we rushed away, me pulling you along, you kept glancing behind us.

The next day you said you wanted to visit the beach again. I knew why. And I admitted to myself that I was drawn back too. We were poking a wild dog, but something about him felt familiar to me as well. It might have been his recent loss, or simply the frightening loneliness in his anger.

He was fishing at the same spot, accompanied this time by his son, who, like his father, was shirtless and had a pole in the water. They each sat on a separate rock without talking or acknowledging one another.

We watched them in our own rapt silence, though this time from a more concealed spot beneath some trees. It felt strange, the fact that you and I were finally sharing something. I was pleased by it, but also saddened.

The boy jumped to his feet. He had a bite on his line and was trying to lift it carefully out of the water. Son watched him without saying anything. The boy struggled with the pole and seemed on the verge of success, but when he grabbed the line with his hand, it went limp. He turned immediately to his father, who came over to inspect the line and promptly rapped his knuckles on the boy's crown and admonished him loudly.

The boy sat back down, rubbing his bowed head.

I felt sorry for him. He had seen his mother drown and watched his father lop off another man's fingers. What must have filled his head at night?

Son returned to his spot and to his fishing and seemed, once again, absorbed in the deep waters of the sea, oblivious again to the boy.

Their bare backs looked bronzed in the sun, the son's a smaller and more delicate facsimile of the father's.

We visited the promontory twice more that week. Son and the boy never seemed to change. It was as though we were returning each day to look at a painting.

They fished mostly in silence, but every now and then Son's loud voice broke upon the air and he'd begin talking at length. He could easily have been talking to himself. I understood very little from our distance, but I could see that the boy, who hardly spoke at all, hung on every word. He clearly feared his father and might have loved and admired him too. How much of that had he inherited from his mother?

Her memory hovered around them. The boy often sat with his face turned toward the sea, the pole forgotten in his hands. The first time I saw him cry, his father scolded him and he had to set down the pole and wipe his eyes with both hands. The other time it happened, Son merely looked over and watched until the boy recovered himself. Then Son started speaking. His tone was even and gentle, whatever he was saying.

I tell you all this because I saw a love there that was circumstantial and yet more real because of it. In another life, had they not lost the woman they both loved, they would not have tried at all.

For as long as an hour, we'd watch them as the trees swayed above us. Once or twice, the boy glanced up in our direction. If he saw us, he made no mention of it to his father.

It was around this time that I started having nightmares of us back on the boat, except it was just the two of us and we were drifting on the ocean, sitting under moonlight by the stern until we heard something crawling up the side of the boat, and finally a wet hand reached over the gunwale.

I also had dreams of you drowning in the nearby well or eaten by rats in the night, or your body washing up on the beach after a terrible storm. Strangely, in the dreams of us on the boat, you were always alive, and in the dreams of us on the island, you were either dead or missing.

Not coincidentally, it was also around this time that you began going off on your own. We shared our hut with seven people, and I would come back from an errand or wake up from a nap and find that you had disappeared without anyone noticing.

The first time it happened, I was frantic, those dreams of you inflaming my worst fears until I finally found you at the chapel watching people pray. I scolded and spanked you. It did no good. You continued your daily excursions into other people's huts, peeking through the windows of the sick bay, exploring the cemetery on the hill. At sunset one evening, I found you sitting on the beach looking seaward as metal skiffs shimmered on the horizon.

It made no sense. You were hardly five years old but had no fear of being on your own, of getting lost or hurt, of me punishing you. Each time I found you, I seized your arm and shook you and even threatened you, only to have you look up crossly at me as though I had interrupted something important. I began to wonder if you weren't trying to escape me, or punish me for whatever it was I had done or hidden from you in my heart.

I finally asked you why you were doing this. I did not expect a real answer.

We were inside our hut, and you peered at the empty doorway and murmured to yourself, I was looking for Father.

A voice awoke me one night. I sat up and found everyone in the hut sound asleep.

You were snoring beside me. I had started tying rope from my ankle to yours, to alert me if you ever wandered away at night. I untied it and stepped outside to listen again for the voice.

I walked barefoot around the camp, beneath clear skies and a full moon. Rats the size of cats squeaked along the empty pathways. I heard a few faint voices from nearby huts, though none that sounded like the one that had awoken me. I was aware that I was following a sound from the depths of sleep, yet I felt compelled to hear it again, as if mute and searching for my own voice, and I continued walking until I found myself outside the camp, headed slowly in the direction of the beach.

The sea was calm that night, lapping the empty shore and washing cool and soft over my ankles. I let the swirling sand bury my feet and looked out into the night, past the lonesome jetty, at the gray moonlit waters. Vietnam was somewhere out there. It might as well have been the moon.

A sound drifted toward me, like someone slowly paddling a boat. It was hours past curfew, so I thought at first that a patrol boat had spotted me. But all I saw was a dark figure about twenty meters out in the water, moving parallel to the shore. I started down the beach to get a closer look without wading in any deeper. I made out her long tangled hair, her white blouse drenched and clinging to her skin. The sea was up to her waist, and she was taking one long, slow stride after the other, dragging herself through the water with her head bowed, searching for something in the shallows.

She had not yet noticed me.

Are you okay? I called out to her. She brushed her hands across the surface of the water as though parting curtains.

I called her a second time. She turned around with a start.

Her long face was unmistakable, that howling still there in the stark eyes that regarded me now with outrage and eagerness. She began dragging herself toward me, rising out of the water with her small gray breasts visible beneath the translucent blouse and its neckline ripped and her hair dripping over those outraged eyes. And I saw again in my mind that flash of her head and arms, frozen forever in midair, when she stepped off the gunwale and plunged into the sea.

I wanted to run away, but my feet were planted in the sand.

She stopped about five meters from me. Have you seen my son? she said.

No, I said immediately. I wanted to tell her that he was alive and safe and probably asleep on the floating hospital moored somewhere out there in the darkness, but I was afraid she might make me take her there.

He's just a little boy, she continued and shook her head. She gestured around her. I can't seem to find him anywhere out here. Where could he be if he's not out here?

How did you lose him?

She peered down the shore and said, It feels like forever ago. She started wading away, the water slashing her knees. But then she turned back around. She looked at me carefully. Are you sure you don't know where he is?

I felt my heart beating again. I have no idea, I told her. I'm sure he's okay.

Her face turned hard. She said, I don't care if he's okay. I left the world because of him and now I find he's not here with me like he's supposed to be? Tell me, is that fair?

I shook my head.

She waded away again, this time toward the rocky end of the shore. What will you do if you find him? I called after her.

She looked over her shoulder, still moving, and said, I'm taking him with me. What else?

My feet shifted finally in the sand and I took a step forward. Wherever she was headed, her son would not be there. Yet I felt compelled to follow her, to see what she would do if she ever did find him. She seemed both terrible and beautiful in the moonlight.

I made the sign of the cross and watched her figure fade slowly into the night until all that was left was the distant sound of sloshing water.

You fell ill with the flu the next day. I brought you to the sick bay and they gave you medicine, but your fever got worse. You spent two days lying on your cardboard pallet, hardly eating a thing. Each time you awoke from a nap, you started crying for your father. No matter how I tried to soothe you, you kept mewling his name.

I understand it now, your love for him. He never scolded you as I did, never lifted his hand at you except to caress your head. In his brief time as your father, he took you on walks nearly every day, held you as you slept, even fed you at the dinner table though you were old enough to feed yourself.

But more than anything, I think you missed having him there when you were upset, to look upon you with eyes that forgave you all your tears, all your questions and sorrows. The moment he arrived in your life, despite being gone for most of it, he instantly filled a space that *you had always reserved for him, for the promise of him, and he filled it with a devotion that he had already prepared in his heart before you were ever born. Perhaps that is the only way that true love can work, when it is prepared for and embraced without thought, without choice.*

It struck me, while you were sick, that if I ever told you the truth, you would blame me and then hate me for not staying behind and letting him take my place.

Soon after you recovered, you disappeared again. While I was away at Mass one afternoon, you went out to the latrine and never came back. Our housemates offered to help find you, but I insisted on going alone. I was afraid my anger would betray me when I finally found you.

I searched all over the camp, every single place I'd ever caught you, including the waterfall where some man had recently fallen and broken his neck. I ended up at the beach, where I had to fight the impulse to grab every child who remotely resembled you.

I do not deserve this, I thought to myself, though it was still unclear what I did deserve.

A commotion soon interrupted my search. People began crowding the shore as yet another refugee boat came bobbing into the shallows, sunk by its occupants and slowly heeling as they jumped overboard and staggered, the healthy carrying the young and elderly, onto the beach.

I watched an exhausted man drag himself ashore with a frail old woman on his back and her arms locked so tightly around his neck that it seemed she was choking him and bringing him to his knees.

The prospect of you being lost forever washed over me then. It had never come to this, all those other times you disappeared. Perhaps my exasperation had numbed me to the panic, to the worry, because suddenly nothing mattered but that I never feel this way again. Never finding you was preferable to finding you dead or hurt. For the first time in my life, I could live with not knowing.

I thought of my encounter on the beach a few nights before, my vision, whatever it was. I had entirely forgotten it until that moment. It did not feel like a dream because I could hear again in my head her impatient voice, her bitterness.

Only then did I start walking toward the promontory. It had crossed my mind from the very beginning, but it still seemed incredible, you going there on your own. Perhaps the truth was that at that point I no longer wanted to find you at all. The closer I got, the less I knew what I would do if you were there. Was I to scold you yet again? Beat you until you stopped all this?

When I arrived and saw you sitting alone on the rocks below, I was struck calm. I can't say now if it was relief or disappointment. You were there waiting for Son, for something I couldn't give you myself, and part of me wanted him to find you and take you away for good. Where to? I kept thinking. Where to?

I started slowly and quietly down the path. You were sitting on your haunches and glancing around yourself, unable to stay still, dissatisfied with your own company. I saw then what I had always been unwilling to see. Your likeness to me, as stark as the waters below. That's when I stopped, about halfway down the path. Every part of me felt exhausted, heavy with surrender.

You hadn't noticed me yet. You crawled to the edge of the rock and leaned over to peer at your reflection. You gazed at it for a long time, unable to look away, leaning closer and closer to it, until suddenly your hand slipped. Before you could cry out you had tumbled headfirst into the water.

How can I explain what happened next? It was as though I had stopped breathing. My mouth was open, but nothing came out. My arms tried to reach out for you, but they felt petrified like my legs and every other muscle in my body.

Your arms were flailing in the water, your white face breaking the

*surface before going under once, twice. I might have been holding my
breath the entire time because my heart was exploding in my chest and
thudding in my ears as your yelps pierced the air.*

*I must have closed my eyes at some point because a loud splash
forced them open. You had drifted farther from the rock, but he was
already under you with his arm wrapped around your chest and your
face lifted above water. He swam to the rocks, heaved you onto them
before dragging himself out of the water.*

*My legs were finally moving by then, as if thunderstruck into
action, and I stumbled down the path, only to freeze again a few
meters from him as he was turning you onto your side while you gasped
and coughed and cried all at once. I opened my mouth but did not
know who to call out to. To you? To him? Was I now to pull you from
his arms and hold you in mine, thank him as I wept over you, hoping
he hadn't seen what I had just done, what I had almost let happen?
All I wanted was to close my eyes.*

*He looked up and saw me standing there, and his drenched face
seized with recognition and then with a fury I'd only ever seen in a
barking dog.*

*He left you there on the ground still crying and coughing and
stormed up to me, and before I could step away he seized me by the
arms and shook me and slapped me hard across the face. What is
wrong with you, woman? he shouted and slapped me again. Open
your goddamned eyes!*

*I took the blows blindly, feeling all at once the relief and the shame,
the finality of what I had done, what I had failed to do. I felt his thick
hands clutching my arms and my body weaken as I pressed my face
against his chest and began to sob.*

*He let go of my arms. His chest stiffened. I expected him to push
me away, and found myself sobbing harder when he did not. He must
have thought me a madwoman, overcome by what I had nearly let*

happen to you. But I was not thinking of you at all. I was crying for myself, for everything I had lost, for your father, your ridiculous father, who would never hold me or forgive me anything ever again.

PART THREE

PART THREE

6

'SHE'S MY WIFE,' I said to the girl. 'My ex-wife. You don't know anyone named Suzy?'

She shook her head uncertainly, holding the edge of the door, half hidden behind it. She seemed caught between seeing me as someone with vital information and someone who'd knocked on the wrong door. Behind her, a column of light from the window sliced the dresser in half.

'Are you alone?' I said.

'Why are you asking?'

'You're right – I'm sorry. I'm looking for Hong Thi Pham. I call her Suzy. Do you know her?'

She waited a beat before nodding knowingly, like she'd been waiting for me to say the name. She pronounced it in proper Vietnamese for me, surname first. 'I don't actually know her. But I know who she is. She's my mother.'

'Yeah,' I said. 'I see it.'

We exchanged a moment of quiet recognition, aware that we had each just discovered something profound. I was still too stunned by who she was, too distracted by who she looked like, to know how exactly to act – trapped between a sentimental stirring inside me and dismay at her sudden existence in the world, which explained so many things about her mother at the same time as it explained nothing.

'Is this her room?'

'I don't know. I guess so.' The girl glanced behind her as if to check that the room was still empty. 'I was told to come here. Why are you looking for her?'

'She's been missing from home since Sunday. Her car is gone, so we think she left on her own, but she didn't tell anyone. Who told you to come here?'

'*She* did. She's been sending me letters.' Her demeanor hardened suddenly like she was remembering herself, and she narrowed her eyes. 'Look, I'm sure you are who you are, but I don't know you any more than I know her. Shit, a month ago I didn't even know she was alive. Now I'm here in an empty hotel room for God knows what reason.'

'Hey, it's okay. Here, let me show you something. I'm just going for my wallet.'

I pulled out an old photo of me and Suzy at Fisherman's Wharf, our backs to the ocean. We were a week away from getting married. Though I was beaming with my arm around her, her face was as solemn as the gray skies behind us. Smiling in pictures made her feel fake. *We smile for who?*

It came back to me then – how awkward and cold she'd get around children, how she'd always refuse when people offered their baby to her to hold, how adamant she'd been when I mentioned kids just a month before this photo was taken. She would have been about ten years older than the girl was now.

She held the photo close to her face and momentarily forgot me. That stirring inside me, I realized, was an outlandish urge to protect her. She had her mother's beauty, except hers was distracted and uncertain: her chewed nails, her scuffed cowboy boots, the *Rosemary's Baby* haircut framing her crinkled brow.

'You even stand the same way she does,' I said. 'Here –' I handed her my driver's license. 'My name is Robert Ruen. Your mother and I were married for eight years. We lived in Oakland. It's where I met her.'

'Guess she never told you about me. Why would she, right?'

'I'm sorry. I'm sure she had her reasons.'

'Don't we all?' She gave me back my license. 'Someone should apologize to you too.' She opened the door a little wider now. 'You came all the way from Oakland to look for her?'

'She moved here a couple years ago. After our divorce. Her new husband here… I'm helping him find her.'

I could see more questions popping into the girl's head. She said, 'Is she in trouble?'

'I don't know. That's why I'm here.'

'But how did you know to come to this room?'

'It's a long story. You mind if I come inside?'

She glared at me like she was trying to peer into my soul, but there was also an eagerness in the way she pursed her lips and tapped her fingers on the door. She finally held it open for me.

The room was identical to mine. It was made up, pristine, no sign whatsoever that anyone had been here except for the girl's purse on the dresser.

I asked her, 'Were the curtains open or drawn when you came in?'

'Drawn. Had to let in some light. The rooms in these old casinos feel like tombs.'

I walked to the far wall without showing myself in the window and pulled the curtains close, plunging us into the room's bronze light. I clicked on another lamp. She stood in the hall by the door, still holding my photo in her hand, thoroughly intrigued by all the stealth. I noticed a piece of paper by her purse, the one I had slid under the door. It must have mystified her until I came knocking and hollering. And even then.

'Listen,' I said, 'I'm as confused by everything as you are. But before I tell you what I know, I need to ask you some questions. Is that okay?'

'You're a cop, aren't you?'

'I am?'

'You talk like one. No offense. I've run into a few cops in my life.'

'I guess you have. Don't worry, you've done nothing wrong.'

'I know. That's not what I'm worried about.' She approached me and gave back the photo. 'You look happy there.'

I returned the photo carefully to my wallet, deflated by her composure. She didn't want or need protecting, not yet. And even if she did, who was I to offer it?

She walked over to the dresser and retrieved her purse. She pulled out an envelope. 'I got this yesterday in my mailbox. The letters always come in the mail, but they're not stamped or addressed or anything. Just my name on the front.'

I opened the letter: *Mai, Please go room 1215 at Coronado Hotel. 2:00 tomorrow. I leave something for you. Tell front desk your name and they give you the key. Your mother.*

It was Suzy's elfin handwriting. Her robotic English.

I didn't hide my relief. 'At least we know she's alive and still in town. Yesterday, anyway. That's all there was?'

132

'Yeah. Her other letters aren't that much longer. More like notes really. I don't have them with me.'

'You started getting them – a month ago, right?'

'A month exactly. This is the fourth one. The first one confused the hell out of me. No one I know would write me in Vietnamese. I had to get some random waitress at a noodle shop to translate it for me.'

'Sounded like you knew Vietnamese just a minute ago.'

'I can speak and understand it okay. But I might as well be reading Chinese. Anyway, in the first letter she says she's my mother and has wanted to write me all these years, she's never forgotten me, and she wants me to know she's watching me now. That was it. Kinda freaked me out. First, I had to believe it was her. Then I had to imagine her out there watching me. Like, how the hell was she doing that?'

'Do you frequent the casinos? Do you work there, I mean?' She had glanced at me as though I'd just accused her of something. She seemed both leery of my questions and anxious to answer them. 'You can say that. I play poker for a living. Don't look surprised, I make more at cards than I would at anything else.'

'I ask because Suzy was a dealer briefly when she first got here. At the Horseshoe, I think. She might have seen you there. Even dealt to you.'

'I've played there, and I'd remember her if she dealt poker. She must have done the table games.' She stopped and squinted at the floor. 'Jesus, how many times did I pass her?'

'She'd never written you before? Even when you were younger?'

'She was dead, for all I knew. She left when I was five, a few months after we got to the States. Just disappeared one day without saying a word to anybody. Guess she has a habit of doing that. I have barely any memory of her. She left two weeks before Christmas. Right about now, come to think of it.'

I was ready to say something consoling, but a flash of bitterness in her eyes told me she didn't want the sympathy.

'Do you know your father?' I said and found myself wincing inside at the thought of whoever he was, someone long before me, someone secret and original.

She shook her head casually. 'He died in Vietnam not long after my mother and I escaped. Cancer or something. I can't remember a thing about him. All I know is that he fought with the Americans and was sent to the reeducation camps after the war and got real sick there. My uncle – *his* uncle, actually – told me all this. He's the one who raised me in LA after my mother left, he and my grandaunt.'

'They've never heard from her?'

'Wouldn't have told me if they had. They were hard-core Catholics – unforgiving as hell. She was dead to them, and when I dropped out of college and took up gambling, they cut me off too. Probably started seeing a bit too much of her in me. They weren't way off, because after my granduncle died a few years back, I left for Vegas and haven't spoken to anyone in the family since.'

She was sitting on the edge of the bed and talking mostly to the dresser. I could sense that she had wanted to tell someone these things for a long time.

'So there were two other letters.'

'Yeah. In English, actually. It was weird – her English

wasn't that good, but that made it easier for me to read, you know? Less intimate maybe. Less of her real voice. I wasn't ready to hear that yet. In the second letter, she says she called up my cousin in LA two years ago and pretended to be an old friend of mine, and my cousin – that twit – tells her I'm a drug addict and a gambler in Vegas, which is only half true. So anyway she moved here and tracked me down. She says she doesn't like it here, but it reminds her of Vietnam for some reason, and she starts going on about the mountains and the skies in Vietnam. Bad poetry, honestly. She says she hopes I quit the drugs and the gambling and visit the homeland some day. It'll help me. Who told her I needed helping? I kept thinking of her living here all this time, driving past my apartment, then putting shit in my mailbox – when I'm at home, even. She came here to look for me and she found me, and for two years she didn't do anything. So why now?'

Her voice had gotten small, and she was picking at a thread on the bedcover. She became a child all of a sudden, as though she'd been spending the last ten minutes suppressing any part of herself that might seem young or feminine or weak. She was a clarified version of her mother, with all the carefulness but none of the mystery, and that somehow eased my mind amid the shock of all she was telling me.

The moment passed and she stood from the bed, stuffing her hands into the pockets of her jeans. 'By the way – what did you mean, "at least she's alive"? Were you afraid she was dead?'

'Not exactly. I just want to find her as soon as possible and make sure she's okay.'

She was studying me again with that hard burrowing stare. 'She divorced *you*, didn't she?' I must have shown some annoyance because she said, 'I'm sorry. I don't know why I said that.'

I swallowed and waved away the apology. 'It's all right. Your mother did leave me. And yes, I've never stopped caring for her.' She nodded sheepishly, so I pressed on, 'Tell me about that third letter.'

'That was the oddest one. It came last Saturday. She says she's going somewhere, and that before she leaves she has to give me something. She also says that one of these days everything will be explained to me. Still not sure what she means by "everything." I don't know if it's me or her English or if she's just trying to be the most mysterious person on earth.'

'She had a habit of that too. Don't take it personally.'

The girl almost smiled, which startled me, made me aware of how intimate our conversation had become.

I said, 'Did she give you any indication in her letters that she wanted to meet?'

Her face fell, again that childish demeanor, that instant smallness, eyes averted and lips pursed. 'No. I figured she might be here, waiting for me. I was all ready with things to say.'

I looked around the room. 'So what did she leave you?'

She shrugged. 'Didn't have much time to look before you started knocking on the door.'

I walked into the bathroom and started searching the cabinets, the tub, the hamper. Mai was picking through the nightstand drawer when I came back out. 'The dresser has nothing either.'

'Have you checked the closet?'

She shook her head.

The brown carry-on suitcase stood beside the ironing board in the closet, with a notecard taped to it. *Mai*, written in red marker. I carried it to the bed. It weighed a good thirtysomething pounds and looked brand-new.

'I'll do it if you want,' I said, but she was already trying to unzip it. Then we both saw the small silver lock.

She grabbed her purse and rummaged through it until she finally fished out a tiny chrome key. 'This was also in the envelope.' She shrugged apologetically. 'I didn't know yet if I should tell you.'

She inserted the key into the lock, and it opened. She hesitated a second before unzipping the carry-on and flipping it open.

'Jesus fucking Christ,' she whispered.

It was packed with jumbled bricks of cash. She picked up one and flipped through the twenty-dollar bills. I did too. Fifty bills a brick. It took me a while to count all the bricks. About a hundred in all.

'Goddamn,' I said. 'There's got to be a hundred grand here.'

'They're real,' she muttered, inspecting a bill under the lamplight and feeling it between her fingers. She plopped herself on the bed beside the carry-on. 'She left this all for me?'

'I don't think it's hers to leave.' I gently took the brick from her hand. She gave me a defensive look. I replaced the money and zipped up the suitcase and went through the outer pockets and sleeves. Nothing but a few silica gel packets.

I turned to her. 'Mai, listen to me carefully. Do you know a man named Sonny Nguyen?'

She shook her head.

'Are you sure? He plays a lot of poker in town. Short, bald, about fifty. Mean-looking.'

'Half the Vietnamese guys that play are balding and trying to look mean. One at every table.'

'How about a Jonathan Nguyen?'

'Am I supposed to know these guys?'

'Well, Sonny is your mother's new husband. Jonathan is his son. This is their money.'

'You know this for sure? Why can't it be hers?'

'A hundred grand? Your mother had nothing when she left me, and she stopped working when she married Sonny. I doubt he's this generous. She took this money from him. No wonder they're desperate to find her.' I banged my fist on the suitcase. 'Goddamn it, how can she be this stupid! She didn't think they'd come after you too?'

Mai gave me a moment before saying, 'Maybe I should be scared, but I'm more confused than anything. Who are these guys?'

I turned away from her so she couldn't see my face and that exasperated flush that only Suzy could inflict on me.

'I guess you can call them businessmen,' I said. 'High-class smugglers, actually, gamblers in every way. The father's got an ugly temper and has had more than a few run-ins with the law, so the son seems to run everything – a restaurant, a pet store, black-market shit, who knows what else. Anyway, it's not about who they are. It's about what they're willing to do to get what they want. And now I know what they want.'

'But you said you were helping them.'

'I didn't have a choice. Listen, I don't have time now to

explain. You need to leave this hotel. They can't know you were here or who you are or that you even exist.'

She glanced again at the carry-on. 'And what are you gonna do – stay here?' She gave me a stiff look, unsure of the accusation she was making but making it anyway.

'Hey, I don't want any part of this. Trust me. If I had a choice, I'd be on the 15 back to Oakland.'

Her face tightened. I was using my severe-cop voice, but she wasn't having any of it. We had a hundred grand in cash staring at us, and I was still as much a stranger to her as her own mother. That's when it hit me, with relief but sudden melancholy, that Suzy had already come today and would not be coming again – that I no longer had a reason to be here.

I softened my tone. 'How about this – I go with you. You barely know me, I know, but I need your help getting out of town, and you need my help too. We can't be too careful about this. And the sooner we both go, the better.'

'Wait – you want me to leave town? Like, just up and go right now? And you're just gonna explain this all later?'

Her voice was more shrill than it needed to be, like she was trying to convince herself not to take me seriously. I could see her mother's stubbornness in her. All that loneliness that comes with refusing anything sensible the world gives you. And there it was again, my protective urge, heroic and sincere and ridiculous all at once. I wanted to shake her.

My father came to mind again. The same man who used to seize my mother by the neck in an argument, slap her hard sometimes if things got nasty – he once cuffed me on the back of the head for not holding the door for a woman at the store. 'Be a man, would you?' he said.

I pulled out the surveillance photo of me and placed it on the bed in front of Mai.

'This is what they got on me. That's Sonny on the floor. I put him there. Doesn't look good, I know, but… last year he threw your mother down the stairs, broke her arm, nearly killed her. I came to Vegas five months ago to teach him a lesson. Turned out to be a pretty dumb idea. I put a gun to him here because he went at me with a kitchen knife. Asshole tried to plunge it into my fucking heart. You'll just have to trust me on that one.' I pulled up my sleeve to show her the scar on my wrist. 'The son did this and also broke all my fingers to warn me away from his father. I didn't listen. Now they're blackmailing me with this surveillance footage so that I'll find your mother for them – though it's apparently the money they really want. They might know nothing about you, but they might know everything, and until I can figure out what is what, you and I need to go somewhere where they can't find us. And believe me – they'll find us in Vegas.'

Her eyes darted back and forth between me and the photo, blinking back the questions. A gambler's knee-jerk skepticism. Or maybe she was finally scared.

'You don't have to believe that I'm an upstanding guy,' I said. 'But at least you know I'm not crazy. I wouldn't make us both walk away from a hundred thousand dollars if these guys weren't dangerous.'

'So we're just leaving it all here?'

'Have you been listening?' I grabbed her purse off the dresser and handed it to her. 'Now please tell me you fucking drove here.'

140

'Okay, okay. Yeah, my car's in the parking garage. Casino level.'

I put the lock back on the suitcase and carried it to the closet. I remembered the five hundred dollars Junior had given me and stuffed it in an outer pocket, then grabbed the notecard with Mai's name before closing the closet. I made a point of giving her back the tiny chrome key and also offered her the notecard. She gave the closet one last glance as she followed me out of the room.

Once we arrived next door, I started throwing all my stuff into the duffel bag. She looked around as though she'd been led into some labyrinth. She tried the knob of the adjoining door like a child poking a mannequin for signs of life. I went to get my Glock from the nightstand and she watched me stick it in the back of my jeans. I think it hit her then, the gravity of the situation.

'Ready?' I opened the door.

She didn't move. Again, that stare. 'You never told me how you knew to come here.'

I sighed and let the door slowly close. 'Your mother,' I said. 'She's been coming to that room every Thursday night for a few months now. They had her followed but never found out what she was doing here. I can't even begin to guess. She liked being alone. Always has. So maybe that's all it was – a room to be alone in. Anyway, they were hoping she'd show up today since it was booked again in her name. She did, apparently.'

I had missed Suzy in the last few hours. In fact, she might have passed me and made herself invisible somehow, as was her way. She might have even read my note, left it there on the floor.

'She's still in town then,' Mai pointed out.

'Maybe. But she's made as big a mess as I have. I can't clean up both at the same time. Not with you in the mix.' She was about to say something else, but again I opened the door. 'We need to go. You can tell me once we're on the road.'

At the elevators, I took a moment. 'Describe your car for me. In detail.'

'An old black Jeep, a CJ7. Big fat tires, ragtop. Real dirty. The passenger door is scraped pretty bad.'

'Okay. You shouldn't be seen with me, in case Sonny has eyes here. Once we get down there, start walking to the garage. I'll follow you from a ways back. Just go to your car and then drive up to the casino entrance in the garage, and I'll wait for you there.' I tapped the elevator button.

She was looking askance at me.

I dug out my badge for her. 'Here.' I placed it in her hand. 'In case you're still wondering.'

She weighed it in her palm as though weighing its authenticity, and mine. It occurred to me that I was supposed to be the good guy in all this whether I was wearing that badge or not.

The elevator dinged open. The cell phone in my pocket rang.

7

'WHO IS IT?' Mai whispered.

UNKNOWN CALLER appeared on the phone's display. 'It's the son.' I nudged her into the elevator. An old couple stepped aside and nodded at us with polite smiles, and the doors closed. I silenced the phone on the fourth ring.

'I'll call him once we're out of here,' I said under my breath. She was peering at the breast pocket of my jacket, where the phone was.

The old woman leaned over and tapped my arm, the gold bracelets on her wrist rattling. 'Pardon me, sweetie – have you-all tried the buffet?' she asked, her southern accent as frail as her hands.

'Not yet, ma'am,' I said.

The old woman glanced at Mai and smiled, still talking to me. 'I hear they got Chinese food too. And Japanese and Mexican and Italian. Little bit of everything.' She chuckled sweetly.

I tried to look impressed.

Her husband ignored her and so did Mai, who had taken out a pen and was scribbling something on a business card. When the elevator opened, she handed me the card and murmured, 'The number to my cell – just in case,' and we walked out separately. I stood to the side and lit a cigarette as I watched her thread her way through the swarm of afternoon gamblers. It was a card for some place called the Midnight Room. Her number was written on the back.

Everyone had a cell phone in this town, even people who had no one to call. Always on the move, these people. Always ready for the next destination.

The old woman tapped me again on the arm, smiling and squinting through her owlish spectacles. 'What a pretty oriental wife you got.'

Her husband, who was dressed in a bolo tie and a pea-green suit that looked as old as I was, pulled her by the hand. 'Thelma, let's go.' As they walked away with her holding his arm, I could hear him mutter to her, 'That's not his wife, dear.'

The cell phone was ringing again and I ignored it and started across the casino floor. Mai's figure turned the corner and vanished. She moved like someone accustomed to walking away from people at the slightest provocation. She didn't know how to trust people, or maybe she just didn't on principle. My father once told me he was glad I was a boy because girls were either too trusting or too suspicious, and he had no patience for either thing, especially if he was to teach someone how to survive the world.

A waitress, all legs and bust, was approaching me with an empty tray, mistaking my stare for thirst or desire or whatever it was that men usually eyed her for. What I really wanted was to toss the cell on her tray and make a clean run for the city limits, cut my losses and abandon everything to this desert dust, consequences be damned. Knowing I couldn't and wouldn't do that pissed me off all the more.

Suzy had always been rash like this, blindfolded half

the time – a hungry infant one day, a sullen child the next. And now she'd left her daughter a poisoned gift and somehow contaminated me as well. For two years I had mislaid that anger she was so good at stoking, and locating it again made me at once nostalgic and bitter, as helpless as I'd always been, and now with more questions than ever. Maybe getting Mai out of town was me protecting myself from all that old impotence.

I weaved through crowds of people whooping and high-fiving each other around the table games, then passed solitary men roaming the floor as though adrift on their cigarette smoke, deaf to the singing slot machines. A casino, I'd always thought, was a carousel of hope and hopelessness. I'd been to a few in California. They were all the same. You come for your drinks, your music and dancing, and of course your spin with fate, and then you win or lose, and then you either leave or go right back and seek shelter at another game, another chance at fortune. But when you're there, you can't hide. Not for long. Not with so much hope everywhere.

Maybe that's what drew people like Sonny and Mai to this place. Its endlessness. The thought quickened me toward the exit.

In the lobby, a gaggle of young women in tight skirts and high heels were snapping photos in front of the giant glittering Christmas tree. One of them accosted me with her camera and begged me to take their picture. In the viewfinder, they raised their drinks and blew me bright lipsticked kisses. I walked away annoyed by my desire for them.

Outside the casino entrance, I waited several minutes

before Mai's Jeep finally lumbered up, tires as high as my waist. She was dwarfed by it, a schoolgirl behind the steering wheel. The Jeep was dusty and pockmarked and had a rusted foot-long gash on the passenger door, which creaked open.

'I need your room key,' I said, tossing my duffel bag inside. 'Why?' She was gripping the steering wheel with both hands. 'The money is all they want, and we're giving it back to them. We'll need to leave them the key somewhere here.'

She looked confused but fished the keycard out of her purse. I walked to a row of potted ferns by the wall and slipped the keycard into one of the large stone pots, pushing it into the dirt. Mai watched me carefully from the Jeep.

As soon as I got back inside, my cell started ringing, and again I silenced it.

'You're not answering?'

'Not until we're miles from this place. He'll call again. Head for I-15 going south. Once we're on the highway, I'll answer and tell him how to get the money, and we'll see what he says from a safe distance.'

We exited the parking garage and the desert sun hit us like a camera flash. I peered through the rear window, checking all the cars behind us. The facade of the Coronado went white in the sunlight, quickly receding as Mai barreled down the streets.

I was escaping a burning house again, I thought – but was I also abandoning someone inside?

Mai played with the heater, but it didn't seem to be working. She spoke up, 'There's something I haven't told you.' She stared hard at the road, shifting gears like she was restraining an angry animal. 'On Tuesday a woman came to my door. Vietnamese woman. Woke me in the middle of the afternoon with her loud knocking. I'd never seen her before in my life. She had glasses on and was wearing a casino uniform and a baseball cap low over her eyes, and she asked me, real serious, if I was Mai. I noticed a cut on her lip and a bruise under her eye that she tried to cover up with makeup. When I said yes, she asked if my mother had contacted me. I was too stunned to say anything, but I guess she could see the answer on my face. She told me that if I saw my mother, if I had any way of reaching her, I had to tell her to leave town at once. Tell her Happy said this, she told me. Tell her Happy means it.'

Mai was gauging my reaction. 'I didn't get that it was her name at first. Had to repeat what she said over and over to myself. You know this woman, don't you?'

I nodded tiredly. 'Your mother's friend. Her best friend, actually. We knew her in Oakland, but she lives here now. I have no idea where.'

'That's why I didn't totally trust you at first. I thought you might be the reason my mother needed to leave town.'

'Did Happy tell you anything else?'

With her free hand, Mai began rummaging blindly through her purse and finally pulled out a prescription bottle. 'She gave me this. She said my mother needs it. And then she hurried away before I could say anything.'

The bottle was Suzy's prescription of anxiety pills. Something she'd been taking in the final few years of our marriage.

Mai's face was soft in the sunlight, fine-boned. Her short hair accentuated the size of her eyes, which – when they gazed at you – seemed to want everything and at the same time give you nothing.

'I'll be honest with you, man,' she said, 'I don't give a shit about anyone in the world. But this is my mother, you know. I've stayed up every night for a month thinking about where she could be, why she's writing me. Everywhere I go now, I'm looking for her, and I don't even know what she looks like. It makes me sad, but it also pisses me off. It's like she's always just around the corner and at the same time on the other side of the world. Actually, that's how it's felt for twenty years.'

We kicked onto the highway, the Jeep rumbling now as she shifted into high gear. She was waiting for me to say something, but I wasn't ready yet to say it. Her patience embarrassed me, made me understand that I was a grown man, a cop no less, asking a young girl I barely knew to help me escape the city, to save me from my worst self.

The phone started ringing again. I looked at Mai and put my fingers to my lips.

I took a breath and answered after the third ring. 'Yes?'

'I've been trying to reach you, Officer Ruen.'

'Who is this?'

'Me and my brother brought you here this morning.'

I twisted around in my seat and scanned the cars behind us. Mai was giving me curious looks. All I could do was gesture for her to keep driving.

'I'm not following you,' the voice continued. 'Mr Nguyen doesn't know I'm calling. No one knows, not even my brother.'

It was the older brother. His voice sounded distant. It

reminded me of his sad eyes in the rearview mirror the previous night.

He said, 'We should talk.'

'Why?'

'I know the girl is driving you in a black Jeep. I know she's Mrs Nguyen's daughter.'

He let that sink in for a second. 'There's a bar called the Cottage on Paradise Road, just north of Flamingo and a few blocks from the Stratosphere Hotel. Small white building with a chimney, right next to a strip club. Meet me there now, both of you, and I'll explain everything.'

'Explain just what exactly?' I struggled for a way to tell him he was crazy if he thought I'd actually go meet him face-to-face, let alone bring Mai with me.

But then he said, 'You left the money, didn't you?' When I didn't reply, he added, 'The money in the room. In the suitcase.'

'If Sonny wants it, it's all there. We want no part of it.'

'Okay, you're fine then. For now. As long as he doesn't know where it is.'

'So it *is* Sonny's money.'

'Every last dollar.'

'And all you want is to talk.'

'You'll both want to hear what I have to say.'

'You're trying to help us?'

'I'm trying to help Mrs Nguyen. Look, I helped her steal the money. Now meet me at the bar as soon as possible. Remember, the girl comes in too.'

He hung up. I palmed the phone and let my hand fall to my lap.

'Well?' Mai said impatiently.

I peered at Suzy's prescription bottle in my other hand with a mixture of relief and old dread. 'All right,' I said. 'We're not leaving yet.'

8

As Mai drove us up Paradise Road, with the Stratosphere Hotel looming in the distance, a giant alien scepter, I told her about her mother's most recent episode with Sonny. Twenty minutes was barely enough time to state the facts, let alone explain the truth of the matter, which after ten years still felt as far away from me as ever.

'She used to be like that with me,' I said. 'Scared me shitless. I didn't know what to do half the time.'

'Jesus,' she muttered with a disbelieving chuckle and a shake of her head. 'Woke up this morning thinking I'd meet my long-lost mother. Now I find out she's a thief *and* she's crazy.'

'Don't say that,' I told her. 'Your mother's not crazy.'

What she was, I could not say. The doctor – her physician actually, the only doctor she ever saw – called it acute depression. I would always think of it as a sadness she carried around like something she needed.

Mai slowed down as we passed Flamingo Road. We started looking for the bar. It was frigid in the Jeep, but the sunlight warmed my cheek, made me think of warmer days in the past when I'd go driving with Suzy by the ocean. I was never the passenger with her. I drove us everywhere, even when we took her car. It was my role and I insisted on it, and to some degree she did too, though I know now that

I drove because I simply didn't trust her to do it.

Had we the time, I would've told Mai about my honeymoon with her mother. I would've told her about how we had gone to San Diego, a drive that took us an entire day, and how her mother got carsick and vomited several times onto the Pacific Coast Highway.

It was July, traffic was horrendous, and the car's air conditioning was weak and intermittently didn't work at all, not to mention I had forgotten the cooler with all the drinks and snacks she prepared. She spent most of the ride with her seat reclined, staring out the window at the ocean as the tape deck played her yowling Vietnamese ballads.

San Diego was my idea. We could go to the zoo, eat authentic Mexican food, visit the beaches and see Tijuana in the distance. She agreed but seemed less than thrilled. I suspected a honeymoon in our living room would have suited her just fine. She had this irrational fear of leaving town and being unable to come home, of us somehow getting lost and never finding our way back. That's what she told me, anyway.

Even before I was old enough to understand my parents' arguments, my father used to tell me – usually after one of my mother's fits throwing dishes or books or whatever – that women lose control when they're afraid and that men lose control when they're in love. Naturally I took all this on faith until I finally fell in love myself and realized, with some horror, that it was often no different than being afraid, and that my father had been simply confessing how little he loved my mother and how much it terrified her to know that.

When we finally got to San Diego that evening, I

decided to take Suzy to an expensive and secluded seafood restaurant on the shore, a place I once took a girlfriend years ago. She was quiet throughout dinner. She still looked a little white but was also, I knew, silently blaming me for everything that had gone wrong that day. I ordered all her favorite seafood – oysters, squid, lobster. I must have spent half a week's salary. She ate some bread and pasta but barely touched anything else, so I let her sulk and stuffed myself, nearly finishing everything on my own.

When the bill came, she got onto me for spending so much. I told her to calm the hell down, which was when she snapped and demanded that I drive us back home. I suggested she walk home if she wanted to because I wasn't driving another goddamn mile, and that's when she flung her fork onto her plate, shot up, and stormed out of the restaurant, abandoning me to a restaurant full of curious glances. I hadn't yet paid the bill and had to toss my card on the table as I hurried after her.

I'd had women do this to me before and was already rolling my eyes when I saw her marching alongside the dark windy road that led away from the restaurant. The key was to let them cool off, to avoid forcing anything. So I followed, calmly calling after her, insisting that we should drive to the hotel and get some rest, that she'd feel much better after a night's sleep. She continued down the side of the road in silence until we had walked nearly half a mile.

Finally I decided to catch up, and I grabbed her arm and she turned and looked through me, as though at something frightening behind me.

'I want to go home,' she muttered in a distracted voice and wrenched her arm away. 'I need to go home,' she kept repeating to herself as headlights from a passing car illuminated her dress and her petite figure and yanked her shadow across the two-lane road. Even in that moment, I desired her.

We had known each other for only four months then. I was humoring her not yet out of understanding, not yet out of exasperation, or resentment, or a lack of options. My love was still too new for me to see this as anything more than a problem I could always fix later, a nuisance that came with the territory.

So I continued following her, hoping she'd just tire herself out. We could have easily been mistaken for a couple on an evening stroll along the shore, with her leading the way as the ocean waves mesmerized us and kept us silent. And in fact, they did. I was bone-tired from the drive and busting at the seams after eating so much, but the moonlit evening was breezy and the rumbling waves were lulling me into a calm that I found more pleasant than anything we'd experienced that day.

The road turned lonelier, just the ocean on our right and hills on our left, and very little light save the moon and a single dim streetlamp every quarter mile. Suzy veered away from the road, climbed casually over the guardrail. She approached the edge of a grassy cliff that overlooked the dark beach below us.

I came up beside her. 'What are you looking at?'

She said nothing for a few moments. Then she took another step forward and pointed, almost sadly.

I squinted and finally made out a solitary figure strolling alongside the water's edge. I couldn't tell if it was a man or a woman.

'Do you want to go down there?' I asked. 'I'm sure we can find a path.'

'Yes,' she murmured but did not move. A moment later, in a wounded voice, she said, 'I don't want to bother them. Maybe they want to be alone.' She had a habit of referring to an individual in the plural, almost like it was rude to refer to anyone as only one person.

'The beach is big enough for all three of us. I'm sure they won't mind.'

The figure began wading out into the water, dipping hands into the ocean.

'Come on, let's go,' I said. 'I'll find the path for us.' I tried to take her hand, but it was balled into a fist. 'Why are you crying? Come on, it'll be nice down there. The water will do us good. And the sand –'

But she was shaking her head, her shoulders trembling a little now. She started backing away.

'What is it now?' I tried to check the annoyance in my voice. 'Come on, it'll be fun.'

'No,' she replied and climbed back over the guardrail as I moved toward her.

'Well, then we should get back to the restaurant. I left my card there, you know.'

I was raising my voice again, a thing I would always have a problem controlling with her. But she was moving faster and farther away from me and still murmuring 'No' to herself and shaking her head and crying in her muffled way.

'Where the hell are you going?' I shouted after her, before screaming out a moment later when I saw the lights of an approaching car. She was still rushing toward the road, and then her feet hit pavement and she sprang back just as the car's headlights set her ablaze, and in an instant the car swerved, screeching its tires, and crashed headfirst into the guardrail on the other side of the road.

Suzy stood there like she was lost. As I raced past her, she turned to me in horror, clarity returning to her eyes, and I knew she had come back to earth. I would confront that face many times again with both relief and anger, but at that moment I was much more concerned with whoever was in the car.

It looked like an older man, his body slumped over the deployed airbag, face turned inward under a mop of strewn white hair. He had not been wearing his seat belt. His car's front end was embedded in the gnarled guardrail, headlights doused, but I saw no smoke or sign of leakage.

'Sir?' I called through the half-open window. 'Can you hear me, sir? Are you okay? If you can hear me, don't move. Do not move any part of your body! We'll go get help!'

I ran to the passenger side, reached in, and took the key from the ignition. It was still too dark to see his face or any blood. I felt his neck and found a pulse. My hope was that the impact of the airbag had only knocked him out.

I remembered Suzy and looked up and she was standing on the other side of the car, peering in with frantic eyes. She said, 'I killed them.'

'No, you didn't. But I have to call for help. We passed a gas station down the road.' I rushed over to her. 'Baby, I need you to stay here and watch him. Do not move him, understand? If he comes to, tell him he has to stay completely still. If the car starts smoking or anything, run away as fast as you can. Do you understand all that? Do you? I'll be back as soon as I can.'

She was startled out of her trance and started shaking her head at me. 'No, no, don't leave me,' she pleaded quietly.

'Someone has to watch him in case he comes to. I'm coming back, all right?'

She took hold of my wrist and kept insisting I not leave, and finally I had to wrest my arm away. 'Stay, goddamn it!' I thrust my finger at the motionless man. 'I need you to stay! I will be right back!'

Her arms fell and she looked at once chastened and desperate. Before she could say anything else, I raced down the road.

When I got to the gas station, it was still open but no cars were out front and I couldn't see the attendant at his counter. Instead of running inside to find him, I ran directly to the pay phone.

I gave the dispatcher the location of the accident, but when she asked for more details, I pretended to have been a passerby in my car. Maybe I already sensed then what Suzy would do. Maybe I was already acting out of shame. When the dispatcher asked me for a number and a name, I hung up and started racing back.

The driver's body still had a pulse but had not yet moved. Suzy, on the other hand, was gone.

I started calling out her name, screaming it at one point despite knowing it would make her less likely to respond. She was probably as terrified of me now as she was of the accident she had caused. I'd never seen her look at me that way. She might still, I thought, be in the throes of whatever emotion had seized her and thrown her out onto the road. I knew I had to abandon the driver.

Up the road, the grassy cliff beyond the guardrail dipped and a rocky path revealed itself. I scrambled down the slope, out of breath at that point, until I landed on sand and began running across the beach and again yelling for her.

I soon heard sirens swarming in the distance, no doubt a fire engine, an ambulance, and the accompanying squad cars, all in case the accident was severe. They would probably block off the entire road. Unless we wanted to be questioned, we'd have to find another way back to the restaurant.

By the time I made it down the length of the beach, my shoes were filled with sand and grating my feet and I could see the glow of flashing emergency lights from above. I was hidden under a canopy of trees crowding the hillside, tramping through the sand in darkness. The beach was desolate. All I felt, more than worry or exhaustion, was this helpless rage at what Suzy had done to me that day. In our first months together, she'd shown glimmers of how emotional she could get, slamming doors and cabinets and crying even at our silliest arguments, but she had not yet revealed this side of herself.

I considered returning to the accident to explain everything and report Suzy's disappearance, so perhaps then they could help me find her. But I'd also lied to the dispatcher, making the call anonymously, leaving the scene, and I wouldn't be able to explain all that away, not as an officer of the law myself. Knowing this just made the rage worse.

My only option was to walk back in the direction of the

restaurant and hope to find her on the way, and if not, I could go searching for her in my car.

It took me nearly half an hour to find my way up onto the road, far enough away from the accident to not be noticed, and then back to the restaurant. Only a few cars were left in the parking lot, my Chrysler one of them.

I saw a lone figure in the backseat. She was sitting still in the darkness, hugging her legs to her chest. She jumped when I opened the door.

'What the hell were you thinking!' I hissed at her.

She was peering up at me stark-eyed and shaking her head again like she was shivering. 'Don't let them arrest me! Don't let them take me!'

'I told you to stay there, goddamn it. Why did you take off like that?'

'I killed them. I killed them!'

'You didn't kill anyone,' I snapped at her.

She was tearing up again and trembling, pushing herself farther into the car.

I took a long breath and went down on a knee. I softened my voice. 'No one's going to arrest you. It was an accident, and you didn't do anything wrong. I'm sure that man will be fine. He was just knocked out, is all. Come here.'

I got into the backseat with her and closed the door. 'Come on,' I whispered and put my arm around her. 'Everything's okay.'

Her hot face pressed against my chest, and she curled into that space that had already become hers, like she was wrapping herself into the folds of a coat. I felt then the dampness of her dress and hair, the bits of sand on her arms, strewn also over the car seat.

'You are sure?' she said, hugging me tightly now.

'Yeah, he's fine.' At that point, I was convincing myself of that too. I could call the nearest hospital the next day and confirm it. 'The police and the medics are there and they'll take care of him. Let's go to the hotel now and get some sleep, okay?'

'And the woman?'

'What do you mean?'

'The woman. In the back. She is okay?'

'The woman...' I repeated to myself. In the darkness, I could feel her staring into me, her breath warm against my chest. 'She look like she sleeping. But then she open her eyes and she look at me.'

The hair on my arms bristled, and the darkness felt stifling. Again I heard sirens wailing from afar, like she and I were in a cocoon and the world outside was burning.

Had she hallucinated some phantom woman in the car, or was I the one who'd gone crazy and somehow overlooked another human being in the backseat? But why would the woman sit in back and the man in front? Did I even once glance back there?

I said, 'I'm sure she'll be fine too. I promise you they're both fine.'

After we finally got to the hotel that night and showered together and then lay our wet heads down on our pillows, Suzy fell instantly asleep and I lay there blinking at the ceiling, promising myself that I would call the hospitals in the morning.

When I awoke at dawn, she rolled over and embraced me and apologized for everything that had happened. We made love in the gray light.

Afterward she wanted to describe the dream she had had that night. I braced for something terrible, for her to start crying as she recounted it. It turned out to be the one beautiful dream of hers that I know: of her living in a three-story house drifting on the ocean. You could reach outside the many windows and caress the waves that lapped the walls day and night. Her entire family from Vietnam lived there with her, even those who had died. Everyone had their own room, her mother and father, her aunts, her uncles, her sisters and cousins, and every room was colorful and unique and connected to the others so that you could walk through them all like you were walking through a garden of rooms. Only years later, thinking back on this dream, did I wonder if I had a room in this house, or if I was even there at all.

In the afternoon we went to the beach and swam in the ocean and ate a lunch of grilled fish and oysters. I took her shopping afterward and bought her a new dress, then we saw a matinee showing of *Dances with Wolves*, which moved us both to tears, and in the evening we had a delicious dinner at a Vietnamese restaurant downtown. We made love twice more that night, and she cried the final time.

Perhaps I made myself forget, but I never picked up the phone that day.

9

THE COTTAGE, which had white wooden shutters and a white chimney, stood facing the road, flanked by a strip mall of restaurants and a strip club called Paradise Palace. The tiny parking lot out front was empty, but I told Mai to park in back. We walked under a red awning and through a red door and stepped into a room cloaked in rusty light.

All the tables stood afternoon empty, snugged up against button-tufted leather booths that looked proudly worn. Wood paneling and crimson wallpaper surrounded us, above us a low canopy of ceiling fans spinning lazily. The place had a saloonish quality, a cowboy gruffness despite all the dolls encased in glass cabinets along the walls. They stood side by side, dozens in each cabinet, some a foot tall, decked in period dresses and garish hats and hairstyles: a showgirl, a cowgirl, a geisha, an English wench, a French lady. Mai stepped up close to one cabinet and glanced at me to see if I shared her bemusement.

A young couple were arguing quietly at the bar, their faces close, their lips moving swiftly. The girl was luxuriously blond and wore a green dress, and it took me a second to realize that the guy, who had on jeans and a T-shirt, was a girl too, her slender left arm covered in colorful tattoos as she gesticulated at the blond, their voices muted by Lee

Hazlewood crooning 'Some Velvet Morning' over the jukebox.

At the other end of the bar sat an old bearded guy sucking on a cigar beneath his Stetson, too engrossed in his video poker to care about the girls or us. He was the one who looked out of place.

Behind us, the front door opened and two men in suits and open-collared shirts walked in, both taking off their sunglasses to look around. They must've mistaken the bar for the strip club and promptly turned and walked back out. I couldn't imagine Sonny setting foot in a place like this either, which explained why we were there.

'We should probably order something to drink,' I told Mai. The bartender, a sturdy middle-aged woman, stood watching the TV on the wall, her short inky hair gleaming beneath the white Christmas lights strung above the bar. When she turned to greet us, her casual smile felt like the first genuine thing I'd seen in Vegas.

'Getting cold out there, huh?' she said, her voice cigarette raspy. 'I should put on a sweater, but my tits like to breathe.' She grinned innocently at Mai. Her blouse was low-cut, her leathery bosom less sexual than a proud badge of all her years in the harsh desert sun. 'What you having, baby?'

'A Coke,' Mai replied and turned to me.

'Whatever you got on tap,' I told the bartender. I asked Mai, 'Too early in the day?'

'I don't drink. *Or* do drugs. My cousin's an idiot. Can't do that stuff if you want to be good at cards.'

I went for my wallet, but she had already set a hundred on the bar.

'You play every day?'

'When I'm not sleeping.'

'Why poker?'

'The money,' she replied dryly.

'Bartender at the Coronado told me poker players are an honest lot. Very proud.'

'He just means we're control freaks. It's great to be lucky, but it's better to be in control. When you're good, you can control the luck.'

She tipped the bartender the price of both our drinks, and then she turned and noticed what I had not.

Nested in the far corner of the bar was a small stage with a black piano, above it an unlit neon sign: DON'T TELL MAMA. A few tables stood against the wall by the stage. The older brother was sitting at one with a pitcher of beer, staring at us patiently through his cigarette smoke.

'Don't tell him your name,' I muttered to Mai.

We got our drinks and made our way to the table. He couldn't take his eyes off her, but then I remembered that he must have known what her mother looked like.

As we sat down, he nodded at me and said 'Hello, sister' to Mai in Vietnamese. On the wall above him was a cabinet of dolls dressed like old Hollywood starlets, their lipstick smiles made vulgar by the shadows.

There were three glasses on the table, though only his was filled. He intended for us to talk a bit. Beneath the table, I noticed, leaning against his leg, was a small black backpack.

'My name is Victor.' He pushed his cigarette pack toward me, the same one from this morning. Again he offered me a light. His name and a cigarette: gestures of goodwill. In the car this morning, he must have wondered what it took to earn the trust of a man like me.

'Has he called you yet?' he said.

'Your boss? Not if you're the one who called me the last four times.'

'He probably won't, then, unless I report something. And I haven't.'

His voice had a cold, quiet edge to it that these young tough types cultivate nowadays, though I could see that it was shyness too that hardened his face. It was easy for him to intimidate. Much harder for him to look people in the eye and talk to them earnestly.

Mai was peering at him as I imagined she would another poker player. She had yet to touch her Coke.

I gestured at her. 'They know about her?'

'I would've already visited her if they did.'

'Like you visited Happy?'

He went silent, then blinked a few times at Mai. 'She came to see you, didn't she?' To me he said, 'Mr Jonathan – the son you spoke to – he was there. I had to do my job. Don't worry, she gave up nothing. That's why we had to go visit you in Oakland.'

Mai said something in Vietnamese to him. His face crimsoned. 'What was that?' I said.

'I asked him if he liked hitting women.'

'Of course not,' Victor replied. He recovered his calm and added, 'Not even when they deserve it.'

I jumped in, 'So what are we doing now, Victor? You and your brother broke into my home yesterday and put a gun to my head and then drove me here to do something I don't want to do. And now you say you want to help me.'

'I said I want to help Mrs Nguyen.'

A glass shattered somewhere, and we all looked up. The

bartender, her hands on her hips, was peering irritably at the floor behind the bar. Patsy Cline was playing now, and I noticed that the two girlfriends had stepped away to slow-dance by the jukebox, the blond with her head on the other girl's shoulder, their argument doused. They had caught Victor's attention too. I couldn't tell if he was bothered or intrigued, but when Mai swiveled in her chair for her own glimpse, I saw him give her a lingering look.

He coughed hoarsely into a fist and drank his beer. 'It's Mrs Nguyen I want to help,' he repeated.

'Then tell us everything you know. Start at the beginning. How much time do we have?'

He flipped open his cell for a quick check and then set it back on the table. 'It's a bit messy.'

'Only a bit?'

He put out his cigarette. He'd only smoked half of it. 'First thing you got to understand is I rarely know their reasons for doing anything. I do what I'm told, I don't ask questions. Me and my brothers, we've been doing that for years now. We started out washing dishes, and now we do whatever needs doing. They like that we can take care of ourselves, that we send money home to our mother, that my brothers do what I tell them. Knowing your place and what you have to do – they expect that of everyone, especially people they trust. They put us through school, you know. That's the other thing you got to understand. Me and my brothers came to America on our own. Our father died on the way, and we haven't seen our family back home in thirteen years. So Mr Nguyen and his son, they're all the family we got here.

'But like I said, certain things they don't talk about.

When Mr Nguyen got married two years ago, we didn't know he was with anybody. We were curious, of course. But we never saw her. She didn't come by the restaurant, and when I drove Mr Nguyen home or picked him up, I had to park by the curb, stay in the car. So I only ever saw her from a distance, standing in their living room window usually. I think he wanted it that way, her not knowing about his business, us not knowing about her. But some things you can't help knowing. He started arguing with her a lot on the phone, spending more and more time at the restaurant, at the casinos. I lost count how many times he'd storm out of the house when I picked him up in the morning, all red-faced and cursing to himself. Drunk. He's always been a drinker, but I'd never seen him start that early in the day until Mrs Nguyen came along.'

Victor kept his hands in his lap like they were handcuffed under the table. I noticed he didn't gesture when he spoke, even when there was emotion in his voice. And it was strange to hear so many words come out of his mouth. He wasn't that taciturn after all. He just had remarkable self-control.

'Then one night last year,' he said, 'I get a call from Mr Jonathan, telling me I have to come to the house at once. I figure I'm in trouble or something. But when I get there, he's waiting at the front door and waves me inside. First time ever. He looks nervous, which isn't like him. When I walk into the living room, I see why. His father's sitting slouched by the staircase in his underwear and no shirt on, and he's holding his hand like it's broken. He looks at me with bloodshot eyes, like he doesn't know me. Mrs Nguyen's lying beside him at the foot of the stairs. She's not moving. Her hair's a mess. Her nightgown's ripped at the shoulder. I can't see any blood, but at the top of the stairs is an overturned lamp. Mr Jonathan's on the phone with 911, and when he hangs up, he hands me a pair of pajamas and orders me to put them on. He says Mrs Nguyen has fallen and is unconscious, so when the paramedics come, I have to tell them I'm a family friend who was staying over and woke up and found her this way, that she accidentally fell down the stairs. I'm not to say anything else, or move her, or let her move on her own if she wakes up. He's gonna meet me at the hospital shortly. I get even more freaked out now because I know he's trusting me with her life. He grabs his father's good arm and gets him to his feet, like he's a stubborn child, and he starts hurrying him to the garage door. Mr Nguyen hasn't said a word yet, but suddenly he pulls his arm away and smacks his son across the face with his good hand. Mr Jonathan glares at him like he's ready to choke him. But then he just says, "Let's go, Dad," and his father looks back one more time at Mrs Nguyen and stumbles out the door on his own.

'So they leave, and I do exactly as I'm told. An hour later Mr Jonathan arrives at the hospital. He's alone, acts real concerned with the doctor and the nurses, even holds back a tear when they tell us that Mrs Nguyen broke her left arm and suffered a concussion. She was lucky she didn't break her neck. After that I'm told to go home.

'A week later, I finally see Mr Nguyen again. He's got a metal splint on two of his fingers. Him and his son act like nothing happened, but for the next few months, he's a lot calmer and nicer on the phone with Mrs Nguyen. He's drinking less, brings food and flowers home to her. They even go to Hawaii for a week, and I know how much he hates flying.

'But once she gets better, things go right back to how they were. I pick him up one morning and he's got a big bandage above his left eye. Few days after that – this was about a month ago – she comes storming into the restaurant during dinnertime and demands to see him. Mr Jonathan tries to calm her down, but she swipes a glass from the counter and smashes it on the ground. That's when Mr Nguyen comes rushing out of the kitchen, grabs her by the arm, hauls her into the kitchen. There's a lot of yelling at first, stuff flying around, but then his office door slams shut and we don't hear anything for hours. Even after the restaurant closes, they still don't come out.

'So I wasn't all that surprised when Mr Jonathan took me aside the next day and told me to start following her. It was now my full-time job. Rent a different car every day, park down the street, wait for her to leave the house. Anywhere she goes, I go. She didn't work anymore, so I was usually following her to the grocery store or the shopping mall, sometimes to the movies. One thing she liked doing was going to the casinos in the afternoon and just walking around, gambling a little, watching people. Sometimes she'd go driving for an hour and then come straight home. I reported all that.'

Victor had been telling his story mostly to me, but now he turned thoughtfully to Mai. 'What I didn't report was her visiting you. One afternoon she parks across the street from your complex, crosses over on foot. She walks directly to your apartment, drops an envelope in your mailbox, and doesn't stop until she gets back to her car. I guess you got that letter.'

Mai gave me a knowing glance but offered Victor only coolness. 'You just kept that to yourself? Respecting her privacy all of a sudden?'

I expected someone like Victor to bristle at sarcasm, but again he seemed surprised, more hurt than annoyed by her tone. 'I was respecting the situation,' he insisted. 'I figured I was following her because Mr Nguyen thought she was cheating on him or something. This felt like something else though. The way she looked after she went to your apartment... When she got back to her car, she sat there for a long time with her hands gripping the steering wheel and just stared at your complex. It was like someone had died. I went back to your apartment that evening and waited on that bench by the pool. You passed me, actually, when you came home. You were wearing exactly what you're wearing now. I knew at once who you had to be. It'd be obvious to anyone who's seen your mother. And I don't know – something about the whole thing... it felt so *private*, I guess. I admit I was curious, but I didn't want to say anything until I knew more.'

He tried to look Mai in the eye, searching for some approval, and I could see now why he was doing all this. The first time he saw her, she must have inflamed his curiosity just as her mother did to me ten years before. He probably went back to that bench the following night and every night after that. Might have even fantasized about this very conversation, in this bar, with her and only her sitting across from him.

'I watched her mostly during the day,' he went on. 'Mr

Nguyen was home in the evening, and she rarely went out after sundown anyway. The one night I had to keep watch was Thursday night, which has always been Mr Nguyen's long session of poker. He plays at the casino from seven in the evening to seven in the morning, so she spends that night alone, and recently she started going to the movies. That didn't surprise me. I had already followed her one afternoon to a showing of *Castaway*. Sat four rows behind her and saw her cry several times, even during parts of the movie that weren't sad at all.'

His face softened. He spoke to Mai with sudden confidence, an intimacy he seemed sure she would reciprocate: 'You and her left Vietnam by boat and were at sea for a long time. Awful things happened, I'm sure.' He said a few words in Vietnamese, as if reciting some adage she surely knew too. Then his voice leaned into her. 'Mr Nguyen and his son were also on that boat. All four of you went to the same refugee camp.'

Mai appeared to withdraw from him in her seat. In a small voice, like she was claiming innocence, she said, 'My uncle said my mom and I were on Pulau Bidong.' She pronounced the name with Vietnamese inflection.

He nodded. 'That's where she first met him,' he added delicately. 'You must have met him too. We were there, actually, me and my brothers. Seven years later, long after you guys left. I think that's how he first felt he could trust us. Knowing we'd been to the same place, and that our father died there.'

I'd become the stranger at the table. Victor fell silent, and Mai was speechless, cupping her Coke with both hands. I wanted her to know what Junior had told me about him and his father in that camp, how Suzy had loved Sonny long before she met me. I wanted to tell her that as bad as it is to have no memory of something significant you were a part of, it's much worse to know you were never part of it at all.

'Anyway...' Victor turned back to me. 'I was actually looking forward to going to the movies, but when Thursday came around, she drove to Fremont Street instead. To the Coronado. It was suspicious for sure, her going to the one place in town where Mr Nguyen and Mr Jonathan are blacklisted. Anyway, she checked herself into a room with nothing but her purse, and that's when I got real nervous for her. I had the front desk put me through to the room, but she answered, so I hung up. If someone was in there with her, I knew I had to report it, and there was no telling what Mr Nguyen would do about that. Then five hours passed and nothing happened. At midnight she came out, checked out of the hotel, and drove home. I tried calling the room again right after she left, but the front desk said it was vacated. So that's what I told Mr Jonathan – that Mrs Nguyen had been alone in there the entire time.'

Victor refilled his glass with the pitcher. He drank like he was thirsty. It seemed to embarrass him, telling us all this, hearing his own voice so much. I wondered if this wasn't some kind of confession for him, one he was ashamed yet eager to give – more to Mai apparently than to me.

'Do me a favor, Victor,' I said. 'Don't call her that.'

'Mrs Nguyen? You want me to call her Hong?'

'Whatever. Just don't call her that.'

He shrugged his assent, and he and Mai exchanged a brief private look like they both understood my pain.

His cell phone chimed and startled all three of us. He picked it up, his eyes gathering Mai and me carefully before he answered it. His voice was low, his Vietnamese soft and slurred, a southern accent. He appeared to be answering questions.

When he hung up a minute later, he said, as if issuing us a warning, 'That was Mr Jonathan. He'll check on me every two hours.'

'You said something to him about a gun,' Mai said.

'I told him a few weeks ago that I saw your mother buy one at a pawnshop. I was just reminding him there.'

'So she's packing heat too? Jesus, is this woman seriously my mother?'

'But she hates guns,' I said to them both. 'Never even touched one. She bought a gun?'

'Not exactly,' Victor replied. 'But she does have one.'

'So you lied to him?'

'About her buying the gun, yeah. She'd actually taken one of his.'

'Then why mention it at all?'

'Because she wanted me to.'

In the silence that followed, he put a fresh cigarette between his lips, then changed his mind for some reason and inserted it back into the pack before returning to his story.

AFTER THAT FIRST TRIP to the Coronado, he spent most of the following week sitting in his car, watching their house from his curbside seat. The only time Suzy left home was for groceries, the mail, or takeout at the nearby Chinese place. Through his binoculars, he could see how unkempt her hair and clothes were and how stark her face looked, like she was perpetually waking from a nap. I knew that face from all her long melancholy spells, going to bed as soon as she got home from work, sleeping until two in the afternoon on her off days, sometimes spending the entire day in bed watching television. Victor said she moved like an old woman.

When Thursday evening arrived, however, she came out of the house in a dress with her hair brushed and her face made. She was carrying a red knapsack. As she had the previous week, she drove to the Coronado and checked herself again into room 1215.

Victor tried to stay out of sight, but just in case she spotted him, he had also started wearing baseball caps and sunglasses, which must have got to him. I could see it now on his face. It wears on you – watching someone who doesn't know you're there, who doesn't know they should be hiding from you. After a while, you start feeling like the one hiding from them.

But did Suzy know he was there that entire time? Sitting in his anonymous rental by her curb, the same guy who picked up her husband every morning in a funereal Lexus, that dark figure behind the steering wheel and the tinted windows? Had he made some sort of impression on her from that distance, even before this mess started? Her world was hardly big enough for the people in her life, let alone those on the periphery. So how did Victor get in?

To look more like a hotel guest that night, he wore a suit. He sat in a chair across from the elevators, just around the corner from her room. Anytime he heard someone approach, he lifted the magazine he was reading. He must have wondered how long he could keep this up before she started noticing him there every time she left her room, or before some hotel staffer or security camera noticed too. Maybe it was that night that he realized how tiring it was to hide. Maybe that's why he was careless.

Nothing happened for a couple of hours. Hardly a soul passed him in the hallway except for the hotel maids rolling their cleaning carts.

At some point, he dozed off. He didn't know for how long, but when he opened his eyes, Suzy was sitting on the edge of the chair next to his and eyeing him like she'd been waiting for him to awake.

She spoke to him in Vietnamese, a proper northern accent, which often makes southerners feel inferior. She told me that once when I laughed at her English. I'm not a dummy, she chided me. In Vietnam I speak beautifully.

Tell me, little brother, she said to Victor. What is your name? He told her his Vietnamese name. Perhaps he was still in shock, because it never occurred to him to lie or deny anything. You've been following me. For my husband.

When he nodded, it felt like a confession.

He believes I'm crazy, she said. His son does too. You've been watching me for some time now. Please tell me the truth. Do I seem like a crazy person to you?

She had asked the question so sincerely that he knew she'd see through a lie. So he said, A little.

Why? What makes you think that?

Because you always seem like you're looking for something that isn't there.

She sat back in her chair.

It's good that Son chose you, she finally said, her eyes

calmer now. Instead of your brother. You seem like someone who thinks long and hard before you do anything. I think that's why you have a sullen face. And why you smoke all the time. You should stop that, by the way. You're so young and yet I see you coughing all the time.

Suzy waited for a hotel maid to reach the end of the hallway before she spoke again, her voice lowered:

I decided tonight. Just now in my room. I want to ask for your help. You can say yes or no, of course, but from here on it's all in your hands. There's nothing I can do about it after tonight.

Victor knew she was about to tell him things she couldn't take back, but he must have been burning to know what else she meant by that. Suzy had a habit of putting things in that way, as though she had accidentally set your house on fire and had no choice now but to stand back and watch it burn.

She said, You followed me to that apartment I visited last week. That's my daughter who lives there. I haven't seen her since she was five. I've been writing her letters. She has no memory of me, I'm sure. It's quite possible she hates me, or doesn't think of me at all. Twenty years ago, I left her with her granduncle and went as far away as I could. I'm still not sure I can explain why – to you or to myself. I don't regret it though, as difficult as it was to do. The strange thing is that I've never stopped thinking of myself as a mother. You must think that's ridiculous. How can a woman give up her child and still see herself as a mother? But that's why I'm here now, talking to you. You're the first person I've ever told this to.

Victor remembered her taking a breath after she said that.

'WAIT A MINUTE,' I stopped him. I had to check the disbelief in my voice. 'Why you?'

Victor shrugged slightly. 'That afternoon at Mai's apartment. She recognized me. She saw me in her rearview mirror, smoking out of my car window, and immediately realized what was going on. It really worried her, of course – Mr Nguyen finding out about Mai. But when she got home, he didn't act any different with her. If he knew something, she would've seen it. He's not very good at hiding his feelings. So that really shocked her – that I hadn't reported anything. Somehow she just knew it and decided to trust me.

'There's another reason. She told me this at the hotel. The night I waited for the ambulance with her – she opened her eyes at one point and started moaning, murmuring to herself. I figured she was too out of it to see or think clearly, but she remembered me kneeling beside her and telling her not to move, that help was coming. She said I held her hand until the ambulance arrived. I guess I did do that.'

Mai spoke up. 'So she told you about me, but did she ever tell Sonny? If he met me back on the island, he must have asked her about me. Hey, where's that daughter of yours? What she doing nowadays? The subject must have come up at least once in two years of marriage.'

Victor didn't reply immediately. He glanced at me like I already knew the answer. 'She told him you had died in a car accident when you were six. She didn't want him knowing anything about you. To protect you.'

This brought on an exasperated chuckle from Mai as she sat back in her chair. In the dim light, she resembled the dolls on the wall behind Victor. Her smile was as baffled as theirs, and it both stiffened her face and made it seem brittle.

'Why did she start writing me, then? Did she tell you that?'

'Well, she asked me to follow her to her room, and that's the first thing I saw, the letters on the desk. She said she'd been coming to the room for months to write you. Long letters, apparently – that she hadn't sent yet. It was the only place she could do it. I figured she wanted me to deliver them to you or something. But then she reached into her knapsack and pulled out a gun and set it on the bed in front of me. She said the hotel was the only place in town she felt safe. And she needed to feel safe, if only for one evening a week. Then she told me that she was leaving Mr Nguyen, that I knew what he had done to her that night and that he had done other things too and would never ever let her go. She'd have to leave town without him knowing. She could manage that, but she had to do something else before she left. Something for you. For that, she needed my help.'

'The money,' Mai said.

'She knew about Mr Nguyen's safe at the restaurant, inside his office. Where he keeps cash from business dealings and all his gambling. I've seen him put tens of thousands of dollars in there at a time. She had figured out the combination, and all she needed from me was the code to the alarm and copies of the keys to the restaurant and the office. She offered me twenty thousand. The rest she was leaving for you.'

Mai sat there stiffly. 'One hundred thousand dollars,' she murmured, as if to herself, and no longer with that gleam of shock and desire she showed at the hotel. She was appraising, it seemed, the price of her forgiveness.

I could have told her that money had always been about freedom for her mother, that she had made me return her engagement ring so she could put the money in the bank instead – but I felt out of place at the moment sharing something like that, or saying anything at all.

Victor was massaging his brow, adjusting himself in his chair. He'd been recounting everything with a self-assured, strangely nostalgic calm, but Mai's mention of the one hundred grand had plummeted him back to earth, where the implications of what he'd done must have hit him hard again.

'She had a plan, if that's what you want to call it.' He sounded impatient. 'In a week, once I got her the keys and the alarm code, she was gonna go get all the money in the safe, leave it in a suitcase in that hotel room for you, then leave town. She kept insisting it was all very simple. All I had to do was pretend I didn't know anything. Just keep following her like normal, like I still didn't exist to her, and when everything went down, just do whatever Mr Nguyen and his son ordered.' Victor's voice tightened, like he was straining to understand his own story. 'I told her, though. They already knew about the hotel room. Was it really the safest place? All she said was that it had to be that room. And that she trusted me.'

He put up a hand like one of us had tried to interrupt him. 'I know what you're thinking. Why me, right? How was she so sure I'd go along with all this? That I would trust her and go betray a man I'd been obeying for – how many years now? He'd cut my throat if he had to.'

He was shaking his head feebly now.

'Do you need the money?' Mai said.

'Who doesn't need the money? The money had nothing to do with it. It still doesn't.'

Fleetwood Mac's 'As Long As You Follow' had started playing on the jukebox, the opening guitar chords tingeing Victor's last words with a melodramatic air.

The bartender was leaning over the bar and chatting quietly with the cowboy, like old friends, like co-conspirators. They were the only other people in the place now. The two young women had left some time ago, and their absence somehow reminded me that I was in the desert, in a bar among strangers.

'Why did you do it then?' Mai finally asked Victor. She had dropped her interrogating tone.

I couldn't quite manage her sincerity yet. When he didn't reply immediately, I said, 'You know he's a bad man. You always knew that.'

Both of them turned to me like they'd forgotten I was there. 'What is a bad man to you, Officer?' Victor said.

I saw then why he was good at his job. He could slip on that coldness like it was a second face.

I'd forgotten about the small black backpack by his feet. He unzipped it and pulled out a videotape, which he set gently on the table.

'I haven't told you the whole story.'

10

VICTOR, I COULD SEE NOW, was a reluctant criminal. He enjoyed his job as much as I enjoyed Vegas but kept at it for that most Asian of reasons: obligation. To his brothers probably, who looked up to him. To his family back home, who relied on the money he sent them. And of course to Sonny, who had taken him in and made him a man, programmed to honor duty over desire. I could see it in his eyes every time he looked at Mai. The kid had never truly desired anyone, and this strange new thing he felt made him both defiant and naive. The most annoying kind of criminal.

He nudged the videotape closer to us, like it was some sinister artifact, and I could imagine it all from there: years of him thoughtlessly obeying orders, doing whatever needed doing and looking the other way, and suddenly one morning from his car he sees his boss's wife, whom he's never met before, standing in the window of their home. She's watching her husband, his boss, walk to the car that will whisk him away to all the ugly things he does during the day, without her, and she knows this. Her arms are crossed, her stare cold and yet strangely tender, like she is saddened by something she also hates. She frightens him actually, though he feels this inexplicable urge to protect her. She reminds him of his mother or his sisters back home, and maybe also those desolate women he saw in the refugee camp. Every morning he comes to pick up his boss, she's standing in that window like some troubled ghost haunting the house.

Then one morning, though he's far away behind sunglasses and tinted windows, she sees him. He can feel her judging him. Her arm is in a cast and she knows now that he has hurt people, stolen from them, perhaps even killed them – all for his boss who's done terrible things too, including all the things he has done to her.

So when he is ordered without any explanation to follow her, he does so with redemption on his mind. It's the naive hero in him, the good son. Every day he trails her down the aisles of grocery stores, through the afternoon crowds at shopping malls and casinos, and into half-empty movie theaters, until one afternoon she leaves a letter at someone's apartment, and when he returns that night and sees who this someone is, he finally understands. All that wandering through the city has been a circling around this young woman, her long-lost daughter, who's even more beautiful and perhaps more alone.

And so maybe he falls in love with this younger version of her. Or maybe the whole thing makes him think of his dead father and the mother he might never see again. Or maybe it just makes him angry, that people have to carry around secrets like this.

When she appears at his side in the empty hallway of the Coronado hotel, it feels like they've been silently speaking to each other all this time. She starts telling him the story he's been waiting for. In room 1215, she reveals the letters on her desk, the gun in her knapsack, and the fear in her heart. One day soon, she says, intentionally or not, his boss will kill her. She has to leave him, but she wants to punish him too, this man who's probably given Victor everything he has. When she asks for his help, he refuses, so she reaches again into her knapsack and pulls out the videotape, puts it into the VCR. She goes into the bathroom with her rosary and asks him to knock on the door when he is done. He must watch it all, she says. To the very end. And then she'll tell him everything else.

THINGS HAD STARTED GOING BAD a year back, when Sonny's poker game went sour. He'd come home from his sessions moody and drunk, starting arguments and slamming doors for no reason. She had no idea how much he was losing, but the thing he always blamed was his luck. It baffled him, enraged him. He kept telling her about it, repeating the same bad-beat stories in different ways, like he was trying to convince her of how outrageous it all was. She tried to sympathize but had to steel herself against anger that felt directed more and more at her, like he believed on some level that her presence in his life had somehow affected the way the universe was treating him.

She admitted to Victor that she'd blamed herself too for a time, that her own dark moods often scared her more than Sonny's did and had come to pollute both their lives. A year in the desert had dried up whatever hope and happiness the move there initially promised. She felt walled in by all the mountains, oppressed by the barrenness of the land, the emptiness of the sky, and all that constant sunlight. She told me once that she preferred the nighttime to the daytime because at night most things are hidden, and it made her feel safe. Back then, that made no sense to me.

She went back on her old medication, but it no longer helped her sleep as it once had, so she turned to sleeping pills, even during the day. Mixing that with alcohol made things worse, and she was doing that daily now, just as she had with me. Two or three beers at lunch. A bottle of wine every evening.

Her bad dreams returned. They crawled around inside her all day. She started seeing the people from her dreams. They would walk past the bedroom door or the bedroom window, trail her on her walks through the neighborhood in the middle of the night, vanish behind trees and fences and into shadows. She dreaded the nighttime now – a choice between not sleeping at all or taking pills that would unleash all the terrors inside her.

But Sonny didn't care. He had no interest in her nightmares or her visions. He slept soundly, I imagine, through all her trembling in the night, her nonsensical murmuring, her waking up with a start and grabbing your arm, your hand, ready to tell you all the horrible things she'd just dreamed. She had no one to tell them to now. Maybe that's why she got to hating him so.

She started arguments over things she barely cared about, like which lights should stay on or how hot the tea should be. She couldn't stop herself. As soon as she began antagonizing him, it was like some pulse inside her would quicken and overtake her with an intensity she no longer felt for anything else. I remember it well. That dark eruption of fire in her eyes. A rage I've since suspected felt good on some level. She used to lock herself in the bathroom after our arguments and weep quietly for as long as an hour, and

I wonder now if – more than shame or sadness – it was out of relief that she was still alive inside.

I doubt Sonny had patience for talking things through, for seeing doctors or finding solutions. They simply stopped doing whatever it was that had made them happy that first year of their marriage, if they were ever happy. They even stopped making love, an urge that had apparently dried up in her. With me, she used to blame her medication or her drinking or her period. Who knew what reasons she gave Sonny, but I doubt if any would have made a difference.

The night of the fall, she awoke to him kissing her hard on the mouth. He'd come home late from the casinos, his breath reeking of alcohol. She pushed him off her, and that's when she saw the kitchen knife in his hand. He stood up, completely naked. He demanded she take off her clothes. When she refused, he plunged the knife into their mattress. When she tried to run from the room, he seized a handful of her hair and dragged her back to the bed. In their struggle, she grabbed the baseball bat he kept by the door and whacked the knife from his hand. He screamed out in pain, cursing her as she fled the room. At the top of the stairs, he caught her again by the hair, but she turned and kicked him in the groin, which was when he grabbed her face and shoved it like he was taking off her head. She remembered stumbling back and gripping the top of the bannister, then losing her grip and nearly all memory of what happened thereafter.

She awoke on a hospital bed with Junior sitting beside her. He looked even more severe than usual. He insisted his father was devastated, had not known what he was doing, would never do anything like it again. Junior would see to it. He'd make him quit drinking. He'd move back into the house with them both if necessary. She just had to try to forgive him and say nothing to the police. He swore to protect her from then on.

Who knows whether she actually believed him, but in that hospital bed she must have already been planning her escape from them both. She told Victor that the first time Sonny saw her at the hospital with her arm in a cast, he knelt and wept in her lap. For months, he stopped raising his voice around her, came home early to eat dinner and watch TV with her, and went to bed with her every night. He treated her again with that quiet kindness he showed no one else, not even his own son. But she knew it wasn't going to last. She was just biding her time until her arm healed.

And then, out of the blue, I charged into Vegas with my death wish and must have wrecked all her plans. Was she lying to Sonny when she promised to stay with him if he spared me? Or was she trying to contain the damage, the rage I had reawakened? No wonder she never reached out to me. No wonder she put all her trust in a confused Vietnamese kid, a reluctant thug.

What finally broke her, of all things, was perfume. She'd never worn it in her life, and one day she smelled it on his clothes in the closet. It could have been knee-jerk jealousy, residual love even, or simply one betrayal too many – but this rage, her own, she could not contain. She drove at once to the restaurant to confront him, and only when he vehemently denied everything was she sure that it was true. He was a liar, but he'd never been able to lie to her.

She went mad. She threw things in the kitchen and

screamed and cried until finally he seized her car keys and forced her into his office and onto the couch, and then he held out her pills in his hand. When she refused, he shoved them into her mouth.

He must have treated those pills like I used to, like they were magic. Take them and *voilà!* you become your old self again, or someone else entirely, someone new and preferable – though the truth is that that broken person inside you still lives and breathes and merely hibernates until reawakened.

Hours later, she opened her eyes and found herself alone in the office, lying on the couch in darkness. She'd never been in that office before. The door was locked. It was one in the morning and everyone in the restaurant must have gone home hours before. There was no telling when anyone would come for her. For the first time in a year, however, she felt safe.

All his drawers were locked, so she started sifting through the papers on his desk, opening random books on the shelf and peering under the couch. She told Victor that she was not searching for anything in particular, just seizing an opportunity to rummage through his things and maybe see him in a way he did not want to be seen.

That's how she stumbled upon the safe, concealed behind a painting of storks. It didn't surprise her at all since he liked hiding things the way they do in movies, and also because he had installed a similar safe at home, a smaller one hidden in their bedroom closet where she kept all that jewelry he bought her that she never wore.

She tried the same combination on this safe – the date of his release from the concentration camps. It didn't work. She tried other dates: his son's birthday, the day he left Vietnam, the day he first arrived in America. She knew about his obsession with dates. It was a gambler's superstition – a way to hold on to the past, I guess, so you can control the present and the future.

She tried everything she could think of, forward and backward, with no success, and it was finally in giving up that she punched in one last-ditch combination, which turned out to be the right one. Her own birth date.

The safe was a mess. Hundreds of cash bricks stacked every which way, tossed inside like the ziplock bags full of colorful pills and the five or six handguns piled on top of each other.

She counted as much of the cash as she could without moving anything, and that's when she noticed the videotapes at the very back of the safe. Six of them, labeled only with dates from the past six months. She knew about his closet of surveillance tapes at home, so it immediately intrigued her that he was keeping these six here. At random, she chose one and put it in the VCR.

It begins with her standing in their kitchen at home and washing dishes. The date onscreen is from two months ago. It's morning or maybe the afternoon. The only sound is running water. You can't see her face or understand at first why he would keep video of her doing something ordinary like this. Then you fast-forward two minutes, then five minutes, and slowly you see it. For a good quarter of an hour, she washes the same glass over and over without rinsing. She stops only to pump more soap onto her sponge.

The video cuts abruptly to her standing at the living room window, still in the same clothes, arms crossed and staring not so much out of the window as *at* it, like she is praying to her reflection. Again she stands there for twenty minutes without once turning away. As the video fast-forwards, her body hardly moves.

Then it is evening, still the same day, and she's sitting empty-handed at an empty kitchen table, then brushing her hair on their bed, then watching the snowy TV screen in their bedroom, all for extraordinarily long periods of time.

What must she have thought when she saw herself this way? Perhaps it's the grainy footage, the distance and the bad lighting, but in each new scene she looks more and more unrecognizable – her body too long, her skin too dark, her face too angular. It's like Sonny videotaped an impostor in their home, a famished twin of her pantomiming these mindless acts. If she did indeed see those people from her dreams, then maybe this is what they looked like, this creature, this unfamiliar shade of her.

The next footage is dated a week later. There's only darkness until suddenly a light flicks on and it's from the bathroom in their bedroom. You can see Sonny lying facedown in bed, with only his pajama pants on, sound asleep. Then you hear the toilet flush and you see her appear in the doorway of the bathroom in her white nightgown, the same one she always wore with me. She used to wake up three or four times at night to go to the bathroom, sometimes locking herself in there for God knew how long. But now she is just standing in the column of light that spills onto their bed and onto Sonny's broad naked back. She's staring at him, her profile barely visible. Maybe he looks kind when he's asleep and she's rediscovering a tenderness for him. Maybe she's imagining him suffocating under a pillow. Whatever is on her mind, she seems entranced by it, and it probably doesn't go away after she clicks off the light.

The tape cuts to another day, another afternoon of her rearranging the same twenty or thirty books on the bookshelf for over an hour, more of her standing by the window and brushing her hair and wandering naked around the house, like she's looking for her clothes.

Then it's nighttime again, and this time it's Sonny standing by their bed and her lying asleep. The small lamp on their nightstand is the only light, but you can see that he's naked as he stares at her, and you can see very clearly the kitchen knife again in his hand. It seems at first that this might be the night of the fall, but the date is months later. And after a minute, though only his backside is visible, you realize that Sonny is touching himself. You can barely hear him groaning under his breath as he holds the knife, pointed at the ground, in his other hand. Finally his body trembles, and then he is still. She has not yet moved on the bed. He continues staring at her for a long time, swaying ever so slightly. Then he trudges into the bathroom, knife still in hand.

You wonder now why he would include this footage of himself – why stitch together all this video of her bizarre behavior, alongside his own, and keep it locked up in a safe? It's like a secret affirmation of their connection to each other. An act of communion with someone he has already lost.

The video stutters, and you skip to the next scene, which

is again at night and looks at first like a replay of the previous scene. Sonny is naked again, his back to the camera, the knife again in one hand as he's touching himself with the other. But it's another night. She's lying on the bed beside the long pillow she always hugged in her sleep, her slender arms visible atop the blanket though her face is obscured in the shadows.

A moment later he sets the knife on the nightstand and draws back the blanket. Slowly he lifts her nightgown, drags her underwear down her legs. He crawls on top of her. His movements are careful, unhurried, soundless. His broad back conceals her face entirely, but you can see that her body has not yet moved, not on its own.

THIS WAS THE MOMENT, she told Victor, that stopped her heart. She wanted to turn off the video, throw the remote at the TV. But she couldn't look away. She forced herself to keep watching, to confront it all no matter what new horror came into view, until suddenly it did: she saw those thin arms beneath him move and snake themselves around his back, the hands clawing now at his head, his neck, his spine. The legs were moving under him too, wrapping themselves around his backside. She heard a voice groan in the video, a distant sound, and realized it was her own voice, though it sounded deep and throaty and alien.

When at last he finished and moved off into the bathroom, the body fell still as though it had never awakened, the face a shadowy blur. He returned with a towel to clean the body, but it might as well have been a corpse on the bed.

Only then did she flip off the TV and rush to the light

switch. She retched into the wastebasket. The office door remained locked no matter how much she wrenched the knob. The room must have felt a mile underground.

They had not touched each other in over half a year. The last time he kissed her, she insisted to Victor, was the night he threw her down the stairs, months ago. The last time he saw her naked was when her arm was in a cast and she couldn't bathe herself. She was convinced of all this, that she could not have tolerated being intimate with him that entire time – except for the possibility that she had somehow forgotten, or been drugged, or been out of her mind. Was that truly her on the video? What else had he done and what else had she forgotten? What else was on those other five tapes?

She didn't have the stomach to see anymore. What made her most ill was her last reaction, when those thin arms awakened and started touching him all over and she found herself more horrified than if the body had not moved at all.

It was now two in the morning. He must have locked the office and expected her to sleep through the night – that deep and impenetrable sleep of hers that was more an affliction than a rest from anything.

She ejected the tape. She put it back inside the safe, but then changed her mind and pulled it back out, along with one of the handguns. She buried both at the bottom of her handbag.

She turned off the lights and lay back down on the couch after swallowing two more sleeping pills. The darkness swam around her, she said, for hours.

It was Junior who woke her in the morning with a bowl

of ramen, a cup of coffee, and another apology for his father.

VICTOR WAS LOOKING from Mai to me, gauging our thoughts. 'Anyway,' he concluded. 'That's what finally did it for her. She said she had to leave after that – no matter what.'

He fell silent, averting his eyes like he'd run out of things to say.

Mai drank from her watered-down Coke. His story had disturbed her, and she was trying not to show it. She wiped her mouth with her fingers. 'So you believe her, then. That Sonny's capable of killing her.'

'Mr Nguyen is capable of anything. But your mother was afraid of herself too.' He nodded at the videotape in front of us. 'Especially after she saw that. She told me to keep it in case something bad happened to her. As proof, I guess. I'm giving it to you now.'

Mai shook her head slightly. She nudged the tape toward me. 'You've told me enough.'

I fingered the tape, inspected it, and knew I would have to watch it, that I both wanted to and was afraid to. I imagined Suzy sitting alone in that dark locked office, petrified in the white glow of the TV screen. What horrified her most about seeing herself in the video – what she had forgotten, what she didn't know, or what she recognized?

'Proof of what?' I said. 'This tape doesn't prove anything – except that she's sick and that your boss is a perverted fuck. What use is that to anyone? Victor... why have you been telling us all this?'

The question startled him. He seemed sheepish for a

moment, as though realizing that he'd gotten carried away with what he'd divulged, even with what he felt.

'She wanted me –' he replied meekly before beginning again. 'The last time I saw her, a week ago in the hotel room, before she disappeared, she asked me if I was sure I wanted to help her. When I nodded, she asked me to kneel on the floor and close my eyes, and then she prayed over me. I didn't like that. It made me feel like all those people, the ones I've had to hurt, begging me not to hurt them.'

He spoke haltingly, and it made his face appear pathetic. 'Before I left, she gave me an envelope. She asked me not to open it until I was home alone. It was a letter. Things she couldn't say in person, I guess.' Victor looked at Mai. 'The last thing she wrote was that if something happened to her, I had to protect you. And no matter what, even if it meant hurting her, I had to make sure you got the money. Every last dollar.'

Mai wasn't even blinking, probably thinking about the money again, but no doubt reminded of her own letters too, wherever they were. I could see it clearly now, the orphan in both of them.

'So where is she now?' she asked.

'She didn't share that part of her plan – and I have no way of reaching her. We figured the less I know about that, the better.'

'Your mother's probably long gone then,' I said.

'I'd say yes,' Victor agreed as he pocketed his cell phone. Mai sat up. 'You never told us how you got your share of the money.'

He shook his head. 'I didn't want it.' He rose heavily from the table to put on his jacket, then stood before us with a philosophical air. 'She said something. That she'd been asleep all these years, ever since the night she left Vietnam. Got me thinking, I guess – of my last night in Vietnam, the last thirteen years of my life here.'

A ceiling fan spun slowly above his head, dragging shadows across his face. Who knew if the kid truly regretted the shit he'd done for Sonny, but it was clear he didn't enjoy it anymore. It occurred to me that Suzy had not only been exposing his boss to him, she'd been confessing all the dark ugly things about herself too, the same thing that Victor – maybe without intending to – had just done with us.

He checked his watch and said to Mai, 'I'd say you have until eight thirty tonight. At nine my brother and I will be replaced at our post. Mr Jonathan's orders. Go home, Chi Mai, and get everything you need, then go back to the Coronado. Park on Ogden Avenue and use the south entrance. My brother won't see you there. Get your money in room 1215, all of it, and leave town. Go somewhere far away. I'm heading back to the hotel now to do my job, but I will see to it that you're safe. On my brothers' lives, I won't let anyone stop you.'

He ended with something else in Vietnamese, saying it like some soldier going off to war.

I was stirring now, and he turned to me with some of that toughness he'd shed in the last hour or so. 'You can't go though,' he said. 'Not yet. Our orders were to watch you tonight and, if nothing happens, let you go in the morning. If you return to your hotel room now and do nothing, then nothing's going to happen. I'll give you your car keys at noon tomorrow.'

'That's it – they just let me go?'

'Miss Hong – she isn't coming. You'll be useless to them, don't you see? And you're a cop. They can't hold you here forever.' He looked at me for the first time with something approaching pity. 'You've been an insurance policy, Officer. That's as much as I know about it.'

He grabbed his backpack and gave Mai one final glance before walking toward the exit.

11

WE'D BEEN IN THE BAR for almost two hours, and the sun was already setting, the Strip lit up now and aglow amid a sky of sudden gathering clouds that smeared orange below and tinged the air blue.

The bar's back lot was still mostly empty. A few men had parked their car near us only to wander over to the strip club next door, where the neon lights had become a flashing signpost in the twilight.

The Jeep's flimsy vinyl top did little to keep out the cold. I zipped up my jacket and asked Mai if it was okay that I smoked.

She was sitting behind the steering wheel with her keys in her hand, her eyes focused on the Stratosphere Tower in the near distance, rising above the surrounding buildings. It was a copy of the Space Needle in Seattle except much taller, both more regal and more vulgar.

I wasn't sure what we had to discuss first. If Victor's last words were to be believed, then I'd been given a reprieve, possibly absolution – at the very least a little time now to consider our next step. But my unease had deepened. Leaving town was still a no-brainer. The thought of leaving behind everything Victor just told us, though, was like tugging at a shackle.

Mai spoke up. 'Did you believe all that – about my mother?'

'A lot not to believe.'

'Yeah, but that she *sees* things? Forgets she's fucked someone?' She glanced at the duffel bag at my feet. I had shoved the videotape in there, buried it in my clothes.

'God, don't say it like that,' I said, but I could see she was asking me sincerely, as if for confirmation. 'What do you want me to tell you? I went through similar shit with her for eight years.'

She seemed ready to say something, but then gestured for a drag of my cigarette. She exhaled smoke through her nose, holding on to the cigarette as she continued eyeing the Stratosphere. The neon lights next door flashed red and blue across her face.

'I've seen things too,' she finally said. 'Things like that. When I was a kid, I used to see my dad every once in a while. Standing in the doorway of my room at night. Or by the tree below my window. I never saw his face exactly, but I knew it was him because he was bald. Didn't scare me. Over the years I got used to it. That's one thing she and I have in common.'

She handed back the cigarette. 'You think I'm fucked-up too, don't you?' She wasn't looking at me. 'It's been less frequent the last ten years. I sometimes forget that it happens at all. But every time he appears, it's like she does too, and I end up thinking about them both. Usually happens around the holidays. My very own ghosts of Christmas past.'

Her smile was vacant. She dragged her finger along the top of the dash and left a clean trail in the dust.

'You ever go talk to someone?'

She chuckled. 'You mean like a therapist? You kidding?

Vietnamese don't believe in therapy. I vaguely remember my uncle taking me aside about this time twenty years ago and telling me that my mother had to leave town and would be gone for a long while. It took him all of five minutes. He said it like it was something I already knew. I don't think it upset me at all though. I forget what happened in the following months, if he or my aunt ever explained anything more to me, but I do remember it feeling natural to be without her. "Gone for a long while" meant she'd come back at some point, so I didn't think any more of it. It's weird, right? That I would just accept the unexplained disappearance of my mother? That's how it was for a few years.

'It wasn't until my fourth Christmas there, when I was watching the end of *It's a Wonderful Life* – you know, when Jimmy Stewart gets his old life back and runs home and hugs and kisses the hell out of Donna Reed and all his kids on the stairs? That's when it hit me that she was gone for good. No one in the family ever mentioned her. It was like she never existed. I started crying then and got real angry – at her, at my aunt and uncle, at my cousins too. Everyone thought I was crying because of the movie.'

She stuck her key into the ignition but left the key chain dangling there.

'That's rough, kid,' I said. 'I can't imagine.' I offered her the last of the cigarette.

She shrugged, finished the cigarette, and put it out in an ashtray filled with gum wrappers and loose change. She nodded at the Stratosphere. 'You know that's the tallest observation tower in the country? At the top they got a moat and two tall metal fences to keep people away from the edge, but last year some guy still managed to climb the fences and jump off. Fell over a thousand feet. His body hit the roof of the parking garage before landing in some bushes by the valet parking. God knows why he did it. There's a story going round about people seeing his ghost in the elevators. I rode them up to the top a few weeks ago, to see if I might bump into him. Then I realized I had no idea what he looked like. He could've been one of the men in the elevator.'

Her eyes went again to the top of the Stratosphere and followed the phantom falling body down the tower's white walls. She was playing with a casino chip, blindly flipping it across the knuckles of her right hand so that it seemed to move on its own.

'More suicides here than anywhere in America,' she mused. 'I hear about hotel maids finding dead guests in their rooms all the time. In bed, in the bathtub, on the toilet.'

A green minivan pulled up to the strip club and a middle-aged guy stepped out in jeans, sneakers, and a sweatshirt and walked to the entrance like he knew the place well, like he regularly went alone to ogle tits and ass at five in the evening. He could have been my father thirtysomething years ago, heading to the store for milk and coming home with a bottle of Jack.

I said to Mai, 'We should get going.'

She turned to me. 'What did Victor mean at the end there – you being an insurance policy?'

I'd been waiting for her to ask, though I was loath now to explain it out loud.

'Means that if your mother shows up and they had to

hurt her to get their money back, kill her even, they can always blame me, the jealous and bitter ex-husband – tell the police what I did five months ago, that I came back to steal his money, steal his wife, whatever. The story's adaptable. That's why my car is here and the hotel room is in my name, paid with my damn credit card too. Just in case they need a story. And if they don't and your mom doesn't show, then I *am* useless to them like Victor said. Sonny would've at least had some fun with me.'

Mai was staring out the windshield and still knuckle-rolling the poker chip, her face alive now with concentration.

'I don't know,' she said. 'Seems like you're much more a liability than insurance. Say my mother shows up and you find out about the money and everything. There's no way you send her back knowing all that. You sneak her out of the hotel and out of town in a cab or something – and with the money too. They end up losing everything.'

'Yeah, but if I sneak out your mother, I flush out the money. That's when they swoop in. The money's what they want, don't you see? Sonny doesn't give a shit about getting your mother back. They *need* me to disobey them.'

'Aren't those all unnecessary risks? They'd know that. Sonny's a poker player, after all. You gamble when the odds are in your favor, when the payoff is worth it. If the money's all he cares about, bringing you here makes no sense. Victor and his brothers could have easily waited at the hotel for her themselves. Why add another potential liability if it's not absolutely necessary?'

I was startled by how thoroughly she was thinking through all this. Part of me appreciated it. Part of me was annoyed.

'Sonny's a poker player all right,' I said. 'You think he won't do anything to get back a hundred grand?'

She looked at me sharply. 'You think gamblers care only about money?'

'This one shoved a woman down the stairs and tried to put a kitchen knife in my fucking chest. You know he once chopped off a guy's hand with a cleaver?'

'Even Hitler had a pet dog, a woman he loved.'

'What exactly are we arguing about here?' I glanced at the time and felt like snatching the keys from her and driving the Jeep myself.

'If it's just about the money, then Sonny would be smarter than this.' She spoke clearly, as if this was what she had intended to say all along. 'So maybe it's just about my mother. He might actually love her enough to take all these dumb unnecessary risks.'

'That's some logic.'

'It's *not* logical. That's my point. He's on tilt. He's the guy at the poker table who's been losing big in bad ways, and now he's playing emotional. He's making decisions he'd never normally make because all he cares about is getting back what he lost – and that's not always money. What I'm saying is: this whole thing only makes sense if Sonny really does want you to bring my mother back to him.'

'And so what if he does? It doesn't matter anymore. It's got nothing to do with what we do next.'

'It does. It makes it easier to trust everything Victor said.'

'I trust no one,' I said, realizing at last what she'd been working toward – and what I had to do now. 'I'll stay,' I declared. 'You go. I'll make sure Sonny gets all his money

202

back, and then he'll have no reason to care about me or you or anyone.'

She was wielding her sudden silence with one hand gripping the steering wheel, staring past it like a sulking child.

'Come on now,' I told her. 'Do I really need to tell you that taking the money is a horrible fucking idea?'

'It's simple.'

'It's insane.'

'Victor – the way he talked to me. It's a Vietnamese thing. I trust him.'

'Doesn't matter. I don't trust the situation.'

'You wait it out at the hotel until tomorrow like Victor said. What can they possibly do to you there? I'll take the money with me tonight and go to LA and wait somewhere for you, and when you get there, I'll split it with you.'

'Jesus Christ, I don't want the goddamn money. And have you forgotten I'm a police officer?'

'You told me you already did some bad shit here.'

'What, am I on some downward spiral? I'm not some good cop gone bad, kid.'

'I leave with nothing, then. I let these guys drive me out of town – these guys who think I died twenty years ago.'

'That's exactly what you do. Look, even if Victor was telling us God's truth, you take that money and you're asking for them to find out about you. Remind yourself what they did to Happy – what *Victor* did. How the hell is he protecting you by telling you to skip town with stolen fucking money? Take me back to the hotel and let me handle this. And forget LA. It's not far enough. Go to Oakland. A police buddy of mine will put you up. He won't ask questions. Once I get home and this all blows over, we'll figure out what to do next.'

The poker chip was now buried in her fist. Her eyes still averted, her voice calm again, she said, 'You think it's just about the money. And it is. Of course it is. But that money *means* something to me, Robert.'

Her using my name, like we were familiars, reminded me that we had only met three hours ago. She had seemed fully American to me, but what I heard now was that melodramatic tone that immigrants can't help sometimes, the Vietnamese especially, like a lament for their old country haunting the back of their throat. In her mother's story, she saw more than just her own ghostly visions, she saw her own loneliness too, her mother's true legacy.

I swallowed and tried my best not to sound condescending: 'I get that. I do. But you can't be sentimental about this.'

She was shaking her head slowly. 'No, you *don't* get it. Stealing that money… it's the only thing she's ever done for me. And she owes me, goddamn it. For twenty years, she's owed me. If I don't go get it and that asshole gets it all back, then everything that's happened the last two months, everything I found out today – it won't mean anything. It'll be like the last twenty years all over again, except now I'll know exactly what I've lost.'

For once, I had no response. It was like being full and arguing the ethics of stealing food with someone dying of hunger.

She said, 'I'm going back to that hotel room and hauling that suitcase out of Vegas with me. You can help me or not, but I'm doing it.'

She turned on the ignition and the Jeep roared to life,

trembling violently. She turned to me and her expression was part wary kindness, part obstinate bravado, like she was both asking me to help her and telling me to fuck off.

I sat back in my seat and sighed. 'Let's go get your stuff first.'

Without another word, she thrust the Jeep in gear and we lumbered out of the parking lot. But then she braked at the mouth of the exit, despite the road being clear. She sat there gripping the steering wheel, staring up the road as the blinker flashed the other direction.

'What is it now?' I said.

She raised her voice above the engine. 'Happy. She knows I exist.'

'Don't worry. She took a beating to protect you. If she didn't tell them then, she'll never tell them.'

'But what else might she know about my mother? Where she's going. What else she's done – or might do. We don't even know if she's left town yet. We're just assuming she has.'

'Make up your mind, girl. You want the money, don't you? Then let me worry about everything else.'

'You want to know too. You're dying to know. We could ask Happy.'

'I told you – I don't know where she lives or even what her number is.'

'But I know where she works. She was wearing a casino uniform that afternoon.' Mai pointed up the road at the Stratosphere. 'There's a chance she could be there right now.'

I looked at the tower, its neon-red antennae piercing the thick clouds. I was shaking my head, but I wasn't sure at what.

'What if she ends up disappearing too?' Mai persisted. 'This might be our only chance to talk to her. You want to risk losing your only chance to find out the rest of the story?'

'What rest of the story?'

'You haven't figured it out yet. She's the woman Sonny was having an affair with. She's my mother's best friend – her *only* friend – and yet my mother goes to Victor for help instead of her?'

Mai had turned on her other blinker, and her eyes flickered at me with certainty now – with enthusiasm. I thought of how her stubbornness was a kind of fearlessness, a reveling in the unknown.

We tumbled out of the parking lot and onto Paradise Road. I was clenching the Jeep's grab bar. It had never crossed my mind that Happy might be involved with Sonny, but deeper than my shock was the suspicion that I'd been wrong about this and possibly many other things.

'Some best friend,' Mai said as she steered us toward the Stratosphere.

'I should've known,' I muttered, though I suspected it would always baffle me why that stupid woman – or any woman – would take up with a man like Sonny.

PART FOUR

PART FOUR

This man who once saved your life, he is not a bad man. Nor a good one. I have long given up on what it means exactly to be either, but I am confident now that you must know one to know the other. Perhaps this is the other reason why I've often thought of him alongside your father. You did too, long ago.

How it turned out then that he, who saved you, ruined me is something I must also explain to you, except I don't know how. It feels like it happened twice without me knowing it. Even as I sit here writing these words decades later, a world away in America, in a desert far from the sea, I am still living on that island where he first met me and I first came to need him. Everything that has happened since seems a shadow of what happened there. Even everything that has led me here to this quiet room.

But let me say one thing. Let me write it down so that it will never again be a question in my own mind. If I have suffered, it has been because of myself. I blame nothing and no one else.

The Sunday after he fished you out of the ocean, I took you to Mass at the island chapel, and during communion I remained seated, abstaining for the first time in my life. You wouldn't stop looking at me, confused that I wasn't doing something you'd always seen me do. You had no understanding yet of the sacraments and how communion is only for those in a state of grace. You had no idea that days before I had closed my eyes while the ocean was swallowing you whole.

I watched communion end and realized that no priest or prayer or ritual could ever make things right, not because what I did was unforgivable but because forgiveness suddenly meant nothing to me. As we walked home afterward, I felt a lightness inside, like an absence, as though some spirit had burrowed into me and then burrowed back out, taken part of me with it and left me unrecognizable to myself.

We passed the junk woman who roamed the camp asking for

people's discards and sold them out of two plastic milk crates at the market. I reached into my pocket for the jade rosary, your father's first gift to me, and was ready to hand it over to her, but then I remembered that you had taken it from my limp hands during Mass. You were now holding it, wrapped around your palm, as you rummaged through the woman's crate of empty jars and mismatched sandals. The woman gave me a disapproving look, nodding at you, and remarked that rosaries weren't toys, but I paid her no mind.

You picked up a dusty red book and flipped through its blank pages. It was a journal. Only the first three pages had handwriting.

Mother woke up coughing this morning, *the first sentence read,* and it was raining so she called for me to open the window.

I bought the journal and brought it home with us. Although I'd been a reader all my life, I'd never written anything outside of a few letters to my sister when your father and I lived in Pleiku. It seemed strange now to write something to myself, for myself. So I turned to the first blank page and began an overdue letter to my mother. I could get no further than a description of our hut. I started a letter to my sister but managed only a halfhearted greeting. Finally, I wrote down your father's name. Only then did the words come.

An hour later, I had written six pages, recounting random stories from my youth that were unknown to him, things that had happened when he was in prison, thoughts I never shared with him because I did not know how. Every word, however, instead of bringing me closer to him, moved me further away, so that it also seemed I was writing stories about someone else, a letter to a stranger about another stranger.

I think it was then that I stuffed the jade rosary into the cigar box, where it would remain for almost twenty years.

I sought out Son that afternoon. I left you in the care of our housemates and went to Zone A, where I'd heard he and his son lived.

It took over an hour and cost me some suspicious looks from people I asked, but I finally found their hut. The boy was sitting outside on a large tree stump, his back to me. He was peering up at the hilltop where the bell from the Buddhist temple had been tolling only minutes before. Midday chants now filled the air from a lone monk somewhere in the trees, and the boy was listening with his hands in his lap.

I remained still until the chants ended. When he stood from the stump and saw me, he withdrew a step. I'd only ever seen him from a distance at the promontory, and I noticed now how handsome he already was, much more so than his father, who seemed hewn out of stone. He must have been no older than eight at the time.

I asked him if his father was there. He said, No ma'am. Then I asked if his father had gone fishing, and recognition flickered in his eyes. Perhaps he had seen us at the promontory after all. He said, My father never tells me where he goes.

I took a step closer, smiling as best I could, and asked if he was hungry and showed him my plastic bag. It contained three eggs, a can of sardines, and a baguette.

Let me fry some eggs for you, I said. Your father did something kind for me the other day, and I want to thank him. Do you have a pan?

The boy considered my face for a moment as if searching for a reason to distrust me. Finally he said, Yes, ma'am.

Inside their tiny hut, a fishing net turned hammock hung above a bed built expertly out of tree bark and planks from the sunken refugee boats. I remembered being impressed by that bed, by the cardboard box of neatly folded clothes beside it, and by their dirt floor, which looked swept, even around the stone fire pit. Atop the stones was their frying pan. I noticed no cross on the walls, no Buddha or altar or anything.

I fried the eggs with the sardines and made two sandwiches out of the baguette. I watched the boy carefully eat one sandwich as he sat on the bed.

I said, That monk chanting… it's very nice, isn't it? So beautiful and calm.

He finished chewing and swallowed before saying, Yes, ma'am. I listen every afternoon. He was about to take another bite but then added, as if pointing out something pleasant, It sounds like the dead are singing.

His sincerity startled me and I found myself smiling. I wrapped the other sandwich in newspaper and said, This one is for your father. Please tell him I came by, the woman with the little girl he helped.

He won't like that you were here.

He won't? Then why did you let me in?

You asked if I was hungry, and I was. You wouldn't have left anyway. I saw it in your face.

He was speaking matter-of-factly, almost kindly, but it still felt like an accusation.

Tell him I insisted on coming in, I said. And that this sandwich is my only way of thanking him. I'll stop by again tomorrow afternoon, and he can yell at me then.

I left before the boy could protest, but as I was walking away from the hut, I heard him call me from the doorway. He was holding his half-eaten sandwich.

My father didn't mean to hurt you the other day, he said. He just didn't know how scared you were. I saw my mother drown at sea, and there was nothing I could do either.

Many months later, after you and I arrived in the States and came to live with your father's uncle in Los Angeles, I saw the boy at a grocery store. It had to have been him. He was alone in the canned soup aisle, looking through the shelves. It took me a moment to realize that he was actually rearranging them, lining up the cans and turning the labels face-out as though it was his job. There was so much purpose on his face.

I was at the other end of the aisle and thought about approaching him to say hello, at least to make sure that it was really him, but then his father's voice somewhere nearby, calling for him, made my heart jump. I rushed away and told your granduncle I had a headache and went to wait outside in the car.

The boy and his father, I knew, had also been sponsored to Los Angeles. For months after that encounter, until the day I finally left for good, I looked for them every time I stepped into a grocery store.

The following afternoon I found them both asleep, Son in the hammock and the boy on the bed. Son's eyes opened a moment after I stepped inside the doorway.

I've brought you all some pork, I said. My bag also contained a bunch of spinach and fresh garlic and ginger.

He sat up in his hammock. Go cook for your daughter, he said. I don't need you to thank me.

The boy was awake now and peering at my bag. For the two months they'd been at the camp, they had probably eaten nothing but fish. The Malaysians, mostly Muslim, outlawed pork in the camp, but I had bought some that morning from smugglers who secretly visited the island every week. I traded in one of three gold rings that I had sewn into the waistband of my pants, and still had enough money to make a week of meals. As many as it would take.

I avoided Son's eyes and asked the boy for their ration of fish sauce and rice. He turned to his father, whose only response was to climb down from the hammock and walk past me out of the hut.

I sliced the pork and sautéed it in fish sauce with ginger and some

213

salt and sugar, stir-fried the spinach with garlic, and made rice. I
fixed a bowl for the boy and told him to eat, then prepared a second
bowl. The smell brought your father's ghost into the hut. I had to hold
back my tears when the boy looked up, chopsticks in hand, and asked
me if I wasn't going to eat with him.

Outside, Son was sitting on the tree stump and whittling a long
bamboo pole to fish with. He didn't look up until I was standing
beside him. With his small knife, he gestured at the bowl of food in
my hands and said, I don't know what was wrong with you that day,
and I don't care. Maybe God or whoever cares but I don't, so doing all
this makes no difference to me.

He returned to his whittling. He would have been thirty-one at the
time, and I twenty-four, both of us impossibly young it seems to me
now, though in that moment I could see that we had each aged years
in a matter of months.

I set the bowl of food beside him on the stump. Anh Son, I said
and waited for him to look up. You lost your wife and I have lost my
husband. I am here to help us forget that for a little while.

I brought you with me the following day. Neither Son nor the boy
appeared surprised. The boy made room for you to sit on the bed,
right beneath his father who remained in his hammock, staring at the
ceiling as you stared at the cocoon of his body above your head. Only
the boy watched me as I cooked lunch.

After we ate, the boy helped me clean up. He was like a woman
that way, thoughtful and thorough in how he tidied everything. I asked
him to please take you outside to play. I explained that I needed to
talk with his father. You sat put and looked suspicious of the boy's
obedience to me. But when he offered you his hand, you softened and
let him lead you outside. Those eyes of his must have convinced you.

Son and I sat staring at the open doorway, the white sunlight outside. *His silence made me hold my breath, but I know now that what frightened me was myself. For days, I'd been driven by the sensation that I was once again the person I'd been before you came into the world, only touched now by a profound loneliness that that person never knew. This loneliness, though vast and terrifying, was the most genuine thing I'd ever felt. If I had become someone worse, someone undeserving of forgiveness or understanding, at least it was someone I had created.*

I went to pull the drapes over the doorway, casting us into darkness. Son was already beside me, his thick fingers around my neck, pulling me to him.

Every day you and I arrived before noon and would not leave until dark. I cooked lunch and dinner, combining all our rations with the fish they caught and the extra food I bought at the market. I ended up selling all three of my gold rings. We ate well, and it took no time for Son to start talking more and even smiling. Whatever he still felt about what I'd done, he had either set it aside, close beneath the surface of his contentment, or simply absorbed it into the sudden familiarity between us. He was quick to upbraid me when I overcooked the fish or didn't comb my hair, and in these moments his voice betrayed tremors of his outrage that day on the promontory. But I soon discovered that placating him was as easy as asking his opinion on something as if only he had the answer. He loved explaining things, himself especially. He was affirming his existence in the world.

After lunch we would all make the long, quiet walk together to the promontory where he and his boy fished and swam and took naps on the rocks. We spent a few afternoons at the remote beach farther down the path, luxuriating in the white sand, but when a few young people started showing up, we decided to keep to the promontory, where we were always hidden. There was better fishing there anyway.

You soon insisted on fishing too, so Son obliged you with detailed lessons that you followed with enthusiasm and care. You didn't want to disappoint him. He even taught you to swim, though you could only go a few meters at a time, the boy always there as your buoy.

I often sat in the shade and wrote in my journal. More letters to your father. Long letters that I would start one day and finish the next. Certain afternoons, I hardly looked up from the journal. The boy once asked me what I was writing, and when I told him they were letters, he asked me to whom. I just smiled and said, Someone who will never read them. This satisfied him as though he understood exactly what I meant.

Sometimes I did little more than sit there and watch you all, or listen as Son told stories from his youth about how he caught more fish and swam faster than every boy in town, about his days running with the neighborhood gang, the time he chased down a thief who tried to steal the family bicycle. I suspected these stories were really for me, even though he was telling them to you and the boy and rarely looked my way.

When he and I were alone, I waited for the stories he never told. About his wife or his time as a soldier or his two years in the concentration camps, just like your father. I also wanted to know, from his own lips, about that incident on the island that kept everyone away from him except me and you. He would have told me all these things, I think, had I only asked.

One day you pointed at his right ear and asked him what had happened to it. The top tip of it was missing, an old injury perhaps. In bed, I sometimes stared at the scar while he slept and imagined some animal biting him and him crying afterward.

I hurt it a long time ago, he replied. Nothing you need to know. Why not? you said.

He fixed you with his eyes and called you by your name for the very

*first time. From now on, he said, if you ask me something and I say
no, you don't ask me again.*

*You looked startled and embarrassed and did not say another
word. For the rest of that day, you stole searching glances at him as
though you were invisible and waiting desperately to reappear. I knew
then that a future with him was possible.*

*For weeks, we hardly saw or spoke to anyone. The four of us were
like a conspiracy. People started talking, watching us every day as
we walked off to our secret place. Who knows what aroused their
judgment more, that I was a young mother taking up with a new man
or that the new man was an outcast. What kind of woman forgets
her husband so quickly, replaces him so easily? What kind of woman
falls for a man who hacked off another man's fingers? They must have
imagined me a happy woman.*

*Every Sunday morning I awoke on my pallet like a lost traveler,
unfamiliar with where I had arrived, unaware of how I had gotten
there. The church bell would toll a dozen times, each slow dong a
reminder of what I was doing, and I would try to sleep through them
despite the looks from our housemates who now walked to Mass
without us, and despite you nudging my shoulder to remind me it was
Sunday and then rolling back to sleep once I shook my head or simply
ignored you.*

*Around Son, I tried to appear content, and soon I found that his
presence actually calmed me, filled me with purpose, made me forget
sometimes that I had no idea what the future held. I was more quiet
around him than I'd been around anyone in my life. I spoke only
when I needed to, and with a confidence that disarmed him yet aroused
something fierce inside him too.*

*He would take me the second we were alone. He would not ask.
He would not say a word. At first it frightened me, how he'd grab*

my wrists and hold them down and cast all his weight upon me, dive into me, never looking into my eyes until he had finished and come up for air. His smell, the ferocity in his breath, the pain I felt afterward. It frightened me because I enjoyed it, thrilled in it, because I would often hurry you and the boy away and would forget you both entirely as soon as his hands were upon me. I felt possessed and yet also in possession of myself for the first time ever, though only months before, even as I knew your father was dying, I was still the young girl who could not imagine being with any other man, who prayed every night for miracles she knew could not come to pass. When I was with Son, I was mourning that girl, and I suppose that was what frightened me the most.

In America, I spent years trying to retrace how he and I came to need each other on that island, and it's only in finding him again that I understand that people need each other not for reasons they can measure or explain in detail. It happens in an instant, when life becomes startlingly new and frightening and profound, and you turn to the person next to you and see that they feel it too.

Those were happy days for you. You were eating and talking more and the swimming had tanned you and made you stronger. Sometimes I watched you in your happiness and saw someone else's child. I would see the three of you walking together down that path, you holding the boy's hand and talking up at Son, asking or telling him things in your loudest voice as if to measure up to him through sheer volume, be deserving of him, and he would listen to you and correct you and respond in his long-winded way, and you would all look like a family that I was not a part of, which filled me first with contentment and then inevitably with despair.

You awoke me one night, your fingers grasping my arm. You had heard your father's voice calling us, and when you peeked outside our hut, you saw him by the palm trees. He's just standing there, you said, but I can't see his face.

Don't say such things, I told you. That's impossible. You were dreaming.

In truth, I believed you. I had not yet forgotten that woman on the beach. Some nights her voice still startled me awake, though I never knew if it echoed from my dreams or from the world outside. It terrified me now to imagine your father out there roaming the night alongside her.

You tried to pull me up by the arm. Your eyes were tearing up. For weeks, ever since Son entered our lives, you had not mentioned your father or showed any confusion that we were around this new man all the time, that I was cooking for him and spending time alone with him, talking to him as I had only talked with your father. To my relief, you finally seemed willing to let someone else in.

But that night I realized that your father still shadowed your every thought. You looked both frightened and hopeful that he was out there.

I should have told you then of his death. I should not have waited as long as I did. In your eyes I could see my own sadness, that pang of recognition I still feel to this day when I think of him.

To save our housemates from waking, I let you lead me outside. We stood near the doorway, beneath a full moon, and watched the palm trees and their broad arms swaying in the breeze.

You must have seen a shadow, I told you.

You shook your head and said, It was him, Mother. He stands that way.

When we returned to our pallets, you hugged my arm and laid your cheek against it. You had not slept this close to me since our nights on the boat. A small part of me wanted you to remain this way forever.

Our very first night in America, it happened again. We had moved into a two-bedroom apartment with your father's uncle, who I had only met briefly one other time, and his wife and three teenage children, who I had never met at all. We were sleeping in the living room, you on the couch and me below you on the carpet. I remember waking with a start and finding you beside me, your eyes blinking in the darkness.

You whispered that your father had just wandered through the living room and into the kitchen. You had said his name out loud, but he did not hear you. When you followed him into the kitchen, no one was there.

I think it was a ghost, you declared as though you had just decided to believe in such things. When you rolled over to face me, I realized you were not lying beside me because you were afraid. You had come close to ask a question.

Does that mean that Father is gone? you said.

I did not let my thoughts give me hesitation. Yes, I said, and let that linger for a moment. The rest came out like a slow exhalation. A few months ago, I told you, your father went to sleep and did not wake up. He was very sick. There was nothing that anyone could do to help him. But he's with God now, and he's watching over you. He visited you tonight to let you know that.

Your only reaction was to glance again at the dark kitchen. I had considered never telling you at all, just letting you find out on your own. Now I could see that you had already done that. The old people call it a sixth sense, but I knew it was that mystical connection you shared with your father. On some level, I truly did believe that he was watching over you, that he had passed me over and whispered his farewell in your ear alone. You needed nothing more from me that night than confirmation.

After a while you said, I hope he visits me every night. You climbed back onto the sofa and wrapped yourself in your blanket. I waited for you to start crying to yourself, that distant lonely sound you made, but all I could hear were your cousins snoring in their room nearby.

In the coming months, you would befriend your cousins, play games with them, learn their American ways and bicker with them like a stubborn baby sister, eventually sharing their room while I slept alone on the sofa. You started kindergarten and soon spoke words I could not understand. You enjoyed hot dogs and hamburgers and other foods I could not eat. You watched television and sang songs I did not know. Not once, that entire time, did you mention your father. If you mourned him, you did so in your own way and kept that part of you, as with every other part, closed to me.

I wonder now if he did visit you again in the night. As you got older, did he ever appear at your bedside or walk past the doorway of your cousins' bedroom? Or did you grow up and stop believing in ghosts?

I should tell you now that I am writing these letters in a room that is not my own. I am alone and it is always night when I am here. Outside my hotel window, I see lights glittering and flashing. You've seen these same lights, I'm sure. They never stop, never go out, not even during the day. Perhaps that is why I've remained in this city for as long as I have. Here, the world outside always feels awake and alive with the stories it wants desperately to tell you, so long as you are willing to listen. Nothing here to remind you that the lights will one day go out, that all stories end whether you want them to or not.

Son ended up telling us about his ear. It was drizzling at the promontory one afternoon, and as you and I and the boy sat together beneath some tree branches, Son sat happily in the open, shirtless as always, with water trickling down his lips.

My father loved to drink, he said suddenly. When I was thirteen, he was stabbed in a fight and was too drunk to know how bad it was. I came home from school that day and the house was empty. Everyone

221

had gone to the hospital. The only thing I found was a bloodstain on the couch the size of our cat.

Son was grinning as he spoke. From the way the boy was listening, I could tell he had never heard this story. But Son was not looking at him or at you. He was speaking directly to me, as if sharing the proudest experience of his life.

His father, he said, had fought the North Vietnamese for years, almost half of Son's childhood, and he returned from the war a drunk and a gambler, disappearing sometimes for two or three days to booze and play cards with people who weren't even his friends. He would then come home and pass out on his bed for an entire day.

He had gotten into an argument that afternoon with a man who owed him money from a card game. In their scuffle in the street, the man pulled out a switchblade and stuck him in the belly. People tried to help, but Son's father shooed them away. He walked the two blocks home all on his own, holding his belly like someone with a stomachache, and collapsed onto the front couch. When the family found him, they thought he was passed out as usual. They would have ignored him if not for the blood.

The man who stabbed him owned the bar down the street and had a wife and two young children. He also had ties to the local gang. No one dared report the incident. Son's father, after all, had walked away from the fight as if nothing had happened.

So while his father lay in the hospital and his mother prayed all day at church, Son sat at a café across from the bar for over a week and watched the man eat dinner with his family, beat his kids in the street, yell at his wife, and play cards all day with his buddies. One afternoon, on a full-moon day, after the man and his family had walked off to temple, Son stole into their home through a back window. Even at that age, he was expert at prying open anything with a hinge.

He was carrying a kitchen knife from home, which he used to slash their bedsheets and pillows, their couch, the posters and tapestries on their walls. In the kitchen, he poured out every liquid he could find. Milk, soup, alcohol, cooking oil, fish sauce. All over the floor. He opened their rice canister and urinated into it. He spit into their jars of bean curd and shrimp paste. He did all this as quietly as he could.

The last thing he remembered doing was going to their Buddha shrine and breaking all the candles and incense sticks, shoving the banana offerings in his mouth and spitting out mush onto the Buddha figurine. This was when he felt a hand grab hold of his hair and jerk him backward. He saw the man's calm yellow eyes for only a second before a punch knocked him to the ground. His face felt broken.

Son was chuckling as he was telling this part of the story. I spit out bloody gobs of banana! he exclaimed and glared wildly at me. I tried to smile for him, shaking my head in disbelief despite not knowing what perplexed me more, the story he was recounting or the way he was recounting it.

The man was a head taller than Son and twice his weight. He dragged him by his hair into the kitchen. Son was crying at this point. Bawling. He tried to get up and run but slipped on the wet floor. The man kicked him in the stomach, which knocked the life out of him. Then he planted his shoe on Son's face.

You think I don't see you out there every day? he said. Spying on me like some Viet Cong? Tell me, what should a man do to someone who destroys his home? He unsheathed a switchblade.

Son squeezed his eyes shut, too petrified to struggle as the man seized a handful of his hair and sawed it off, then another handful, then another, so rough and vigorous with the knife that Son hardly felt the blade slice the tip of his ear. Then he screamed, but the man did not stop.

When he finally opened his eyes, the man was standing over him

223

with an unlit cigarette between his lips. He pocketed the blade and tossed Son a towel for his ear. He pulled out his wallet, counted out some bills, and reached down and shoved the cash into Son's mouth.

Stop crying or I'll cut your throat, he said. That's the money I owe your father. I would have given it to him if he had asked nicely.

Son's ear hurt too much for him to know yet that he wasn't going to die. What's more, it spooked him how calmly the man spoke, how clean he looked despite the mess around them.

He ordered Son to stand up. Look at me, he said. Are you satisfied? Is all this enough for what I did to your father?

All Son managed to say over and over was, I'm sorry, sir, I'm so sorry.

The man shook his head. Don't be sorry, you idiot. Be a man. Next time you want to get back at another man, stab him in the heart. Don't piss in his rice.

He called out a name, and a big ugly fellow appeared as though he'd been waiting outside the kitchen the entire time. After he was given instructions, he took Son by the arm and led him away. Son waited until they reached the alley behind the house, and then he threw up all over his own feet.

At this last memory, Son laughed loudest and did not seem to mind that we were all silent and serious, waiting for him to continue. I glanced at you and was reminded of your expression on the boat when that woman jumped overboard. I had been too engrossed in Son's story to see how disturbing it might be for a child your age. But it was too late at that point. And you were never a child your age anyway.

It was still drizzling, and Son wiped his face with his hands. The grin vanished. That ugly man, he said, was the ugliest man he'd ever seen. He remembered staring at his acne scars and wondering if his own face looked worse. The man dragged him to a house at the end of the alley. An old woman lived there. She must have been a nurse or *doctor of some kind because she gave Son medicine and stitched up his ear and bandaged it. She shaved his head and cleaned the cuts on his scalp and face, and then made him bathe and gave him new clothes. She handled him with care but never once looked him in the eye or uttered a word. The ugly man also remained silent until the very end, which was when he pointed at the door and said, Go home.*

When Son's mother saw him, she nearly screamed. She was used to him getting into fights, but he had never come home like this. He told her he crashed his bike and that a farmer had found him and helped him. She didn't believe a word of it, though she said nothing more. Her eyes were quiet with exhaustion. She was still busy waiting for his father to die.

But his father did not die. Nor did he change his ways. Son never told him what happened that day, what he had done for him. And he never gave him the money. It was almost fifty thousand dong, the price of a new bicycle. He stashed it in a pair of old shoes for over three years until the day his father stumbled drunk into the street outside their house one rainy afternoon and was hit by an ice truck. The evening after his funeral, Son took out the money and bought into a card game at that man's bar. He was barely seventeen, only two years away from becoming, like his dead father, a soldier and a killer of other men. The man recognized him immediately but said nothing. Son lost everything to him in less than an hour.

When Son finished his story, he looked at me and shrugged as if none of it mattered. I struggled for something to say. In the silence that followed, he lay down on his back, closed his eyes, and let the rain beat down upon him.

I wonder if he had ever told anyone this story before us. He might have once, before they were married, lain beside his wife in bed and, as they spoke of those things we all share before falling asleep, suddenly excavated this memory with a mixture of pride and shame and muted desire. What did she say to him afterward? Did she take his hand and squeeze it and whisper her astonishment? Or did she turn from him in the darkness and say nothing?

On our way to the promontory a few days later, Son began speaking to me in an unusually quiet voice. You and the boy were ahead of us on the path. Their paperwork had begun, he said, and a Baptist church in Sacramento, California, had offered to sponsor him and the boy. This was great news for them because Son had no family in the States. And also because he knew your father's uncle lived in Los Angeles and was sponsoring you and me.

He said he would make his way to Los Angeles as soon as he could, and find work, in a restaurant or a garage, maybe on a fishing boat, and then he would save up money and open his own restaurant where I could cook and host and do whatever I wanted. He would buy a house for all four of us and put you and the boy through school, and also buy a car, one for me as well. He said all this as if stating facts.

I couldn't tell if marriage had no part in his plans or if it had already become, without my knowing, an unspoken agreement between us. In any case, I held my breath until he finished his daydream. I thought for a moment more and said, I want to ask you for something. You must promise not to think I am crazy.

Son kept his eyes on the path.

I will do everything you say, I said. I will work with you, live with you, cook for you, everything. All I ask is that you give me one year to be on my own. To be alone. Just one year. I will go somewhere, anywhere, I don't know where yet. But I promise I will come back. I just want to know that you will take care of my daughter, and that you will not think I am crazy. I'll come back and we can all be a family, and I will never ask you for anything ever again.

Son would not look at me. His face was unchanged.

I was waiting for his questions. Where could I possibly go? What would I do for an entire year, alone in an alien country, no money, no knowledge of anything? It sounded ridiculous even to me. And yet nothing made more sense. All I needed, I thought, was the chance to know what it was like to be unneeded, unwanted, unfettered. Only then could I return to the world as something other than what I had been for the last five years, this misshapen creature full of bitterness and barren of all desire.

I believed at the time that Son would understand all this. His story the previous day had been a confession, if not out of shame then out of a need for me to see him for the man he was and accept it anyway. So now it was my turn. I was ready to tell him about your father and the years after the war, about the day you were born and what I'd suffered every day since, about what happened at sea with that woman and the boy she thought she lost, about my encounter with her on the beach and how I still saw her every night in my dreams, dressed like me and holding you by the hand, guiding you to the edge of a cliff. I was willing to tell him everything, no matter what he might think or say.

But he remained silent for the rest of the walk.

At the promontory, he went directly to his fishing spot down in the cove and ignored everyone. By then you already knew not to bother him during these moods, so you fished in silence next to the boy while I watched you all from above, sitting in my writing spot beneath the trees.

The waters were choppy that day, and I called out for you to be careful. The boy moved closer to you and offered me a reassuring wave. You ignored me.

Some time later, I saw you jump to your feet. You had a catch on your line, which rarely happened, and you were trying desperately to haul it in on your own. The boy was directing and encouraging you, but a moment later your hands were empty and you were peering into the water despondently.

You turned to Son at once and apologized for losing the pole. He took no notice of you, so you wandered over to the far side of the cove to sit by yourself, as though that was your punishment, self-imposed.

A brown gull soon landed on the steep stairway of rocks above you. You got up to get closer to it, and stood there entranced for some time, watching it preen its feathers. The next time I looked back, you were mounting the rocks.

I called out to you and the boy looked up. You had climbed about three meters when the gull flew onto some higher rocks. This didn't stop you, and again I called out your name. The boy had set down his pole and made his way over to scold you down the rocks. You were out of reach at this point, and still moving steadily up that craggy staircase. Again, the gull flapped its wings and this time alighted on a ledge that was high up enough now to be level with where I was standing on the promontory, watching everything. I had stopped calling you, afraid that my voice might distract you from your climb. You did not seem afraid though. You moved with such purpose and skill.

But then your foot slipped and I screamed out, and that was when I saw Son hurrying along that far side of the cove. He vanished around the corner. A few moments later, he reappeared on the ledge above you. He kicked at the gull and it flew away, and then he leaned over the edge and waited for you with an outstretched hand. As soon as you were within reach, he grabbed your arm and hauled you up onto the ledge.

He was kneeling in front of you now, holding both your arms and chiding you for your recklessness. As soon as I breathed a sigh of relief, I saw him slap you across the face. I heard the slap. It knocked you back a step, and you began crying instantly.

Don't touch her! I cried out.

That's when he finally turned his glare on me. Even from that distance, I could tell that his anger had nothing to do with you, that there was venom there, clarity in the way he clutched your tiny arm and gazed calmly at me.

You're hurting her arm! I shouted, weakly.

You yelled something at him too, fearlessly for once, but he kept his eyes on me. When you wrested your arm away, he grabbed it again, muttering something to you as you shook your head vigorously. He pulled you over to the edge of the ledge and pointed down at the deep waters, more than eight meters below. You flashed me a frantic look and tried to pull yourself back.

Stop it! I was screaming, but before I was halfway down the path, he had already thrown you over the edge.

You hit the water hard and disappeared. The boy leaped in. By the time I reached the cove, he had you above the surface of the rough waters with your arms wrapped around his neck. As he swam you to the rocks, your face was too full of concentration to show any emotion, and when I lifted you out, you were heavier than you had ever been in my arms. You clung to me. I can still feel your violent breathing there on my neck, below my left ear.

Son was peering down at us from above, a dark faceless figure in the bright sunlight. I was waiting for him to say something, to fling down his accusations.

He barked at the boy, who gave me one final glance before grabbing the fishing poles and hurrying away to follow his father. We never saw them again on the island.

Son didn't need to say anything, of course. He had finally figured out that I had come to him not to give myself, but to give you. It was what I wanted from him all along. It was what I believed I needed.

You must wonder why I thought to abandon you with a stranger instead of with your granduncle and his family. The truth was that I was terrified of changing my mind. I wanted the choice to leave and the choice to come back. Asking Son was my only hope. I must have loved him then because I believed every word I said, every promise I made, even ones I should have known would never be kept.

In the end, how much distance lies between the truth and what we believe to be true? Between the things we feel at one time and the things we end up doing?

It still startles me, what he did to you. In the moments after it happened, I went from rage to a sudden numbing clarity, overcome by a sadness I had never experienced, not even with your father's death, because as Son and the boy disappeared into the sunlight and out of our lives that afternoon, I realized that I did not and would not ever know what I wanted, and that in not knowing I would always hurt someone.

So it was on a cold December morning, many months later in America, that I was stricken again by this sadness and knew I could not bear it this time. I stepped onto a bus and let it take me as far away from you as possible. In my mind I kept riding that bus for the next eighteen years, never sure of who I was becoming and constantly waiting for you or someone to reappear like an avenging ghost, until one day Son of all people reappeared. It's outrageous to me now, a fateful trick from God perhaps, that he would be the one to step back into my life. But by then, after so many years, he seemed like a savior to me. By then I had spent two decades burying your father and forgetting you. I had twice made another life for myself. I had even married another man, a good man who helped me disappear into that other life, however briefly, though I ended up hurting him as well and finally realized that other lives are not possible, not for me or him or you or anyone. The life you leave behind never dies. It inevitably outlives you, my daughter, just as you will outlive me.

So when Son once again offered me a future with him, I accepted this time. Out of love and regret and fear and also, I suppose, exhaustion. We forgave each other by not mentioning the past. We conspired against it in our silence. Just as a child might close its eyes in the presence of something frightening. Just as I had done so many times before.

But that is another story. I have twenty years' worth of stories I can tell you, each one inevitably a shadow of the other. Which ones do I tell now?

I've tried to explain myself and lay bare whatever truth I can find in the things I've done and the things I've let happen. Yet it seems the more I explain, the more I muddy the truth. My one story becomes so many other stories that I feel I can never properly tell it to you, that once you finish reading these words, if you ever do read them, you will be worse off.

So what I tell myself is that I haven't been writing to you at all, or even to myself. I've been writing to someone who does not exist, a child of my imagination. That is the only happiness, after all, to tell the truth without making anyone suffer.

The last time I saw you, you were asleep in bed with one of your cousins. It was morning, cold and stormy outside.

Your cousin had pulled the covers away from you in the night. I stood by your bedroom door in my work clothes and watched you toss and turn, searching for warmth in your sleep. Your cousin's old pajamas were a size too big on you and made you look again like the infant I once held to my bosom. I remember rooting for you to take back the covers, but after a while you gave up and settled back into a deep sleep.

On the dresser, beside a photograph of you and your cousins at the zoo, I set down an envelope with your name written on it and $2,500 inside. Your granduncle had gotten me a job at a friend's restaurant, so I had spent six months riding the bus to work every morning, then cleaning and cutting vegetables, bussing tables, sweeping every inch of that place three times a day. I left you half of all the money I had in the world.

All of it would not have been enough, I know, but I should have still left you everything and sought my way in the world naked and empty.

I thought briefly about leaving a long letter for your granduncle, at least to tell him what to say to you, but I knew no letter of any length could properly explain what I was about to do. So under his bedroom door, I slipped a note saying that I was leaving for good and I was sorry to him and everyone. I can only imagine what he ended up telling you. If he lied, he had a right to. I deserve his scorn as much as yours.

In the living room, the Christmas tree stood blinking in the early-morning dark. It was an American tradition that your granduncle, to my surprise, had taken up, and I had slept next to it for weeks with those red and emerald lights blinking in my dreams, as they still do nowadays at Christmastime, even though I avoid the tradition altogether.

All I carried to the bus stop was an umbrella and my old knapsack that held my purse, one change of clothing, and the cigar box of trinkets and photographs I knew I would eventually have to discard, one by one.

Two weeks before this, I had come home from work to an empty apartment. It was the first time I had been there alone. I looked in the bedrooms to see if anyone might be asleep but soon found myself slowly roaming the entire apartment, picking up objects I had never dared touch, looking through drawers and cabinets and shelves, the odds and ends of people who were still strangers to me.

You must know too well now that your father's uncle was a shy and private man. He said only four words to me when I met him at my wedding to your father, and though he provided all he could for me in those months I lived there, I don't recall us having a conversation that lasted more than a minute.

In his bedroom closet, on the shelf above his neatly ironed shirts and pants hanging nestled against your grandaunt's dresses, were rows of shoeboxes stacked three or four high to the ceiling. I started with the topmost ones and worked my way down. I found jewelry, old shoes, candles, music tapes, seashells, various papers, and countless photographs, mostly things that apparently belonged to your grandaunt.

One box contained stacks of old letters that had been written, in his flawless penmanship, by your granduncle to your grandaunt during the four years he lived alone in America, having escaped the country right after Saigon fell. I sat there reading them for almost an hour. Many were about nothing more than what he ate that day or what he had been doing to bring her and the children to America. Some detailed his loneliness and his longing for her, for Vietnam, for his old life back home.

Then I opened a letter that began with him asking for her forgiveness. I did not intend to, he wrote, but I've sinned against you and God. He had been with another woman in America, had loved her deeply, and was now confessing everything to your grandaunt as she was preparing to come to the States with the children. He explained every detail of the affair, how he and the woman had met, how his loneliness had led him to her, how awful he felt the entire time, and how he ultimately ended the relationship out of his duty to God and to her. It was quite honest, I thought. Perhaps too honest. Details no woman would have wanted to know. He ended the letter by asking again for her forgiveness and *swearing to the Lord that he would spend the rest of his days making amends for what he had done. Nowhere in the letter did he say that he still cared for your grandaunt, that his feelings for her had not changed since they parted, that his love for the other woman was just a temporary displacement of his real love for her.*

He sounded like an entirely different person. The man I knew was as devout as a priest, as emotional as a monk. It startled me to imagine him in a passionate affair with another woman. Did he not show his wife affection now because his love still lay elsewhere? Did he not smile or talk warmly to anyone because he had chosen a life he no longer wanted? I've forgotten many specifics in the letter, but one sentence has always stayed with me. You might understand, he wrote, if you can imagine a drowning man suddenly feeling thirst and then having that thirst quenched.

Your grandaunt was just as quiet a person, though more outwardly kind and curious about others. Perhaps you disagree. She must have forgiven him, I suppose, though I'm not sure what that required of her. Did she have to decide that he had not wronged her, or did she have to accept that he had and so choose to live with it? The only true way to forgive someone, it seems to me, is to forget what they have done to you and, in turn, forget them. Whether that is possible is another question.

When I heard the front door open, I quickly returned all the boxes to the shelf and came out to greet everyone. You had all gone to buy the Christmas tree, which your granduncle was now carrying into the living room as you and your cousins beamed with enthusiasm around him.

As he set up the tree and you and your cousins began decorating it, your grandaunt made tea and brought him a cup. Before handing it to him, she blew into it several times. He took it from her and nodded, and amid the laughter of all the children he watched her walk back to the kitchen, and I saw in his eyes a mixture of love and endless sadness.

He was only forty-five years old at the time, still very much a young man, your father's youngest uncle, a man I had never known and would never truly know beyond a confession he had once written to his wife.

It was then that you finally acknowledged me. You had my red knapsack in your hands and you handed it to me. You had been using it as a book bag for school. My mother bought me that knapsack when I was sixteen, the only gift of hers I took with me when we left Vietnam. It had grown worn over the years, the edges frayed, the red canvas faded after all that time in the tropical sun, dragged through sand, soaked in rainwater and seawater as it held everything you and I owned in the world.

You said, Auntie bought me a new bag today, and you gave it back to me as though returning something broken, and then rejoined your cousins at the Christmas tree where your face lit up and you yelped with laughter.

At the bus stop, my normal bus came and went. The rain intensified. When cars thrashed past me on the watery streets and I closed my eyes, I heard the ocean.

As the downtown bus arrived, I thought I might begin crying, but all I felt as I mounted the steps was my breath quickening, a wave of oxygen and exhilaration, what a deep-sea diver must feel when he comes back up to the sunlight and the air.

PART FIVE

PART FIVE

12

MAI WRESTLED THE JEEP into a tight parking spot at the Stratosphere, nearly running over a convertible half its size.

Once she cut the engine, I said, 'Twenty minutes. That's it. We can't find her, we go straight to your place and get your shit and then go back to the Coronado. We put all this behind us.'

She put her hand on my arm before I could open the door. 'Let me speak to her first. You know her, but I speak her language.'

'What's the difference? We'll be lucky if she's even here.'

'You look like you're ready to choke someone.'

Even inside the Jeep, we could see our own breath.

'Just Sonny,' I said, admitting to myself that I was now relishing the idea of taking his money – anything that was his.

We were on the fifth floor of the parking garage. It had taken us some time to find a spot, but as we marched toward the elevators, hurrying past a football field of cars, we didn't see a single person and heard only Sinatra's cavernous baritone blaring from invisible speakers.

I checked the cell phone to see if anyone had called. It was not yet six, but night had already swallowed the city by the time we drove into the garage.

As I tried to keep pace with Mai, a shiver of claustrophobia – of sudden loneliness – ran through me. Driving up into these casino garages, with their stark fluorescence and low ceilings, their serpentine corridors, felt more like a descent, a submersion into something airless.

We got into a warm, empty elevator and Mai stood close beside me, her cheeks pale from the cold. She could have been my daughter, I thought – not without regret and some anger. Before Suzy, I had been a bachelor for decades and thought little of the past and even less of the future, but that's natural when your solitude is intentional. There's so much of tomorrow ahead of you, so much time left to redo and rethink your regrets and forget about the rest of it.

The elevator doors opened, and the din of slot machines jerked me back to life.

Mai had played at the Stratosphere only two or three times but apparently knew the place well. She started us walking the casino floor and circling the roulette tables, then the blackjack tables, the baccarat and craps tables. The floor was bustling, the evening crowd here trading in their afternoon sweatshirts for crisp collars and glittery dresses, their baseball caps for hair gel, their handbags for clutches and high heels. This was a newer casino, higher ceilings and skinnier waitresses, and the perfumed air pumped in from the vents masked the cigarette smoke that clung to the walls of a place like the Coronado.

Some of the tables were crowded enough that we had to stop and search for the dealer. Again, they were mostly Asian. Twice we approached a female dealer with glasses, and each time my face went hot with anticipation.

The thought of confronting Happy felt vaguely humiliating, made me regret our chance encounter in Oakland and all my lustful glances at her over the years. I kept imagining Junior and Victor roughing her up, and as ugly as it all was, as much as it proved what she was willing to take for Mai, all I cared about now was whether her bruises had kept her from coming to work.

'Three days are enough for a black eye to fade a bit,' Mai said knowingly. 'Little makeup like she had on, and you're fine. And you can hide a lot with glasses on.'

I followed her into an area with ceilings painted like the sky, past escalators that ascended into clouds toward the entrance of the Stratosphere Tower itself. A sign boasted thrill rides and the Top of the World restaurant. I thought of the suicide Mai had mentioned and wondered if taking this ridiculous route made it easier, gliding past slot machines and fake clouds and zooming up eleven hundred feet to a roller coaster, where to a chorus of laughter and screams you leap off the edge of the world.

Mai had led me on a brisk, circuitous path to the poker room, which was situated far away from the main floor. We arrived at the four-foot wall surrounding the room and started scanning the fifteen packed tables.

Mai slapped the wall irritably and walked to the front desk, which was attended by an impressively tanned guy wearing a double-breasted suit and an oil slick for a haircut. He didn't look up until she said, 'Is Happy dealing tonight?'

'"Happy dealing"?' he said like it was some foreign phrase. He glanced at me.

'Yes, Happy,' Mai repeated. 'Is she here tonight?'

'Oh. Wrong poker room. No one here named that.

Wouldn't matter anyway since our dealers rotate every half hour.'

'Okay, then.'

'We have the best, though. They'll walk you through if you need help.'

Mai had half turned to go but was now giving him the eye as though admiring his ripe tan. 'Will they?'

'I can sign you up for the tournament. Starts in half an hour. You're only risking the sixty-dollar buy-in. A little less pressure.'

'I play cash games.'

'Oh. You do. Well, let's see… there's an open seat at the one/two game. No-limit hold'em.'

'How about a twenty-five/fifty?'

The guy looked up to measure her seriousness, a little embarrassed but also ready to be annoyed. 'I'm afraid ten/ twenty is the highest we have right now.'

'Too bad. I'll try another room. Maybe I'll find Happy there too.'

Mai turned on her heels and stalked off, leaving the guy to look at me again for an explanation.

On our way back to the main floor, I told her, 'She's not here. We need to get going to your place.'

She continued eyeing the tables we passed. 'Let me try one more thing. Do you still have that card with my cell number?'

'What for?' I checked my pockets and handed her the card. She approached an empty roulette table overseen by an older Asian woman and took a seat.

'Good evening, good evening,' the woman said, her crow's-feet blooming as she smiled. 'Try your luck tonight?'

She was barely five feet and looked elegantly comical in her bow tie and vest. Despite the 'Betty' on her nametag, her accent was strong and unmistakably Vietnamese.

Mai set four crisp hundred-dollar bills on the felt and said, 'In quarters please.'

After flashing the bills to the pit boss, Betty pushed a small stack of blue chips in front of her. Each chip, I noticed, was worth $25.

'Excuse me, sir. If you not playing, I can ask you step back from the table? Maybe stand behind pretty lady here?'

She flashed us both another toothy smile and announced, as if the table were full of people, 'Place your bets.'

I muttered in Mai's ear, 'Is this all necessary to ask her a question?'

'What's your birth date?' she whispered back.

'Jesus. September seventeenth.'

'Of course you're a Virgo.' She took four chips and placed two each on 9 and 17. The minimum bet for the table, a sign said, was ten dollars.

'No more bets,' Betty announced and waved her hand over the table like a magician. She spun the roulette wheel, her smile as empty as her wandering look around the casino.

'My friend Happy deals here,' Mai spoke up, riffling her chips. 'Is she on tonight?'

'Oh, you know Happy?' Betty replied brightly. 'No, she don't work tonight.' The ball landed on 23, and she raked in all four of Mai's chips. She clucked her tongue sympathetically.

Mai again placed two chips each on 17 and 9. 'I heard

she got hurt bad the other day. She's doing better?'

It took Betty two long seconds before she nodded. 'Yes, that's right.' She spun the wheel again and looked back quickly at us. Her beaming had lost none of its wattage, but there was a new depth in her eyes, a stillness.

The ball landed on 17 this time. My heart jumped, but Mai gave no reaction. It was like she had expected it. As she watched Betty count out her winnings, about $1,800, she started speaking Vietnamese to her in a measured voice.

At the roulette table next to us, a gaggle of young dudes in khakis and starched shirts were clapping and cheering. I wondered at first if Betty had heard Mai over the noise, but as she pushed four towers of blue chips toward her, she shook her head like she was apologizing and murmured, 'I don't know anything.'

Mai kept at it, her Vietnamese voice tinged with a formal sincerity I hadn't heard yet. She wasn't asking questions. She was revealing things.

The humor drained from Betty's face. She glanced around us. 'I don't know anything,' she said again, soberly this time, and put up a hand as if declining a gift.

A man appeared behind her, in another impeccable double-breasted suit, the pit boss no doubt, brandishing a ringed hand on the felt. He said politely to Mai, 'Excuse me, miss – mind if I check your ID there?'

She had it ready for him, apparently used to this. He examined it, then handed it back to her. 'Thanks so much. Some people look a little young, is all. You have fun now, miss – but you can only speak English to the dealer, okay?'

'Sorry, sir,' Mai said. 'We have a friend in common.'

'That's fine, but English only, all right? You all enjoy yourself.'

As he walked away, Betty finally looked up from the table, her smile tired now, her silence purposeful.

Mai whispered to me over her shoulder, 'What's my mother's birth date?'

'We need to go.'

'Just one more bet.'

I told her June 15, and she promptly placed an entire stack of chips each on 6 and 15.

'Jesus, how much are you betting?' I asked her.

'I don't know – five hundred on each, I think.'

Betty focused on me now like I'd really been the one interrogating her. When the roulette ball landed, she announced 'thirty-five' in a small voice and cleared the table of more than half the chips Mai had won in the last spin.

'I'll cash out,' Mai said. 'In blacks, please.' She took out the business card I'd returned to her and placed it on the felt, her phone number faced up.

Betty counted out her remaining chips, announced the cash-out to the pit, and set nine black chips – $900 total – in front of Mai. 'Thank you for playing,' she said and mustered one last halfhearted smile for us.

Mai stood from the table, palmed four of the chips, stacked the other five on the card, and slid it toward Betty. 'For you. Please tell Happy to call me at that number. Tell her it's Hong, and that I really need to speak to her.'

Betty looked wary of both the tip and the card.

A man in a black turtleneck and a sport coat appeared at the table with a blond half his age and twice his height, his hand on the small of her back. In one smooth movement, greeting them as she had greeted us, Betty scooped Mai's $500 tip into her tip bin and slipped the card into her vest pocket.

As we walked away, I glanced back and caught her eyeing us. I asked Mai, 'What did you say to her?'

'I told her Happy's in trouble and needs our help. Did you see her face?'

'You can't go around right now giving strangers your number. There's no telling who or what she knows – or if she's even loyal to Happy.'

'She doesn't need to be to deliver the message.'

'You're taking too many chances.'

'I was right, though. You saw her face. A middle-aged Vietnamese woman dealing in a casino? Good odds she's been here a while and knows every Vietnamese woman who works here, who they're married to, who they love and hate. She'll deliver the message.'

We elbowed our way through a thick crowd of people waiting in the lobby for the start of some live music show. Mai bumped the arm of a guy twice her size, who muttered after her, but she kept walking like nothing had happened.

We returned to the elevator, and again we rode it alone. Mai stared at the elevator doors as though she could see some distant destination through them.

It wasn't recklessness. She was too deliberate for that. What worried me was her unpredictability, always another plan or urge withheld. It had loomed inside her mother too, that same shadowy sea creature right beneath the surface of the water. You're alone in the company of such people.

'There was more,' I said. 'You said something else to

her.' Mai passed a hand through her hair. 'I said they'll hurt Happy again if we don't help her. They'll kill her next time.'

When the elevator opened, she marched toward the Jeep. It took me some effort to keep up with her.

13

THREE MILES EAST of the Strip, we disappeared into a dusky neighborhood of low apartment buildings, gravel lawns, and famished pine trees, a few of them lazily adorned with Christmas lights. Mai turned into an alley that led to a small walled-off parking lot behind her complex. She parked beside a rusty VW bus with two flat tires and cut the Jeep's engine. I had to adjust to the quiet, slot machines still ringing in my ears.

I followed her through a gate with a hole where the knob should be. Her complex looked more like an abandoned motel: two stories of crusty peach stucco wrapped around a dusty gravel courtyard and a lit-up swimming pool half filled with greenish water and leaves, its bottom a brown blanket of scum.

Chicano music drifted from somewhere in the darkness.

We clanged up a metal staircase to the second-floor balcony that led around the building. She led me past dark windows, vacant inside perhaps or nobody home. Across the courtyard, two young black men stood smoking on the opposite balcony, leaning out of the shadows, their murmurs echoing across the way in some African language.

We turned the corner and approached a Mexican man on a plastic stool with a beer in his hand and a small boy in his lap, wrapped in his coat. I smelled grilled onions.

When we passed their window, I saw a woman working the kitchen stove and three more children crowded around a small TV on the carpet, beneath a painting of the Virgin Mary framed with Christmas lights. Mai and the man nodded at each other, and the boy watched us intently as we made our way past and arrived two doors down at Mai's apartment.

When she inserted her key, I said, 'Let me go in first. How many rooms are there?'

'Just my bedroom. The kitchen opens to the living room.'

I flipped on the lights, smelled the cold odor of cigarettes. I pulled out my gun and gestured for her to stay by the doorway.

Her place was small, the walls completely bare and the brown shag carpet dark enough to hide stains. The only furniture, shoved into the center of the living room, was a leather recliner, a coffee table littered with a pizza box and soda cans, and a fancy big-screen TV as tall as Mai. In the cramped kitchen, my jacket snagged on the chipped edge of the Formica counter, which looked more yellowed than yellow and held a microwave and a rice cooker and nothing else.

The walls of her bedroom were also bare, her bed a mattress on the floor, a tangle of yellow sheets. Beside the head of the mattress was a lamp and a cardboard box of file folders as well as piles of books stacked against the wall.

I came back out to wave her in. I picked an empty cigarette pack off the floor and set it on the counter. 'You get robbed recently, or did you just move in?'

Mai closed the front door, locked it. 'I live simply,' she said and walked past me into her bedroom. She opened the closet, pulled out a black suitcase, and started throwing clothes inside.

'Take only what you absolutely need,' I reminded her. 'Once everything cools off, we can get someone to come back for the rest of your stuff.'

'I can get new stuff.'

'Won't your landlord wonder?'

'I've always leased month to month. He'll be more than happy to take the big-screen.'

I noticed a bunch of poker manuals among her books, some Hemingway and Chandler novels, a few books on yoga and Eastern spirituality.

My foot knocked over an ashtray and I apologized, picking up the cigarette butts despite it not mattering. I checked my watch. It was nearly 7:00. Victor said we had until 8:30, but I didn't want to take any chances.

'Can I ask a question?'

'Why do I live in a shit hole?' She set the file folders atop the clothes. The top one had 'Bankroll' written on it, the others neatly labeled too, by far the most meticulous things in the apartment.

'You spend money like you have it.'

'Didn't when I got to town four years ago. This was the only place I could afford and it's been good enough for me.'

'Kinda shady, no?' I peeked through the mini blinds at the alley below, shrouded in an orange-tinged darkness.

She shrugged. 'I don't go for walks at night.'

'Pretty sure we passed a drug deal down the street – those two kids on their skateboards.'

'Par for the course around here. Muggings too. A stabbing or shooting now and then. Doesn't make me nervous anymore. If a man can live here with his wife and kids, I can too.'

'Easy to say until shit happens to you.'

'What makes you think it hasn't?'

She went to the bathroom, and I heard her rummaging through drawers.

On the way to her place, she had asked if I liked being a cop. Her first personal question since we met. I told her that it depended on the day, that some days it's just one idiot human being after another. When she asked if I had ever saved anyone's life, I told her about the guy I once pulled from a burning car and how he survived despite third-degree burns to half his body. He'd also just robbed a convenience store, led me on a high-speed chase, and T-boned a minivan, killing a mother and her nine-year-old daughter. I'd wished at the time that he had burned in his car, but I didn't tell her that. Helping the wrong people often felt as bad to me as hurting the wrong people.

She came back with some toiletries and what looked like a wooden statuette of Buddha, which she shoved into the outer pocket of the suitcase.

She finally went to her books, packing first a small stack of worn paperbacks. The Narnia Chronicles.

'I read those way back,' I said. 'Can't remember any of them except that one where they go through the wardrobe.'

'I've read that one eight times.' She snatched a cigarette from a pack on the windowsill and lit up as she picked through the other books. 'This is gonna be tough.'

'Don't take forever.'

'We still got more than an hour, don't we?' She offered me the cigarette and went back to the books, sometimes lingering on a cover for a few seconds before making her decision. 'Yeah, I used to go into my aunt and uncle's closet and look for a door behind their clothes. I wanted so bad to find one. Just walk into another world like the kids in the book. Close the door behind me, never come back.'

'Was that the kid in you, or was that LA?'

'Both.' She threw in a book on meditation, then a book on the stock market. 'LA never felt like home to me. Neither does Vegas, but at least here you can be anonymous. Everyone's from somewhere else. Passing through for a few days, a few years. Being temporary can be a good thing.'

'Maybe. Being permanent ain't possible anyway.'

'Permanence is overrated.'

She zipped the stuffed suitcase, stood up, and looked around. She took back the cigarette. I glanced again at my watch but didn't want her to stop talking. It was calming to hear her so chatty and relaxed, so perversely in denial of the circumstances. She smoked with her arms half crossed, her rigid posture giving her an air of both authority and wariness. The elbows of her leather jacket were frayed like her jeans and cowboy boots, but she wore it all well, with hushed purposefulness, as though she had chosen this uniform – the haircut too, the lack of makeup – to moderate her beauty. Help her blend into the background.

She said, 'Do you miss her?'

'Depends on what's missing.'

'Okay, what do you *not* miss about her – besides all the crazy shit she did.'

'I don't know. I guess I was never a fan of all the praying and churchgoing. All that devotion to God. I indulged her, of course, but I haven't set foot inside a church since she left.'

'It's a Vietnamese thing. Ingrained in all of us. Total waste of time.'

'That wasn't it. Your mother always seemed like she was hoping for a fucking revelation or something. You know what I *do* miss? When she wasn't being so goddamn serious. When we traveled, on our road trips, she lightened up then. She hated leaving town at first, but she got to liking it over the years. It put her at ease – being on the road, seeing new things.'

'I get that,' Mai said. 'Wish I did it more.' She bent down to stub out the cigarette in the ashtray. 'I've been saving up for a trip to Vietnam. I want to travel the entire country. Start in Saigon and go up to Hanoi, maybe find an apartment by Halong Bay. Live there for a year and see how it goes. That'll all be easier now. Shit, I almost forgot.'

She went back into her closet and returned with her hand in the belly of a small stuffed bear. She pulled out a passport, slipping it into her back pocket, and tossed the gutted bear on her bed.

'Finally got one four years ago and still haven't used it,' she said. 'I've never even been to Mexico.'

A cell phone rang, but it wasn't mine. Mai rushed to retrieve hers from her purse and threw me an eager look.

She answered it in a low voice and listened intently. Yes, she replied in Vietnamese and then asked a question. After a long pause, another yes. Then, eyeing me, she said, 'Okay, okay,' and hung up.

'Was it her?'

She nodded. 'She's at a pay phone across the street. She's coming over right now.'

'How did she know to come here?'

'Betty must have described me.' Mai hit the light switch and doused us in darkness. 'Stay in here and I'll answer the door. She sounded nervous. It might scare her to see you right away. Let me talk to her first.'

'She could have anyone with her.'

'Well, if she does, you can come out and shoot them.' She nudged me back a step, leaving the door slightly open.

With my gun again in hand, I watched her through the narrow opening. She stood waiting at the edge of the kitchen. After five minutes that felt like twenty, footsteps finally approached and stopped outside the front door. Two quick knocks. Mai disappeared from view.

I heard the front door open and Mai say 'Hello, big sister' in Vietnamese. A soft voice replied in kind, but I couldn't make out if it was Happy, only that it was a woman.

The front door closed, the lock clicking loudly.

They continued speaking in Vietnamese, their voices closer now, Mai's calm and careful, the other quick and hushed. Mai started explaining something in a reassuring tone. She sounded like someone else entirely when she spoke her mother tongue.

Suddenly I heard my name. A silence followed. Mai's voice called out for me. I wedged my gun into the back of my jeans. My heart was thumping, and for a moment I thought it was possible someone else had come.

When Happy saw me, she looked more confused than frightened. Under her black peacoat, she was wearing a uniform identical to Betty's. Her bow tie was askew, her arms at her side with one hand holding on to the strap of her handbag, which nearly touched the carpet.

'She was at the casino after all,' Mai explained with pride. 'She'd just left her shift and was about to leave the casino when Betty caught up to her.'

I said to Happy, 'How much does Betty know?'

'She don't know nothing,' Happy replied quickly, still eyeing me with suspicion. 'I tell her somebody hit me. That it.'

I inched closer. Despite her makeup and her glasses I could see the shadowy bruises around her left eye and the left corner of her mouth.

'She and me – we not good friend.'

'Then why did you tell her about it?'

'Three day I not leave the house and she come find me. She live in my neighborhood. Why you in Las Vegas, Bob?'

'Sonny. He made me come here and find Suzy for him. I found Mai instead.'

This made even less sense to her, but I didn't feel like explaining.

She said, 'You know she is…'

'Suzy's long-lost daughter? Yeah. Found that out about three hours ago. Don't think Sonny planned on anything like that.'

My mention of Sonny again brought a flash of venom to her eyes.

'Did his men do that to you?' I said.

She blinked away the question. 'Why you try find me? I don't know nothing.'

'Did you know about Suzy's plan?'

'What plan? She don't tell nothing to me. They come

and they say about the money, but I don't know nothing about the money. They hit me and they say they kill me and they kill Suzy too, but I not say nothing.' She looked at Mai. 'That why I come to you Tuesday – to get you tell your mom leave town.'

'You didn't let me explain that day,' Mai said. 'My mother and me have never talked or seen each other or anything. I got a few brief letters from her last month and that's it. I don't even know what she looks like.'

Happy was quiet for a moment. Then she shook her finger at Mai and said something in Vietnamese, like she was gently chiding her.

'Hey, come on,' I said. *'English.'*

'I ask her why she not leave town. That what I say to her Tuesday. She need to go too.'

Mai was avoiding my eyes. She hadn't mentioned that part to me. I couldn't blame her for ignoring the wild exhortations of some strange woman at her door, but even at this point, such dire warnings seemed like invitations to an adventure for her.

I said, 'Does Sonny know about her? Don't lie to me, Happy. Did you say a single word to them about her?'

She dismissed the question with an impatient look. She set her purse on the coffee table and sank into the recliner.

Mai took a step toward her as if to shield her from my intensity. I couldn't tell if she was playing good cop to my bad cop or if she genuinely felt sorry for Happy. It was undeserved either way.

'So my mom did come to see you?'

Happy nodded tiredly. 'She come Sunday night.'

'She say anything about where she was planning to go?'

'No. She come to…' Happy bowed her head like she was about to cry, but when she looked up again at Mai, she seemed baffled. 'How I can explain it to you?'

I let the silence eat her up for a bit. Then I said, 'We know about you and Sonny.'

Her face showed no surprise. Just instant acquiescence. Then she narrowed her eyes at me, and that old glint of knowing amusement returned.

'You think I am horrible person.'

'I do.'

'You think you understand all the story.'

I nodded at Mai. 'She figured it out. I was too stupid to. Never thought you'd go for a crazy criminal who nearly killed your best friend.'

'Robert, come on,' Mai said. 'Go ahead, Happy, what did my mom –'

'Yeah,' I said, 'Go ahead. Explain why you did it.'

'Bob, I tell you something – you think you are good man and you are police and you not like Sonny. But you no different.'

'What? He *cheated* on her. He locked her all night in an office, threw her down a flight of fucking stairs. And who knows how often he hits her.'

'You hit her too,' Happy noted. She asked Mai, 'He tell you what he do to your mother before?'

'That was the first time I ever touched her. You know she's hit me plenty over the years. *That night* she fucking hit me. I couldn't hear out of this ear for a week!'

'You almost break her teeth.'

'Bullshit. I didn't mean to. I didn't want to. No way you're comparing that to what Sonny's done.'

Happy was shaking her head. 'But that not what I mean. You and him – you are both *weak* man. When you not understand somebody, you scare like little boy. You close your eye and you pretend they not there. You not know when you hurt them. Why you think Suzy not call to you for help? She know you still love her. She know what you do here five month before. Sonny hurt her, she almost die, but she *never* call you.'

'She didn't come begging for your help either, did she?'

Happy's scowl deepened as she sat on the edge of the recliner like an alert cat. All those years, she was always the one calming Suzy or me down, the buffer when the three of us were together, making jokes and changing the subject, never an angry word to anyone. It made me wonder now how often she had humored me, held back all the ugly things she really felt.

She turned from me, exhaling loudly as if to relieve herself of my presence.

Mai was standing warily between us. In a composed voice, Happy said to her, 'Your mom – she is difficult woman. She scare just like Sonny and Bob. She hurt them too. I know. Fifteen year I friend with her and she hurt me many time. But she ask me come here because she have nobody, and she help get job for me. I know nothing about Sonny. I know nothing about you. But I know she not happy in Las Vegas. So I come. When I meet Sonny, I see he not good man for her. I tell her, but she not listen. And when they start fighting, I tell her leave but she not leave. What I can do? I just listen to her. But in the summer, she stop talking to me. I call her and she not call back to me. When I go see her, she like other person. So Sonny, he start come every day to my house. He tell me everything. Suzy sleep all day. Suzy not leave the house. She not talk to nobody. He say she not love him anymore.'

Happy's eyes were glistening. Again, she had that inwardlooking, baffled expression.

'How I can explain it? He the one who help get job for me. When I owe money to someone, he pay it. When I date the other man who hit me, Sonny go beat him and make him say sorry to me. I know he do the bad thing, but he always do good thing for me. I thought your mother not love him anymore. I thought…'

She grabbed a tissue from her purse and took off her glasses. As she carefully dabbed at her mascaraed eyes, Mai walked to the refrigerator and returned with a bottle of water and set it on the coffee table.

She sat there slumped with her hands over her knees, clutching at the tissue. She looked fragile without her glasses and yet also, in her suffocating vest and crooked bow tie, ridiculous. I could only half listen to everything, distracted by the memory of her naked in my bed, watching me undress and surely knowing that I could not feel for her as I did for her best friend. And yet she had pursued it, plunged into it as she would again a year later with Sonny. Even if it was not for love, it was still a futile thievery, taking something that could never be hers and offering herself too as something provisional. She must have known all that.

She drank the water, wiped her nose with the tissue. 'Sonny call to me last month. He tell me Suzy know everything. *That it for us.* No more. Good-bye.' Happy glanced in my direction as if reminded that I'd done the same to her. 'I call Suzy twenty time but she stop answer the phone. One month, I not see her or Sonny. Nothing.'

'So you have no idea what she'd been doing?' Mai asked. Happy shook her head. 'I want to go to the house and explain to her, but I too – I have no idea what I can say. I just stay away. But Sunday night, real late, she knock on my door. I almost not open the door, I too scared. She say she want talk to me. She look calm but – it was *too* calm, like when she take too much medicine. I say sorry to her and I cry so bad but she –'

Happy had to stop for a moment. Was it the guilt and shame choking her up, or the thought of what she'd lost in the past month?

She said it felt bizarre, her the one in tears and Suzy leading her to the couch, hushing her. How many times had it been the other way around? For a month she'd been steeling herself for this moment, for all that vitriol she knew her oldest friend was capable of. But Suzy began by thanking Happy. The affair had wounded her deeply, but she was long past loving Sonny and had no room left inside her to hate Happy. If anything, the affair and the subsequent end of their friendship had awoken her from 'the long dream,' she said, 'of these last twenty years' – made her realize, once and for all, that she was alone in the world and had always been, and that perhaps staying that way would not kill her. It could even save her. All she wanted now was to make amends for her sins and leave everything behind for good.

Happy remembered being frightened by the calm finality of Suzy's voice. She asked her if she was taking her medication. Suzy took the prescription bottle from her purse and set it on the table and said she didn't need the stuff anymore. When she stood up to go, Happy knew it was the last time she would ever see her.

Mai asked, 'Did she say specifically that she was leaving town?'

'She not need to.'

'Well what else did she do then?' I demanded. 'She came just to tell you that?'

Happy sat up straight. She dried her nose and eyes and put on her glasses again, then tidied her hair like she was putting herself back together for departure.

Still avoiding my eyes, she said to Mai, 'She tell me about you. She leave you twenty year before and now she find you here in Las Vegas. I can't believe it. Fifteen year I know her, but I never think she have a daughter.'

'She say anything more about me?'

'I ask her so many questions, but she not answer. All she say is Sonny not know about you. She give me your name and your address and…' Happy looked at her hands. 'She say she forgive me. But she make me… she make me promise I watch you. I protect you. Let nobody hurt you.'

'After what *you* did to her?' I blurted out.

Mai put up a hand to calm me down. I turned from them both. It was directed at Happy, but I might as well have been yelling at the walls: 'How could you protect anyone anyway? I mean, why would she tell you all that? Goddamn it, she had to know Sonny would come after you for information!'

'You think she not know that?' Happy replied softly. She rose from the recliner, took her purse, and fixed me with one last frigid look. 'They do come, but I don't tell them nothing.'

Mai glanced at me, and she understood too. Suzy knew Happy would tell them nothing. She had wanted them to come. She had wanted them to do the punishing for her. Confiding in her best friend one last time was Suzy's way of burdening her with Mai's life. A final offer of redemption. The price of forgiveness.

I was shaking my head, but I wasn't surprised.

On her way to the door, Happy stopped and put a hand on Mai's shoulder. They were the same height, though Mai seemed like she was looking up at her.

'Di di, con,' Happy said. *Go now, child.* 'Go somewhere good for you. Your mom, I know she care for you, but she don't know how to be your mom.'

She went to the door. She hesitated with her hand on the knob, melodramatically, and in that instant I considered swallowing my anger and calling her back to apologize for what I'd said, what I'd thought, for everything I'd ever done to her and Suzy. Maybe then she'd tell me the rest of the story.

Another part of me hoped it was the last time I'd ever see her. She opened the door and walked out. I listened to her footsteps hurry down the balcony along echoing clangs, fading fast into the night.

14

SOME PEOPLE you will never know beyond what they give you. To be with them requires a bridge, an interpreter, and even then you're only ever approaching them as you would the horizon.

Happy's visit – though it raised more questions than it answered – finally helped me see that she'd been my interpreter for Suzy, the only recourse I had beyond my own stubbornness and curiosity, my love. She was there for our entire marriage, at our home nearly every week, eating meals with us, sleeping on the couch some nights, on the phone with Suzy every other day. Had I not seen her merely as Suzy's confidante, I would have understood that she was mine as well. How many times had I asked her to explain my own wife to me, what I had done wrong, what secret or foreign custom or female vagary I was not privy to? She always had answers ready for me, and even if they had been lies, they were the only things I could hold on to in the hope that one day I'd get it right.

I suppose it was envy and exasperation that made me lose it back at the apartment. Happy was closer to Suzy than I ever was, but how can you be that close to someone and still not know them?

By the time we'd driven halfway back to the Coronado, my anger had given way to Mai's impenetrable silence. She seemed either crestfallen or still unsatisfied by what Happy had told us. Who knew what she had wanted to hear about her mother? Chances were she didn't know either.

It was 7:45 and we were only a few blocks from the Stratosphere, but the closer we got to the Strip, the worse traffic became. Four lanes bumper-to-bumper with stretch limos and restless taxis jumping lanes, mobile billboards of near-naked dancers creeping alongside us like a prowling peep show. Every other car had a California tag, which only made me more anxious to ship Mai off as soon as possible.

The Jeep's heater finally worked but was fogging up the windshield. Every few minutes, Mai would curse and wipe at the glass with a dirty T-shirt she grabbed off the floor. Those were her only words for the first fifteen minutes of the ride.

Soon we saw droplets of rain. She turned on the wipers, and they squealed across the windshield.

'Stupid things,' she muttered. 'I use them maybe once a year.'

'It's cold enough to snow. Can it actually snow here?'

She looked up at the night sky, bathed in the glow of casino lights, but did not reply.

'Twice I've been here,' I said. 'And each time the weather's been shit. Last time there was a goddamn monsoon.'

A red Mercedes cut us off and she pumped the brakes, immediately laying on her horn for a good three seconds as the guy stuck his middle finger out the window.

'Asshole,' she muttered and glared at the guy as we idled in traffic a foot from his bumper. She checked her watch, the first time I'd seen her antsy about our 8:30 deadline.

A few moments later, though, she was back to being

pensive, her elbow up on the door panel and her head resting on a fist.

'I wasn't lying back there,' I said. 'I only hit your mother that one time. I've regretted it ever since.'

I thought she didn't hear me, but then she replied evenly, 'We barely know each other. You don't need to defend yourself.'

'It matters to me that you know that.'

'Why?'

'Because. I don't want you thinking I'm... like *that*.'

'Like Sonny?'

'You know, it's easy for Happy to say that. She didn't live with your mother for eight years. She wasn't afraid of her like I was.'

'How do you know Sonny wasn't afraid of her too? And what does that mean anyway? What exactly were you afraid of?'

'Victor explained plenty, didn't he?'

'I want *you* to explain it. Were you afraid she'd lose her mind? That she'd hurt herself – or hurt you? No longer love you? I mean, what was it?'

I was quiet for a moment, though I already knew the answer. I'd always known. Traffic crawled forward and we followed and I was glad to hear the Jeep's heaving engine fill the silence in the cab.

'We were always gonna fail,' I said. 'On our honeymoon, I knew it. There was some denial there, but really I knew it was just a matter of time. The longer we stayed together, weirdly enough, the stronger the feeling became, and when it was clear that something was seriously wrong with your mother, I started wondering what was wrong with me.

Why did I hold on? Why did it feel like I needed her more than she needed me? I don't know – I guess I was afraid of the inevitable. And I didn't want it to be more my fault than hers. Turned out it was at the end.'

Another red light. Mai sat there, still not quite satisfied. I was ready to try another explanation, but she said, 'So what happened that night?'

'We were fighting about something stupid. I tracked mud on the kitchen floor. She was yelling at me in Vietnamese, cursing me. I couldn't stand it. It wasn't fair.'

'How did you hit her?'

'I hit her hard, okay? She hit me many times too.'

'No, tell me. You want to defend yourself, so tell me exactly what you did.'

'I slapped her. Twice. Three times. The third time was a backhand – hard as I could. She bled at the mouth. Nearly fell over. You really want the truth? It was like fulfilling a fantasy. Each time I hit her, it felt like something coming true. It felt like a fucking remedy.'

I could hardly believe what I was admitting, but Mai's questioning had been like a challenge. Was I man enough now to lay it out straight to her *and* to myself?

'I knew it was wrong,' I added. 'I knew I'd regret it. But I'd be lying if I said it didn't feel good.'

The light turned green, and Mai revved up close to the red Mercedes like she was ready to roll over it. But then she turned right and we were on Las Vegas Boulevard again, trailing another long line of cars.

Finally she said, 'I've decided I don't care anymore. I care about the money and I care that she gave it to me, but she never wanted anything more than that. So why should I go chasing after her like she's someone I lost? She was never mine to lose anyway.'

For the first time since we met, I had no pity for her, even if she had it for herself. Maybe her moment of clarity was my own too. I looked in the Jeep's side-view mirror to check if my face looked as defeated as I felt.

'What would I have said to her anyway?' Mai concluded.

'Go to Vietnam with the money,' I said. 'Go find yourself a husband somewhere. Have a kid or two.'

She laughed suddenly, a slightly bitter laugh. 'No need for a husband really. But I'd like to have a son. Teach him how to play cards one day. Raising a daughter would be like mothering yourself.'

THE FIRST THING we encountered as we reentered the Coronado was a guy in baggy corduroys and a Christmas sweater hitting a jackpot on the slots. Over five grand. It was one of those Elvis slots, so 'Viva Las Vegas!' was blaring obnoxiously as lights flashed atop the machine, terrifying the little girl in his arms. Heads turned, a swarm of eyes pausing out of envy before returning gradually to their own pursuits.

Mai stopped to watch. The guy was so busy freaking out that he seemed oblivious to his sobbing daughter, whom he cradled in one arm like a bag of groceries as he peered stupidly at the clanging machine. An attendant arrived to handle his winnings, and all the guy could ask, over the little girl's wails, was, 'Do I get it all now?'

'Let's go,' I said to Mai.

She started moving again but kept eyeing the scene until we turned the corner and headed toward the elevators.

The casino floor felt like an endless theater stage swarming with actors, the floodlights glaring, a balcony of eyes watching from somewhere above. I wondered if Victor had gotten anxious about how long we'd taken, if he was still keeping his word. One more question had started worrying me, ever since I retrieved the room key from the potted plant in the garage. It had been nearly eight hours since Junior sent me here, and neither he nor his father had called.

We rode the elevator with four drunk businessmen on their way to some room party. They leered at Mai the entire way, smirking quietly at each other until I started glaring at them. As we got off on the twelfth floor, one of them whispered, 'Sayonara, missy,' and the elevator doors closed on their dumb sniggering.

We walked side by side to room 1215, and I unlocked it. The lamp was still on, the curtains still drawn, and the brown suitcase still standing glumly where we had left it inside the closet.

I opened it with Mai's chrome key to check the money. I took back the five hundred Junior had given me, just in case I had to return it to him in person.

Mai had wandered into the center of the room and was peering at the dark walls and the shadows cast across the ceiling. She stood there with her chin raised like she had smelled something.

'What is it?' I said.

'It's like someone was here.'

'Everything looks the same to me. You see something?' I noticed a trembling along the bottom of the curtains, but it was only hot air blowing from the heater's vents.

'No.' She gave me a sheepish look. 'I just feel it.'

'Got to be more specific than that, kid.'

'I don't know. It's like sitting down in a chair that someone else was just in.'

She remained motionless as though trying to remember something, and I let her do that for a bit, not sure what to ask her or what to make of her sudden clairvoyance, until finally she shook her head and started for the door.

We didn't say a word to each other the entire way down, through the casino, to the parking garage, and finally to her Jeep, where I loaded the suitcase into the cramped backseat, squeezing it alongside her things.

I stood by the driver's-side window as she keyed the ignition. On a faded Chinese takeout menu she gave me, I wrote down Tommy's address in Oakland. I thought of what he'd say to her when she arrived at his doorstep. I thought of how Laura, his beloved wife, was going to have a fit. Then I remembered all the times I'd saved Tommy from himself back in the day, from bar fights and unsavory women, from moments on the job when he'd been on the edge of losing it just as, countless times, I had been.

'It should take you nine hours,' I told Mai, 'but drive the speed limit. You hear me? And drive straight there. Don't stop for anything but gas and food – and take that food with you. When you get there, tell Tommy I sent you and that you'll be staying for a few days. Tell him I'll be coming soon to explain everything. Don't say anything else – about me or Sonny or the money. I don't care how hard he tries to get shit out of you. And stay put, understand? Don't go anywhere until I get there. It should be no later than noon Saturday.'

'And if you're not there by then?'

'I'll be there by then. Remember, stay put and stay quiet. Tell him I ordered you to be a mute.'

Her hands were in her lap.

'What is it?' I said.

She shrugged. 'My mother...' she said. 'Just because you guys were married doesn't mean you have any responsibility to me.'

I just nodded. I checked the time: 8:20. Ten minutes to spare. 'You'll be okay driving for that long?'

'I've done it plenty times before.'

I stepped back. As her window went up, the glare from the fluorescent lamps overhead swallowed up her face.

The Jeep lumbered away, its tires squealing as it turned onto the ramp and dipped away from view.

AFTER SMOKING A CIGARETTE by the elevators for a good five minutes, enough time for Mai to have left the Coronado entirely, I walked back into the casino and made my way as casually as possible to the front entrance. Outside, a new pair of lifeless valet attendants stood leaning against the conquistador. They nodded perfunctorily at me as I passed them and crossed the rain-slicked street.

At night, the Coronado was lit up like a pinball machine, brilliantly reborn out of its dullish daytime appearance. It stood at the mouth of the pedestrian mall on Fremont Street, which went on for blocks beneath a mammoth canopy of white latticed steel, like a cavernous circus tent, flanked by all the old Vegas casinos. A colossal Christmas tree stood at the midpoint of the mall amid a swarm of revelers. It seemed impossibly real, towering over the casinos, reaching almost halfway up to the canopy.

I walked slowly, trying my best to steer clear of the crowds streaming onto Fremont. The rain had stopped but the wind picked up. Nobody noticed. People were too busy sipping at their plastic tumblers and snapping photos, their heads turning skyward when suddenly the lights dimmed and the canopy came alive, like a digital sky, with video of reindeer prancing down the length of the mall and pulling a sleigh manned by Santa and a gaggle of beautiful showgirls. A parade of nonsensical images followed, elves morphing into dancing trees, girls riding candy canes, yin-yangs spinning into flowers into snowflakes into psychedelic whirlpools of color, all as dancy Christmas music filled the mall and the crowds cheered and snapped more pictures.

I stood at the edge of everything, just out of reach of the canopy, and had to remind myself that I was still in the desert, watching this Martian circus come alive before me in the dead of winter. Part of me found it ridiculous, like the rest of the city, while another part of me wanted nothing more than to dive into all that lurid revelry and drown myself.

Some joker in a Santa hat, wearing only a T-shirt and cargo shorts, went skipping around and tapping everyone with a giant candy cane like it was a magic wand. He came close and I saw his bleary eyes, and he slurred at me through his bushy red beard, 'Merry fucking Christmas, man!' When his cane tapped my shoulder, it felt like a blessing.

I finally heard the cell phone ringing at my breast and hurried to an empty wall outside the mall to escape the clamor. I had already missed three calls.

'Yes,' I said into the phone, covering my other ear.

'I thought you were ignoring me.' It was Victor. 'Where are you going?'

'Nowhere. This was the only way I could get you to call me. Listen – I need Happy's phone number.'

'You know I can't give you that.'

'Why not?'

'Stay at the hotel, Officer, and wait things out until tomorrow morning. We went over this. That's the only way you're ever leaving this city.'

I was making my way back to the Coronado. 'I'm not going anywhere. Mai just left with the money and is headed out of town as we speak. She has a safe place to go. All I'm asking now is to speak to Happy. One quick conversation.'

'That's not gonna happen.'

'Victor –'

'Goodnight, Officer.'

'Victor, hold on. Why did Suzy wait four days to give Mai this money? *Four days* she sticks around town when she knows Sonny's after her. What was she doing all that time?'

'You got to stop. Put this all behind you.'

'And why didn't she just bring the money to Mai's apartment? Why go through all the trouble of leaving it here for her – in that specific room?'

Victor was silent.

'Are you there?' I said, nearly shouting over the thousand voices behind me singing 'Jingle Bell Rock.'

'I don't have any answers for you.'

'Well, if you don't, then Happy's all I got.'

I was back in the Coronado and the new quiet of singing slot machines. I lowered my voice. 'Mai just left town

272

with a load of your boss's money. I can't keep her safe if I don't know everything Suzy did to steal it for her. You understand? Victor?'

He finally spoke up, muttering Happy's phone number with quiet reluctance. 'If you take another step outside the casino tonight,' he warned me, 'I'll have no choice.'

I RETURNED TO my room for the duffel bag I'd dropped off, then went back next door to 1215. What Mai had said – that someone had been in the room – still troubled me. Not that I believed her, but that same hush used to pass across her mother's face every now and then, like she had seen or heard something I could not.

I checked the room more carefully this time, even getting on my knees to inspect the carpet. Nothing peculiar finally except a whiff of sweetness in the air which I hadn't noticed until then, like that smell in my apartment from a few days before.

A thought startled me and I searched my pockets for my badge. I rummaged through my duffel bag for a few minutes before finally remembering that Mai still had it. She had forgotten to give it back. I couldn't think of why I'd need the badge at this point, but having it stripped from me made me feel like a shade of my former self, lighter but also less substantial.

I shook it off and sat down beside the telephone on the nightstand.

Happy's phone rang six times. I hung up, waited a minute, and tried again. This time, on the fourth ring, she picked up. Her *hello* sounded small, distant.

'It's Bob,' I said. 'What took you so long to answer?'

'I just get home. How you know this number?'

'We need to talk. Look, I know you didn't give us the full story. I understand why, but I've sent Mai on her way. She's probably already past the city limits. You can tell me now.'

'Bob –'

'Don't deny it, okay? What else did Suzy want from you?'

'Bob...' She uttered my name this time with pity and exhaustion in her voice.

'Happy, listen... I was mean to you back at the apartment and I'm sorry. I don't have any right to be angry. And everything that happened with us – I'm sorry about that too. I've been a mess ever since the divorce, you know that. But all this stuff in Vegas – I didn't ask for any of it. I'm just trying to do the right thing, so please help me out here, okay? I deserve to know everything that happened.'

I could hear her breathing over the long silence that followed. Finally she said, 'She give me a shoe box. It have the letters for Mai.'

'She wanted you to deliver them?'

'She want me keep them. If I hear something happen to her, only then I give them to Mai.'

'If something *happens* to her?'

'I don't know, Bob. I not want to ask her that. She make me promise I not read them or give them to nobody.'

'Well Mai's gone for good now. You won't know where to send her the letters anyway.'

I could see Happy with her phone to her ear, staring at the wall, wondering what else she should tell me.

'I want to tell her at the apartment,' she said, 'but I promise Suzy I not do nothing –'

'Yeah, until something happens to her. That could

literally mean *anything*. Jesus, why does she talk this way?'

'What way?'

'Come on, you know. She used to talk like that to me all the time. Everything was like some fucking riddle. It was like she was constantly trying not to lie to me and not tell me the truth either.'

'But she not mean to.'

'Of course she did. She never trusted me, Happy. With anything.'

'She *do*. She marry you.'

It was the old Happy again, explaining the pain away, dismissing the truth to soften its blow. It surprised me, with everything that had happened between her and Suzy, that she could so easily slip back into this role.

'You know why she married me? I was *safe*. I was a dumb American who would take care of her. Do shit for her. Protect her from whatever.'

'Bob, why you say that? You know Suzy care for you.'

That was all she had for me, and it sounded for a moment like she didn't believe it either. But when she spoke again, her voice was sad, almost a whisper: 'She also write letter for you.'

When I didn't respond, she went on, 'She ask me keep it too. One day I send it to you.'

'You weren't going to tell me this?'

'I *promise* her.'

'Happy, it might say where she's going. I could help her – even save her life. You have it there at home with you?'

'No, Bob, you don't come here.'

I squeezed the receiver tightly, then looked at the time. It was nearly nine. 'I'm at the Coronado, Happy. I'm sitting

275

in the same room Suzy went to every Thursday evening. I know she came here to write the letters. You can keep Mai's, but please come bring me mine.'

I regretted the idea as soon as I said it, but my overwhelming need to get the letter felt justified. In an instant, it had become the thing I deserved all along, after everything that had happened here in Vegas and everything I'd been through all those years with Suzy.

Happy said, 'How you know that?'

'Sonny's boy told me. He sent me here. Put me in the room next door and made me wait in case she showed up one last time. He and his father have no idea why she was coming here. But they're barred from the Coronado. You probably know that. It's just me here. You'll be safe.'

'No.'

'I'm leaving tomorrow morning. You got to do this for me.'

'No way I go to that place.' There was an edge again to her tone. I couldn't tell if she was refusing my request or refusing something else.

'It's a casino. You'll be safe.'

'That place – I can't tell you.'

'Good God, tell me what?'

'You not believe me.'

'I'll believe anything at this point.'

Happy made a sound, like a pained laugh, like she was ready to cry and tell a joke at the same time. 'Bob,' she said in a pleading voice, 'how I can explain it to you? Her husband. Her first husband. He die in Vietnam long long time ago. She think he come to the room. She think he come back to find her.'

I waited a moment before saying, 'Are you kidding me?'

'No,' she murmured, and I could almost hear her slowly shaking her head. She hung up before I could ask the question again.

I called her back, but the line just kept ringing. I banged the receiver on the nightstand and let it drop to the floor.

The heater by the window clicked on. A dull drone permeated the room. I stood up to sniff the air. That smell was still there, and as I looked around the shadowy room, my skin crawled and it made me want to yell at myself for being so easily spooked.

'If you're there,' I said out loud, 'say something. Vietnamese, English, just fucking say something.' I picked the receiver off the floor and slammed it down on the cradle.

I sat on the bed with the duffel bag in my lap and stared at the time blinking on the VCR atop the TV set. Then, like an alarm had gone off, I remembered the videotape.

I didn't want to, but I had to turn off all the lights in the room.

Victor's account had been unsettling, but watching the video with my own eyes – remote in hand, constantly fast-forwarding and rewinding – was like seeing three versions of Suzy at once: the one I remembered, the one Victor romanticized, and this other phantasmagoric shade of her that had descended into Sonny's darkness. Her bizarre behavior appeared harmless one minute, heartbreaking even, but the next minute grotesque. When I got to that final footage, where Sonny is on top of her, I found myself watching it as a stranger might. Could she not be enjoying herself? How could you tell if she had truly forgotten any of it, that what she felt in Sonny's dark office that night was horror and not shame? And yet despite the questions, I still felt sick seeing her on the screen, seeing Sonny there with her, looming like an incubus. I thought watching the video would bring me more clarity, but after half an hour the story felt as incomplete as ever.

I shoved the tape back into the duffel bag and changed into some dark jeans and a black sweater. I washed my face in the bathroom, drank a full glass of water though I wasn't that thirsty.

Leaving all my things in the room, I hurried downstairs to the casino. In the gift shop, I bought a black down coat with a hood and a midnight-blue baseball cap with the Coronado's logo and put them on before leaving the shop.

At the front entrance of the casino, I jumped into one of the waiting taxis and showed the driver the address I had torn out of the phone book from my room. There were over thirty listings under Happy's surname, and sure enough one of them – Tuyet Phan – matched her phone number. The driver said it was thirty minutes away in Summerlin, which was west of the Strip and sounded like some faraway made-up place.

'Get there in twenty and I'll pay you double,' I told him.

As we sped away from Fremont, I peered behind us for any suspicious-looking cars. The driver was playing holiday music and I asked him to turn it off, which he did a little begrudgingly.

In the darkness of the cab, I looked again at the listing and wondered if the first name – Tuyet – was fake, then realized I'd been foolish enough all these years to believe that Happy was actually her real name.

15

WE MERGED ONTO THE 95 going west. Towering sound walls flanked the highway like Native American murals, emblazoned with turtles and geckos and giant scorpions lurking beneath parabolas of shadow and amber light.

Traffic was moderate, easily navigable, and the driver was weaving across the four lanes with a wildness that pleased and slightly nauseated me.

I held the cell phone in my lap, waiting for it to ring, unsure if I would answer it. Victor would have called by now if he had seen me leave. For the first time since Happy hung up the phone, I considered the possibility of this working out, of me convincing her to hand over Mai's letters too. Who else could deliver them at this point?

I could see her standing by the phone with her hands over her ears as it rang and rang. She might have regretted telling me about the letters, but my suspicion was that she had wanted to all along, that all her redemptive promises to Suzy had become too burdensome for her. Happy meant well. Despite what she'd done, she wasn't a liar. But she also wasn't someone who sought the truth or lived very easily with it. Her preference was for the scenic route, the path that skirted the forest and the brush and led circuitously to the sea, and if you were lost she'd draw you a map, or better yet blindfold you and lead you by the hand. That's why she was the perfect friend for Suzy.

What made Suzy good for her was still a mystery to me. The same question I had for myself.

I pictured Suzy bent over the desk in the hotel room, scribbling away for hours to her daughter, to Victor, to God knows who else. All those years of her being as generous as a mute, and now she apparently had words for everyone. Even me.

Was it something I needed to know or something she needed to tell me – secrets she was at last confessing? That she had abandoned her only child twenty years ago because she was too young and afraid, too selfish, to raise her on her own? Because she'd lost that child's father, a man I'd never been able to replace, no matter how happy I had made her in those first few years or how hard she had tried to bury him and their child and that life they had together before she came here, before she ever met me? And now this man had returned. A ghost? A figment of her imagination? An impostor?

I thought of her red journal at the bottom of my dresser at home and all the things she might have revealed in there about the past two decades, or just the past two years, like what had led to her disappearing, where she was planning to go. I had brought it back from Vegas all those months ago with firm plans to translate it all – if necessary, hire someone in the department to do it for me. But I kept putting it off. It was easier to leave it buried beneath my socks and sweaters and not know what she might have truly thought of our life together – or worse yet, that she had thought nothing of it at all.

Her voice came back to me in the silence of the cab and with it a series of events about midway through our marriage. I'd nearly forgotten them.

IT MUST HAVE started with the flu. She spent four days in bed under three blankets, her fever so high that I would have taken her to the hospital had she not refused me half a dozen times. Happy watched her while I was at work, fed her Vietnamese porridge and dabbed her face and chest with that green hot oil throughout the day.

When the fever broke, her color and appetite returned but her mood did not improve. She'd lie on the living room couch with wine in her coffee mug and listen to those old Vietnamese ballads on our stereo, the volume so high that I had to escape into the bedroom and close the door. At dinner, out of nowhere, she started talking about our savings and how much it might cost to fly to Vietnam. Would I mind letting her go on her own for a month, maybe two? When I asked if she still had family to stay with, she said she hadn't spoken or written to anyone in such a long time, and then she promptly dropped the subject.

I stopped home one afternoon during patrol and heard her talking in the bedroom, and since no one's car was in the driveway, I figured she was on the phone with Happy. I knew by then not to disturb their conversations, which could go on for hours.

But something about her voice led me to the bedroom door. She was speaking slowly in Vietnamese, like she was trying to say things as clearly as possible – to a child or a dumb person, someone who was not listening. Her voice kept fluctuating as though she was moving around in the room. We had no cordless in the house at the time.

I nearly knocked several times but ended up returning to the kitchen to check the beers in the fridge and the bottles in our wine rack, which hadn't been touched that day. Carefully, I picked up the kitchen phone and heard the dial tone, and a slow ache traveled down my body.

A few minutes later she appeared in the kitchen and jumped back when she saw me. I tried to act normal. I asked her if Happy was over, but she shook her head irritably, her hand still on her heart, and went back upstairs to the bedroom.

Days later, I awoke in the night without her beside me, which was not yet so common that I wasn't alarmed. I searched the house and finally heard her in our other bathroom downstairs, speaking again in that voice. I knocked this time. She hushed and the light beneath the door went out. I knocked again and the light turned back on and she opened the door.

What do you want? she said. I asked who she was talking to. I was praying, she replied, and when I asked why in the bathroom, she said it was peaceful there and why was I being nosy? Then she walked past me and returned to bed.

Her praying voice was familiar to me, of course, that droning monkish chant that was depressing to hear but never unsettling. What I heard that night was a conversation.

I once asked her, apropos of nothing, if she believed in ghosts, and she replied that everyone believes in ghosts because everyone has memories. I told her I was referring to literal ghosts, not metaphorical ones, which she didn't quite understand, and that's when she told me about the visions she had at night, ever since she left Vietnam. It'd be a man or a woman, never more than one person. Sometimes she knew them. Sometimes they were too far away to recognize. When she saw them on her walks at night, they moved like they had a pressing destination, a thing they were searching for and needed to find soon, and she would follow them for a time, though they never looked at her or acknowledged her in any way, like *she* was the ghost in their world.

I must have looked at her like she was crazy, because she didn't mention it again during our marriage.

I called up Happy the next day. She reminded me that Suzy's flu had been pretty bad and that she had murmured nonsense during the worst of her fever and talked in her sleep several times. And besides, who didn't talk to themselves now and then? This didn't make me feel any better, but Suzy's behavior soon took a different turn.

When I left for work in the morning, she would follow me to the door and ask me when I'd be home. When I stayed up late and didn't come immediately to bed, she'd leave the bedroom door wide open, sometimes coming out hours later to call me in. She was always in the same room as me now, joining me on the couch where I read or at the kitchen table where I finished reports, asking me about work, making conversation out of the blue about customers at her flower shop or horrible stories on the news. I started noticing a childish alarm in her eyes every time I ran out for cigarettes or groceries. I couldn't tell at the time if she enjoyed being around me again or if she simply didn't want to be alone. It bothered me that I couldn't just ask her, that not knowing was something I preferred because I hadn't felt this close to her since the first year of our marriage.

We were making love every other day. After four years together, we'd gone through the cycles, bouts of sudden desire amid the long barren periods, but the one constant was that I was the initiator. Now it was *her* kissing me right when I walked into the house, pulling me away from the kitchen sink after dinner, caressing me on the neck in bed. She would remove my clothes first, immediately take me in her mouth, climb on top of me, handle me violently until I came, then afterward crawl into my arms. We'd made love like this before, but her passion was new and bizarre, and though the shock of it all delighted me at first, gradually it wore on me.

After she startled me one day in the shower, at once kissing and stroking me from behind, I pulled away and asked what was wrong with her. Why was she suddenly acting this way? Even as the shower sprayed her face, I could see her tearing up. She stepped gingerly out of the shower and left the bathroom without another word. I found her on our bed, naked under the covers, her hair soaking the pillow. She was still crying, but I could sense her anger as well. And even as I resented that anger and felt no inclination whatsoever to soothe her or apologize or explain myself – even then, I desired her.

A month into all of this, she awoke me one night after a bad dream. She was always most talkative then, in the middle of the night, in total darkness, when sleep and fear still had a hold of her.

Tell me your happiest memory, she said, as if pleading for a lullaby. The question was so unlike her that I wondered if she was fully awake.

I said it was the day she agreed to marry me, but she dismissed this and asked me to really think hard about it.

Eventually I told her about my father disappearing for three days when I was eight. My mother hurled a frying pan at him one evening. There was hair-grabbing, shaking, screaming. He stormed out, which was normal, but he didn't return the following evening, and my mother explained nothing to me. For the next three days, I blamed her for everything and locked myself in my room. I kept an ear out for the front door creaking open. I'd peek out the window to check for his car on our driveway, and at night I'd wait for headlights to beam across the mini blinds, dreaming later of him drowning in the bay or moving somewhere dark and far away, like Asia or Africa. He finally returned in the dead of night, his hulking form like an apparition by my bed. I did not mind his reeking of cigarettes and liquor, or that he took up most of my twin bed and fell asleep without saying a word. I followed soon after, my arm touching his, the deepest and most peaceful sleep I'd ever had. Years later, long after the divorce and his death, my mother revealed that he had spent those three days with the woman he eventually left her for. He had changed his mind and come home that third night, putting off his permanent departure for a few more years. For what reason, I would never know.

Even Suzy thought this wasn't that happy a story. So I asked for her happiest memory, and to my surprise she told me: about a man she once knew who died a long time ago back in Vietnam, who spent two years in a reeducation camp after the war. They gave him two small bowls of rice a day, mixed with a teaspoon of salt and a little water so that the salt dissolved in the rice. His thirst was so bad that he drank his own urine. When he finally came home after his reeducation, his very first meal was a bowl of his mother's pho. He'd always say that was the happiest day of his life.

I pointed out to Suzy that that was the happiest day of *his* life, not hers. She seemed on the verge of replying, but after a few minutes, I realized she had fallen back asleep.

Over the years, that conversation had been buried beneath what happened a week later, when Suzy started distancing herself once again, no longer even looking at me, until finally I came home to a dark and empty house one afternoon and discovered that her suitcase was gone from the closet along with half her clothes.

I drove at once to Happy's apartment, but Suzy was not there. Happy was as alarmed as I was. We went together to the flower shop, to the movie theaters, to every restaurant and shop in Chinatown that Suzy frequented and every spot on Fisherman's Wharf where she might seek temporary refuge. Happy knew these places well and ended up doing the driving, leading me to sites and habits in Suzy's life that I had not been part or remotely aware of, hushing me every time I lost my patience and cursed my crazy fucking wife in front of her.

We drove around the city until darkness fell and we had exhausted all our options. I wanted to quit then, too worn out and pissed off to care anymore about why she'd up and leave like this or why she'd been acting this way for so many weeks, so many years.

I remembered sitting in the darkness of the car with Happy, feeling as alone as I did now in the darkness of the cab. I finally asked her why Suzy would want to leave me, a question I already had many answers for. She said something about how women get this way at a certain age and maybe all Suzy needed was something new in her life.

Like a new husband? I asked her. Or maybe having a child would make her happy?

She shrugged and thought for a moment, her face contemplative and sad in a way I'd rarely seen. Who know what make somebody happy? she said. It usually not what you think, and it almost never what you want it to be.

That must have triggered something, because she sat up and said she had one last place we could check.

We found Suzy's lone white Toyota in the parking lot of St. Mary's, a mere three blocks from our house. Suzy and I walked there every Sunday morning, even in the rain.

Evening Mass must have ended hours before, though the church doors were still unlocked. Inside, we found no one. There was some light from chandeliers and votive candles along the walls, but at that hour the church was shrouded in dusk and silence.

Happy and I made our way down the aisle, hoping to find Suzy asleep in one of the pews. I suggested we go search the confessionals, but Happy stopped halfway up the aisle. I thought at first that she was pointing at the life-size crucifix above the darkened sanctuary. It took me a moment to see Suzy's small figure below it, standing behind the altar as casually as she would at the kitchen sink at home. One hand kept coming up to her mouth, and as we quietly approached the sanctuary, I could see that she was chewing on something, that it was in fact the Body of Christ. She was picking the communion wafers out of the

Eucharist bowl like they were potato chips. Behind her, the doors of the tabernacle stood open.

Happy and I reached the front pew, where Suzy had left her suitcase. She hadn't noticed us yet. Her eyes were directed at the high arched ceiling of the church. Was there something up there along the shadowy rafters? Something beyond the shadows? If it was God she saw, her face showed no sign of revelation or communion. Each time she brought a wafer to her lips, she bit into it indifferently, chewing it as she would a stale cookie. The way her face caught the pale amber light from the chandeliers, she seemed at once beautiful to me and intolerably alien.

I was too baffled to do anything – to even *want* to do anything. Happy finally called out to her. When she turned to us, she seemed unsurprised by our presence – calm and clearheaded. But then her eyes began to tear up. I remember, before the floodlights abruptly turned on, her saying something in Vietnamese to Happy. It sounded regretful, an apology perhaps, an admission.

A voice boomed behind us. The parish priest was stomping up the aisle in his cassock, shouting, What is this? What are you all doing up there?

He hurried past us and up the sanctuary steps and seized the Eucharist bowl from Suzy, covering it with his hand as he continued chastising all three of us, demanding that we leave the premises at once.

Happy took Suzy by the hand and rushed her out of the church as I stayed behind and tried my best to explain everything to the priest, who knew Suzy and me from Mass but seemed too furious to recognize us. By the time I came out to the parking lot, Suzy was sitting alone in her Toyota and Happy was insisting that I not talk to her, that I should drive home, cool off, and let her take care of everything.

An hour later, when Suzy walked into our bedroom with her suitcase and returned it to the closet, the sight of her instantly drained me of all the questions and bitter words I'd stored up. She peered at me from across the room, unsure if I would yell at her or ignore her. She finally approached the bed and without taking off her shoes crawled onto the sheets and burrowed into my arms, crying softly until we both fell asleep.

There would never be a right time to ask her. We immediately went on with our life together, ignoring what had happened. We started eating out and going to the movies more frequently and even took trips to the Redwoods and other parks that she had always wanted to visit. At my suggestion, we began renovating the entire town house, tearing down the rooms one by one and rebuilding each with our own hands, slowly and patiently and meticulously so we'd not only get it right but also leave ourselves more still to rebuild, to fix and improve. The marriage would end before the renovation was complete, but for four more years we fed off that silent and inexplicable need for each other. That was enough, at least for me.

I did ask Happy once if she found out why Suzy almost left me and how she had convinced her to come home. She would only say that Suzy never truly wanted to leave. I never thought to ask about what she'd been doing at the church. In my mind, she'd simply been trying to talk to a God who wasn't answering – the only kind I've ever known.

I do remember looking through her empty suitcase the

day after her return. Inside an inner pocket, I found a brand-new passport, issued that past week, and an envelope full of cash that must have taken her many months, perhaps years, to save.

THE CABDRIVER was still racing through the night a good fifteen miles over the speed limit. We passed shopping malls that straddled the highway, closed down for the night, then golf-course mansions and sprawling housing estates, then suddenly a lone casino, majestic and brilliant in the night, then more houses and condominiums, lit-up gas stations and cold commercial buildings and all those other badges of suburban peace.

The Strip had long vanished behind us, no sign of the pyramid light or anything.

I asked the driver how much longer we had to go. He said, 'Five minutes max,' and nudged the gas pedal.

I checked the battery on the cell phone. It was still half full. The wipers squealed across the windshield, startling me. In the yellow nimbus of the highway lights, you could see the snow flurries buzzing about like flies.

'Fucking snow in the desert,' the driver said, unimpressed. 'Left Jersey to get away from this.' He didn't seem to care if I was listening. 'Betcha anything people gonna die tonight. People here can't even drive in the rain.'

He said something else, but I was no longer paying attention. I rolled down my window and tossed the cell phone out into the night.

16

THE SNOW WAS FALLING fast by the time the taxi dropped me off at Happy's gated neighborhood. I didn't ask the driver to wait. There was no telling how long it would take to convince Happy to give me the letters, but I'd already decided I wasn't leaving without them. My immediate concern – despite all the others I should have had – was whether I'd chosen the right address.

The security gates were closed. I stood shivering beneath the streetlamp in a chamber of yellow light that felt like the inside of a snow globe. Soon a car approached and I followed it through the gates and into the neighborhood, its tire trail and my footprints the first markings on the fresh snow.

A narrow road led me down a long, winding block of identical onestory duplexes, which were themselves two mirrored halves, each with the same Mediterranean-style roof and pink stucco walls and sometimes the same collection of palm trees and bushes, the only distinguishing feature the color of the front door or the car in the driveway. As I wandered through the falling snow with Happy's address in my hand, I wondered how long it had taken her to not get lost in this maze of sameness.

I passed some kids playing in the snow without coats or gloves. They slid across small patches of lawn that were still green underneath, shook powder off tree branches that still had leaves. This must have been their first snowfall. I remembered a few flurries that instantly melted on the streets of Oakland thirty years ago, when I was in my teens. It stunned me that my first real snowfall ended up being in the desert, of all places, that forty-five years in the world had only gotten me this far from home.

By the time I found Happy's house, I couldn't feel my face or my fingers and had to brush snow out of my hair. Several cars were parked along the curb across the street, covered in a thin layer of snow, none of them familiar. Her side of the street was empty, as was her driveway, her car probably parked in the garage. The blinds on all her windows were closed too, but the lights in one were on. I rechecked the address above the garage. Even as I approached the front door, I kept wondering if I had the wrong half of the duplex.

I knocked and waited, then knocked again. I thought about calling out her name, but all the houses on the block were close together, and even my knocking had sounded too loud.

I tried the knob and it turned and the door opened. I spoke into the doorway, 'Happy? Are you there?'

On the wall of the dark entryway, a painting of a young Vietnamese woman in a yellow *áo dài* smiled at me. She was holding her rice hat against her belly, her long black hair falling over her shoulder. Beside the painting stood a coat rack that held Happy's black peacoat.

I stepped into the entryway and could see part of the living room around the corner and the illuminated red lampshade that ruddied the shadows.

'Happy?' I called out again, my annoyance growing now that I was sure I had the right place. 'It's Robert. I'm coming in.'

I closed the front door and approached the living room. Turning the corner, I saw lit candles on the kitchen counter, then an ivory couch across the way with something long and black draped over its back. Another coat. Beyond the couch was an unlit hallway that led to four closed doors.

When I stepped onto the cream carpet, my wet shoes stained it, so I bent down to untie my laces, and it was only then that I noticed the darker shoeprints ahead of me.

I pulled out my gun and stepped farther into the living room. To my far left, sitting in an armchair beside an unlit Christmas tree, was Sonny.

His head was reclined on the seatback, his dull eyes narrowed on me. He seemed unsurprised by my presence and uninterested in the gun I had on him. His own he held limply, pointed at the floor. It was like my appearance had just awakened him from a deep nap. Beside him on the end table was a half-empty bottle of Johnnie Walker.

'Set the gun on the floor,' I ordered him and moved behind the couch.

He lifted his head. His face was flushed. Tiredly, he said, 'This again, huh?'

He was right, of course. Even the shadows gave me déjà vu. I'd spent the last twenty-four hours wishing I had shot him five months ago, and here I was back in the same spot, made impotent again by fear and curiosity.

'Why are you here?' I said. 'Where's Happy?'

'She not here no more. She gone.'

'Gone where? Why?'

He shook his head as though the questions were too stupid to answer.

'I said drop the gun, Sonny. Did you hurt Happy? Where is she?'

'Where my wife? Where my fucking money? You know that?' He came to life, wincing as he sat up and plunked his gun on the table and grabbed the pack of cigarettes lying there. He lit up and massaged his scalp with his other hand, then ran it roughly across his face like he was wiping off the exhaustion. His smoking hand, I noticed, was shaking slightly. He was an emotional drunk, unsurprisingly, liable to be at his most violent but also, I was hoping, his most sincere.

'Suzy's gone,' I said. 'She's left town for good. I don't know where, but I know she's not coming back. To me or to you.'

'*Suzy*,' he muttered and shook his head. 'You give her that name?'

'Let's bury it right here, Sonny. She's gone, and there's nothing you or I can do about it. Go on with your life. Let me go home and go on with mine.'

'That it, huh? We just say bye-bye, huh?'

'You brought me here to find her, but there's nothing to find.'

'My stupid son – that *his* idea. He don't tell me *nothing*. He say he take care of everything, but he don't get shit done. Look at you. What you do here now? You point the gun at me like this your house. I pay for this house! My son – it all his fucking idea! Me? I want bring you here and fuck you up, man.'

His voice was rousing his body, his fists tightening with each word. I'd been holding on to some possibility of getting him out of the house so I could search for the letters, but my other concern now was how to get myself out without one of us getting shot.

The phone beside him rang, startling only me. After the third ring, Sonny lifted the receiver, killed the call, and left the receiver upturned on the end table beside his gun. The dial tone droned between us.

'Who're you ignoring, Sonny?'

He dumped a couple of cigarettes onto the table for himself, then held out the pack. 'Smoke with me.'

When I didn't move, he flung the pack peevishly at me and it landed on the carpet by my feet. 'Smoke a fucking cigarette, huh?'

'Why?'

'We talk. Like man to man. You want go home, right?'

I had only two choices now: shoot him or humor him. I reached down for the pack, keeping my gun trained on his heart, and shook a cigarette out onto my lips. I lit it with the candle on the kitchen counter behind me and took it in like a long drink.

The phone had gone into its echoing off-hook tone like some distant siren. Sonny stole a swill of the Johnnie Walker and winced again. Then he relaxed, and a wry smile appeared on his face.

'Nowadays, man, I love play poker with American. The old day I sit down at the table and they think I don't know shit. They loud, they laugh, they think they run over me because I small, I talk funny. It don't matter I have good game or bad game. They always think they better. But *now*, man, I talk louder, I laugh louder, make bigger joke, especially when I beat them, take all their money. I love when they don't got nothing to say. It's like I broke their dream, man. It's like I take their money *and* their voice.'

'Why're you telling me this?'

'You fight in the war? I fight with Americans in the war. They get drunk and piss in the street in front of my mother. They drive around and try to pull the pretty girl on their Jeep and laugh when the girl scream and run away. They wanna fuck all the Vietnamese girl, every one they see. Sometime, they fall in love too. One fucking GI, I remember he tall and so white he look like he sick. Always call us "slant-eye" and "Marvin the motherfuckin' ARVN." He make joke we not understand, pat us on our head like we little boy. You know what this guy do? He fall in love with a bar girl, man. He buy her all the gifts and promise he take her home and marry her. He so dumb he don't know she just want go to America and take his money. So what happen? She find another GI who promise her better thing and she leave this guy. And he so fucking sad, he not talk to nobody for a whole week. Nothing. Then one day, he find the other GI in the street. He not say a word. He just walk up and stick his knife right here.'

Sonny made a single stabbing gesture at his throat.

'So I remind you of him.'

'No, man. You not got the balls to do what he do. You the other GI, the one who die.'

'I'm not afraid of you, Sonny.'

'Shoot me then. I let you.' He picked up his gun by the barrel and tossed it on the couch in front of me. 'Shoot me and you can go.' He made a finger gun and pointed it at his temple. '*Shoot me!*' he hissed through his teeth, his chin raised, his bloodshot eyes flaring at me.

Just as quickly as it erupted, his temper vanished and he took another pull from the bottle.

I reached for his gun and slipped it into my coat pocket. I looked around for something I could tie his hands and feet with, keep him drunk and immobile while I looked for the letters.

'She never talk about you, man,' he said wearily.

'All right, Sonny.'

'No, she not talk about you ever, man. You know why?'

'Shut up, Sonny.'

'She feel sorry for you, man. She hate me, but she feel sorry for you.'

His tone stopped me. His bravado had given way to a hush of seriousness, like he was genuinely sad for me. He put the bottle again to his lips, then changed his mind and let it sink into his lap.

Mai might have been right about him after all. I wanted to despise him wholeheartedly in that moment, but it was dawning on me that he not only loved Suzy, but might have loved her more than I ever did – with a depth, with layers, too many probably, that I'd always hoped for but was never truly capable of. Perhaps you need full reciprocity to feel it like he did. Perhaps you have to be willing to hurt and kill and suffer and die for it.

I dropped my cigarette in a glass of water on the kitchen counter, unsatisfied by the hiss, and I wondered if Suzy had asked Sonny for my life also out of pity. There was, strangely, no real anger or envy in me – just the suspicion that I had lost this fight a long time ago, that actually the fight was never mine to win *or* lose.

Sonny was peering at the fake fireplace with its fake logs

and all the candles and picture frames cluttering Happy's mantelpiece. I remembered those same pictures from her old place in Oakland and knew how much family she still had in Vietnam, how none of them had ever made it to America though some had tried. Sonny was looking them over like he knew that too.

Then I spotted, atop those fake logs, the crumpled ashy remains of an envelope. I picked up what survived of the letter inside, a tiny scrap of paper with Suzy's unmistakable handwriting in English, the end of two lines:

never forget.
first time I see

Sonny's heavy-lidded eyes were still pitying me.

'Why did you do this?' I said. 'This was mine.'

'You not deserve it. Don't worry, it just one page.'

'You *read* it?'

'You want know what she say? She say she appreciate what you do for her. She say she want remember you like the first day she see you. She say you a good man. She say she admire you.'

'You're making that shit up.'

'I not lie, man. *She* lie, though. She want to make you feel better. That what I say, man – she feel sorry for you.'

'Where are the other letters? Where the fuck are the other letters?'

He had another cigarette in his mouth. Absently, as though sighing surrender, he said, 'Happy not tell me that.' His hands shook slightly as the lighter lit up his face. That's when I noticed the bright red scratch marks on his cheek.

'Sonny – where's Happy?'

He was staring straight ahead, drowsily, as though waiting for sleep to overcome him.

'Sonny. I called here an hour ago. I was just on the phone with her.'

'I hear you all talk.'

'What the hell is that supposed to mean?'

'I hear every word she say to you.' His head rolled back onto the seatback and he closed his eyes.

I backed into the hallway. With my gun still trained on him, I opened the first door and flicked on the light. It was the bathroom. I pulled back the shower curtain but the tub was empty.

The adjacent door revealed a closet full of stacked shoe boxes and casino uniforms hung in dry-cleaning plastic.

I threw open the third door. The darkness receded into the room: bedsheets pulled onto the floor, an overturned lamp, a whiff of shit. Even before I flipped the light switch, I could already make out the outline of her body, her thin forearm extended over the edge of the bed.

She was still wearing her uniform, her bow tie twisted vertically like he had used that to strangle her, though I could see his purple thumb marks on her throat. Her body was warm, but her face was the color of concrete, her eyes hemorrhaged red and gaping at the ceiling. Her tongue stuck out, a dry slug on her bluish lips, like it was plugging her mouth, and in my mind her pained laugh on the phone became the sound of everything she had ever been to me.

I finally noticed the kitchen knife, streaked with blood, lying on the carpet beneath her outstretched hand. I reached down for it, and it was then that I stepped on her glasses. They crunched beneath my feet.

Sonny had not moved in his chair, his eyes open but looking at nothing. I finally saw the dark wet blotch on his outer thigh, staining the inside of the yellow chair brown.

'I not want to do it,' he murmured and brought his cigarette to his lips.

I slapped it out of his hand. He tried to speak but I swatted his face with the butt of my gun and he fell out of the chair and onto the carpet. He gasped and grabbed his thigh and I stomped on him twice there, on his hand and his wound, and when he screamed out I went down on one knee and slugged him, pummeling his skull, his face, my knuckles scraping his teeth. My hand recoiled and I had to catch my breath, and all my rage went to the pain in my torn hand.

I shoved the gun's muzzle against his temple. His face was half hidden in the crook of an arm, blood dripping from his mouth and onto his chin, crawling down his cheek from the gash above his eye.

It wasn't fear or hesitation that kept me from pulling the trigger this time. Just an animal need to hurt him much more while he was still alive to feel it.

'You motherfucker!' I hissed, still on my knees.

Then I saw the phone cord. I thrust my gun into my coat pocket and ripped the cord out of the phone. I knew exactly what I wanted to do with it.

But I felt his hand seize my leg, and then something hard clunked me on the side of the face. Everything erupted into a black, throbbing vacuum of silence. I came out of it lying on the floor and struggling to open my eyes and finally seeing a bright flare. In my hazy vision, the Christmas tree sprouted a fiery arm, and out of that nightmare came Sonny's shadowy half-form, crawling toward me and raising his arm one last time to bring the bottle down on my head.

I WAS UPSIDE DOWN, draped over someone's shoulder. My arms dangled heavily. A thick hand gripped my thigh. The air was bitter cold and it was hard to breathe, my face thudding against someone's broad backside. We were lumbering across wet, crunchy snow, and in the distance I heard somebody scream.

THEN I WAS LYING in a darkness that droned and trembled. My legs were scrunched against a car door and I could see the highway lamps pass in the window, that sickly yellow light again, the snow still flying about like so many buzzing flies.

The road beneath me felt like it was all around me.

17

THE FIRST THING I SAW when I awoke was the painting of the geisha climbing the staircase. It seemed to me she was floating up the stairs.

I was lying on the leather couch in Sonny's gloomy office, my shoes still on my feet, still slightly damp.

'Can you sit up?' said a voice.

Junior sat behind his father's desk in a white shirt with the sleeves rolled. He looked even younger with unkempt hair, strands of it falling over his eyebrows. Smoke was curling off a forgotten cigarette in the ashtray beside him. He must have been sitting there for some time, waiting for me to awake, contemplating the quiet.

I sat up gingerly and that triggered a nauseating pain that swam through my eyes and swamped my head. I touched the bandages on my cheek and ear, saw dried blood on my sleeve and the front of my shirt, raw cuts on the knuckles of my right hand.

'How do you feel?' Junior said. His serene face amplified the sincerity in his voice. He filled a glass with water from a pitcher.

'Not good.'

'Can you walk?'

'Not sure I can stand. What time is it?'

'Six in the morning. You've been out for most of the

302

night. We had someone stitch up your cheek and your ear. You'll be fine except for the headache. You will need some food, though. Do you think you can drive?'

'Is that something you want me to do?'

'It would be good for you, yes.'

'What about the hotel? And Suzy? What about your father?'

'That is all done and over with now.'

Junior pushed a button on the phone beside him. A voice on the speaker said 'Yes' in Vietnamese, and Junior issued some kind of order and hung up. He opened the prescription bottle on the desk, shook out a few pills. He carried the glass of water over to me and presented it along with the three white pills on his palm.

'For the pain,' he said and set the prescription bottle on the coffee table in front of me and returned to the desk chair. He saw me studying the pills. 'Don't worry, Mr Robert. If I wanted to do something bad to you, I would have left you in the fire last night.'

As I downed the pills, a vision of the Christmas tree ablaze came back to me and with it another wave of nausea. 'There was a fire. You mean the house...'

'Yes. We didn't stay to see it burn to the ground, of course, but we saw enough.'

'And Happy?'

He let the question linger between us for a moment. 'I had to make a quick decision. She was already dead, Mr Robert.'

'Jesus Christ. She didn't deserve that. Even if she was already dead.'

'I'm not sure what you want me to say.'

'Your father – he strangled her.'

'I know.'

'I came there to talk to her and find out where Suzy might have gone. That was it. I had no idea he'd be there. I'd been waiting all day at the hotel –'

Junior waved his hand. 'None of that matters anymore. Frankly, I don't care what you were trying to do. It's all over now.'

'Why would your father do that to her?'

He got up from the chair impatiently and faced the bookshelf, his hands in his pants pockets. His manner seemed defeated, but I couldn't tell if it was from anger or sadness.

With his back to me, he said, 'Do you know what it's like to spend your entire life with someone who must always be held back? Muzzled? Contained? The worst part is that you understand it – you understand everything about them. You're the only one in the world who does. So you live with it. You live with the… It's not fear, really. It's futility. You know they're always on the verge of something you cannot control. It is not wise to go about loving someone in this manner.'

With one hand, he started pressing against the spines of books so that they were all perfectly aligned on the shelf – a habit I indulged at home with my own books.

'Since Sunday,' he continued, 'when Miss Hong disappeared, my father has been on the precipice of one thing after the other. He was convinced she had run away with another man. He was convinced *you* were this man. He was convinced that Happy must have helped her steal his money. Anything would have put him over the edge, but something about Happy cut him much deeper. He had let her in – like he had let Miss Hong in. The thought of the two of them conspiring against him... that was too much. I still don't know what Happy did, but last night I found out that she had quit her job at the casino and would be moving back to Oakland.'

'Who told you this?'

He ignored the question, aligning the books with both hands now.

'It was a mistake to tell him. He went into a rage, convinced it was proof she had deceived him too. He wanted to go confront her himself this time – in the middle of the Stratosphere if he had to. He wanted to hurt her. It took all my energy just to keep him from going to the Coronado to hurt *you*. But I couldn't keep him still forever. There's just so much you can do. You can try to minimize the damage, fix what you can afterward. When he called to tell me what he'd done, I was horrified, I did not think he would go that far – but I was not surprised.'

'Not surprised?' I said. The loudness of my own voice deepened the ache in my skull. 'You could've done something. She didn't have to die.'

'He would have found some other way to hurt her. Sooner or later. I told you, my father is not one for forgiveness.'

'Bullshit. You can't just give up and let someone go crazy on the world.'

'Don't tell me you've never given up on anyone.'

He had started reshelving some of the books, slowly and methodically – stubbornly.

I said, 'So what now? You still gonna protect him? Let him get away with it? They're gonna find out, you know.

Even if the whole place is a pile of ash, they'll figure out what he did.'

He stopped and turned to me, a book aloft in his hand. 'Mr Robert – you were the only person we removed from that house last night.'

He shelved the book and returned both hands to his pockets and stood there with his back to me.

'He was still breathing. I felt his pulse. Right here.' He placed two fingers on the side of his neck. 'My only consolation was that he was not awake to see me walk out the door with you. All my life, even as a child, I've always known that some day I'd have to do what I did last night.'

I was too stunned to say anything. I could see it all in his bowed head, his stillness. What he'd done was a sacrifice, but also a betrayal. There would be no getting away from that. And if there was any relief, there would also forever be regret and shame and anger and, worst of all, doubt. He must have known all this when he walked out of that burning house with my lifeless body. I couldn't help admiring him, despite there being nothing admirable about any of it.

Maybe that was when I accepted that I'd have to give up on Suzy and on everything that tied me to her. A heavy finality fell over me, heavier than what I felt that night I hit her, like I could no longer remember her or any part of our marriage correctly – like a stone door had closed on the last ten years of my life.

A soft knock came at the door. It opened, and Victor appeared, carrying my duffel bag and a small paper sack. Junior gestured for him to come in and close the door.

Victor didn't make eye contact until he was standing above me. If he was upset with me for disobeying him, I couldn't tell. He set everything on the coffee table, including my car keys.

Junior said, 'That is food. Take it with you. It's nearly daylight now. I have no idea how long it will take the authorities to identify my father's body and then contact me. I'm fairly confident, though, that you will not want to be here when that happens.'

The door opened again and this time it was the giant Menendez, his face as expressionless as it had been five months before. I felt a strange tenderness at the sight of him ducking under the doorframe. He must have carried me last night. I wondered if behind that inscrutable face he ever thought about the things he was ordered to do or the people he did them to, if it mattered to him that he had to take one body and not the other.

Victor started for the door, but Junior said, 'Not yet. Mr Robert, before you make your departure, I need to take care of some unresolved issues. One is this.'

He opened a desk drawer and pulled out Suzy's red journal. He held it open, turning the pages delicately.

'Very many years ago,' he said, 'when I first knew Miss Hong, I asked her what she was writing in this book, and she replied that she was writing letters to someone who would never read them. I didn't quite understand that at the time, but I took it very seriously. I still do. You took this from my father's house five months ago. I would say you *stole* it from him, but it wasn't his. Nor is it mine or yours. That's the way it should remain.'

He ripped out a handful of pages, then tossed the journal

into the metal trashcan by the desk. He took the lighter on the desk and lit the pages in his hand, watching the flames grow into a torch before also dropping it into the trashcan. He peered darkly at me as curls of smoke began rising and that sweet burning smell filled the room. All the while I thought about running over and saving the journal, but it was like Junior already knew that I wouldn't, that the fight in me had already been exhausted.

'I've been sitting here watching you asleep on that couch,' he said, 'asking myself why I let you live. My only answer is that letting you die would gain me nothing. I learned that from my father. Don't do something if you have nothing to gain from it.'

Smoke was drifting all over the office, past Victor and Menendez and out the doorway. We all remained silent amid the soft crackling and the swirling haze, watching Junior as he watched the fire. After a minute more, he picked up the pitcher of water and emptied it into the trash can. Then he set the pitcher down on the desk with a loud thud that startled Victor.

Calmly, I said, 'You had no right. It wasn't yours to destroy.'

'Yes, that is true. But I'm doing you a favor one last time, Mr Robert. I'm saving you from futility. It's like my father always said about poker. Even if all the cards are shown, the story is still incomplete. It'll always be incomplete. Live with it.'

'You're punishing me. That's what you're doing.'

'Yes, that is true too. But you're not alone.'

He turned now to Victor and stared at him as if waiting for him to speak first. I would always remember Victor's immediate glance at Menendez, who was blocking the entire doorway. His face, its blank intensity, betrayed too much. Junior was probably only a few years his senior, but for the moment he seemed decades older.

'Victor, I want you to answer me honestly. Did you help Miss Hong steal my father's money?'

I expected Victor to acknowledge me now in some way, but he was too dumbstruck to do anything but stare back at his interrogator.

'I don't care about the money,' Junior told him. 'I don't care about anything else you did. All I want to know is whether you helped her betray my father.'

Victor let the silence swell a moment more before replying, 'Yes. I did help her.' He started to say something in Vietnamese, but Junior held up his hand.

'No, no. Speak English so that Mr Robert will understand.' The look Victor finally gave me was not angry or uncertain or even fearful. It was oddly conspiratorial, like he and I had planned this very moment. 'She was afraid for her life,' he said, 'so she asked me for help. I felt a duty to help her.'

'And your duty to my father? To me?'

'She was afraid. She had no one else. I couldn't say no.'

Junior considered that for a moment, then walked around the desk. 'That doesn't make sense to me. You can always say no. You have a tongue, don't you?'

They were a foot apart now. Victor opened his mouth to reply, but Junior struck him with a vicious upward blow, a palm heel to the chin that flung his head back and sent him stumbling into Menendez's chest.

I leaped to my feet, and the sudden movement made me

light-headed. I managed to say, 'Wait, goddamn it!'

No one paid me any attention.

Victor was bent over, grimacing and cupping his mouth like it was swollen inside. He had bitten his tongue badly. I could already see blood on his lips and his fingers. From behind him, Menendez had both hands on his shoulders like he was either consoling him or propping him up. Then he gently nudged him forward toward Junior.

'What were you going to say?' Junior asked.

Gently, affectionately it seemed, he pulled Victor's hand away from his mouth and lifted his chin with a finger to inspect the damage. Then he put his other hand on Victor's shoulder, as if coming in for a hug, but in one swift motion slipped behind him and wrapped his arm tightly around his throat as the other hand gripped the back of his head.

Victor came alive and grasped at Junior's forearm to break the chokehold, lifting him off the ground for a second before backing him into the bookshelf and knocking books onto the floor. But Junior was glued to him, his hold as tight as a vise. Victor was tucking in his chin and managed to reach behind his head to grab Junior's sleeve, and that's when Junior kneed him brutally in the ribs, which made him gasp. From there the chokehold was unbreakable. His face reddened, his eyes started rolling back, and moments later his body went limp, crumpling to the floor.

I made a move toward him, but Junior threw up his hand and pointed at me like he was brandishing a dagger. He was standing over Victor's prone body, his rolled-up sleeve kissed with blood. I was startled by the sight of him so unrecognizably disheveled and out of breath, flushed with anger as Menendez loomed behind him like his gargoyled shadow.

He nudged Victor's head with his shoe, then nudged it again much harder.

Victor shuddered suddenly, and I heard the violent insuck of breath as his back rose like a tide. He was gasping and coughing into the floor, holding on to his side as he also grabbed at his throat, his legs writhing slowly like he was in the midst of a troubling dream.

I don't know if it was relief or guilt or the throbbing in my own head, but I sank back down onto the couch.

Junior took a deep breath. He stepped over Victor and returned to the desk. I saw him open the drawer again and this time pull out a switchblade, the same one he had used on me. He set it on the desk.

'Please get up, Mr Robert,' he said, slicking back his hair and tucking in his shirt. 'It's time for you to go.'

'What are you going to do to him?'

'It has nothing to do with you. I'm letting you leave. Be satisfied with that.'

'You can't expect me to see this and just go.'

'That's very heroic of you. But I'm giving Victor what he deserves.'

'He doesn't deserve to... I won't let you.'

'You misunderstand. I have no intention of killing Victor. He will be fine – you have my word. He's like a brother to me. He's all the family I have now. But punishment is punishment. We all get our due sooner or later.'

Junior walked over to the wall clock beside the geisha painting. He said to me, 'Menendez will take you to your car. This will be the last time we see each other. As far as I am concerned, I do not know you, I have never met you, and you have never been to Las Vegas in your life. In return, I recommend you never set foot back in this city.'

He turned the hands of the clock in the same combination he did five months before.

As the painting crept open, as Victor continued groaning and writhing on the floor five feet from me, I thought of Sonny and Happy and of all the letters that surely went up in flames alongside their bodies.

Menendez followed me down the dark stairway, but as the painting started closing behind us, I called over my shoulder, 'I was here, though. I was here, and everything happened.'

I could no longer see Junior. I was not sure he even heard me.

18

As I drove out of the city, the sun shone as intensely as it had the previous morning. The sky was the color of the Pacific in July. The farther south I drove on the 15, the less snow I could see. Only a few unmelted patches on the shoulders of the highway, the broken lumps on the tops of passing cars, spitting flurries onto my windshield. It was strange to see green palm trees swaying in the breeze and beyond them the vague warm mountains, because in the bright sunlight, if you squint, it all seems like a vision from some tropical island.

I held on to that thought to lessen the pain in my head. To bury as much as I could of the last two days.

It was my second and my last time leaving Las Vegas. The farther away I got, the more I felt I was shedding some pitch-dark side of myself that the place had awoken. Maybe it was my most genuine side. It doesn't matter ultimately – who you think you are. Sonny and Happy had died, and mourning one and cursing the other made me no more wiser about the things that people do to each other. In the end, good and bad people perish all the same.

I felt inside my duffel bag for the videotape. It was still there, though its value was lost on me now. It would never tell me where Suzy went or what new life she would find for herself. It would never tell me what she had actually written me or what else had happened in that hotel room. All it contained were darkened glimpses of two people whose love for each other somehow lasted for over twenty years.

Two hours out, I stopped at a gas station to fill up my car and change out of my bloody clothes. I threw away the food and painkillers Junior had given me and bought a bottle of ibuprofen, some cold sandwiches and hot coffee, and a pair of cheap sunglasses to cover up my bruised eye and shade myself from the harsh sunlight.

It was still desert all around me, gray mountains behind brown mountains, miles of hoary creosote bushes blanketing the flat land like a bed of thorns. I ate all the sandwiches sitting on the frigid hood of my car and drank my coffee slowly and decided I was never coming back to this or any desert.

Only then did I call Tommy.

As soon as he heard my voice, he said, 'What the hell did you do, man?'

'I can explain the girl,' I said.

'What girl? There's no girl. All I see is a suitcase at my front door with fifty fucking grand inside and a note with your name on it. And oh yeah, your badge.'

He grilled me with a string of questions, but I wasn't listening. I hung up without saying another word.

I sat in the car for a while, sifting through my surprise, my disappointment, and eventually the realization that I shouldn't have been surprised at all.

I considered tossing the videotape then. Run over it with my car first. Burn it and let it melt into the desert dust. If Mai was gone now, why hold on to anything else, especially this?

But I kept it. I would never watch it again, but somehow it felt right to save this one reminder. At least it wasn't some heartfelt memento of something we once had. On the tape was everything I knew about her and everything I would never know. That wasn't enough, but at least it was real.

Acknowledgments

A humble and heartfelt thanks to the following people:

My parents, Son and Nhai, for their love, their sacrifices, and their countless stories.

My sister Mai, who fights crime, is a fount of invaluable information, and has always taken care of me.

My brother Joseph, who has exceptional taste and an exceptionally good heart and is also one of my best friends.

My editor, Alane Salierno Mason, who made this book a great deal better, whose judgment I implicitly trust, and whose tremendous support I will always be grateful for.

My agent, Ellen Levine, whose patience and commitment and enthusiasm over so many years – including the uncertain ones – has meant the world to me.

My 12th grade English teacher, Pat Sherbert, who taught me how to value literature.

My teachers at the University of Tulsa: Grace Mojtabai, Lars Engle, Gordon Taylor, James Watson, and George Gilpin.

My teachers at the Iowa Writers' Workshop: Ethan Canin, Chris Offutt, Frank Conroy, Sam Chang, and Marilynne Robinson. And of course Connie Brothers.

Everyone at the Black Mountain Institute in Las Vegas, including Carol Harter and my indispensable mentors,

Doug Unger and Richard Wiley, who have both given me so so much. Also from Las Vegas: the generous Glenn Schaeffer and the incomparable Dave Hickey, who sharpened my tastes and ambitions and gave me a little necessary edge.

My colleagues in the Committee on Creative Writing at the University of Chicago, especially Dan Raeburn, an outstanding writer and an outstanding friend.

Jenny Swann, a fantastic and crucial reader.

Julie Thi Underhill, who has believed in me since the sixth grade.

Stuart Jacobsen, my first serious reader.

Jarret Keene, who asked me to write the story that became this novel.

Embry Clark, Jess McCall, Aimee Phan, Matt Shears, John Nardone, Jason Coley, Ingrid Truman, and Peyton Marshall – whose friendship has been a refuge.

All the generous and supportive people at the Whiting Foundation and the Vilcek Foundation.

And finally, Kate Hoctor, my best reader and my best friend, without whom so much of this book could not have been improved, figured out, or struggled through into the light of day.

About Us

In addition to No Exit Press, Oldcastle Books has a number of other imprints, including Kamera Books, Creative Essentials, Pulp! The Classics, Pocket Essentials and High Stakes Publishing > oldcastlebooks.co.uk

For more information about Crime Books go to > crimetime.co.uk

Check out the kamera film salon for independent, arthouse and world cinema > kamera.co.uk

For more information, media enquiries and review copies please contact marketing@oldcastlebooks.com